NOW THAT WE'RE ADULTS

A NOVEL

LYNN ALMENGOR

Plaid Core Productions
PHILADELPHIA, PA

Plaid Core Productions
2417 Welsh Road
Suite 21-224
Philadelphia, PA 19114
www.plaidcoreproductions.com

Publisher's Note: This is a work of fiction. Names, characters, places, and incidents are a product of the author's imagination. Locales and public names are sometimes used for atmospheric purposes. Any resemblance to actual people, living or dead, or to businesses, companies, events, institutions, or locales is completely coincidental.

Book Layout ©2015 BookDesignTemplates.com
Cover Design by Domini Dragoone

Publisher's Cataloging-in-Publication data

Names: Almengor, Lynn, author.
Title: Now that we're adults : a novel / Lynn Almengor.
Description: Philadelphia, PA : Plaid Core Productions, 2016.
Identifiers: ISBN 978-0-9974208-0-7 (pbk.) | ISBN 978-0-9974208-1-4 (epub) | ISBN 978-0-9974208-2-1 (mobi) | LCCN 2016936457.
Subjects: LCSH Bildungsromans. | Geeks (Computer enthusiasts)--Fiction. | Family --Fiction. | Friendship--Fiction. | BISAC FICTION / Coming of Age | FICTION / Family Life | FICTION / Literary
Classification: LCC PS3601.L578 N69 2016 | DDC 813.6--dc23

For Fred, my all-time favorite person.

CHAPTER 1

Wade

Everything was exactly how he remembered it, from the rows of tiny desks to the science posters along the back wall. Wade scanned the room. Doing it up front would be weird, like he was performing for an invisible class, but the back smelled foul, like a sandwich was moldering in the lunchbox left on the shelf above the coat hooks. Compelled to check, he flipped opened the latch and almost threw up.

"What are you doing?" Jill stood in the doorway, wearing a short maroon dress and a frown.

"Nothing." He fumbled with the lunchbox, closing the lid. "What's wrong?"

"Your mom needs the money for the organist."

"My bad." He pulled an envelope from his suit jacket and jogged to the front of the room.

"And Ian wants to see you. He's in the sacristy."

Wade rubbed the sides of her arms. She'd been up half the night practicing her speech and was probably nervous. "You're gonna do awesome."

She closed her eyes, taking a deep breath and exhaling slowly. "I just wanna get today over with."

He kissed her forehead, thinking back to that day at nine years old when she'd told on him for drawing a naked picture of Winona Ryder. It wasn't much more than a stick figure with boobs, but the teacher made him stay in from recess. He'd sat there staring out the window as Jill swung high on the swing set, her long brown hair flowing behind her. She'd been an annoying goody two shoes, but he was in love with her even then. And later today he was going to ask her to marry him here in the place where they met.

He grinned. "I have a feeling today's gonna be better than you think."

As she hurried up the hall connecting the school and church, he lagged behind, staring out the window at the swing set. Maybe he'd propose out there instead. With a bounce in his step, he made his way to the sacristy.

The small room smelled of candle wax, its walls lined with cabinets and drawers. Ian stood in front of a closet of white robes, adjusting his shirt cuffs. Seeing Wade, he shoved a crinkled scrap of notebook paper at him. "Make sure I've got it right."

Half the words had been crossed out and rewritten multiple times. Wade grinned. His brother was never one for sentimentality, so whatever he wrote was bound to be hilarious. "Go for it."

Ian wrung his hands as he paced the room. "I remember the day I realized I loved you. We were—stop smirking."

"I'm not." Wade pressed his lips together, trying not to laugh.

"I'm serious. I can't concentrate when you're looking at me like that."

"So turn around."

"Fine." Ian faced the closet, continuing his vows. "We were at the Laundromat playing Puzzle League on our Nintendo DS's while we waited for your clothes to dry. I thought love was supposed to be this big crazy thing, but right then everything felt so normal and so right, and I realized that's what love really is—sharing the everyday moments with someone as amazing as you."

It was actually really nice. Wade didn't have anything even half as good to say to Jill. He crumpled up the paper and threw it at Ian. "Try not to cry too much."

"Fuck you." Ian grinned and smacked him on the side of the head just as white-haired Father K. cleared his throat from the doorway. Wade laughed out loud as Ian dropped his head. "Sorry, father."

"It's time to start. Are you ready?"

Ian nodded. "Yes, father."

The guests had already taken their seats as Wade climbed the altar to stand beside his brother. The church looked nice enough, with ivy vines draped along the

edges of the pews, but it was still so bland. Jill wasn't re-
ligious either, so they could probably have their wedding
someplace more fun. Maybe an aquarium, or even Lahey
Family Fun Park so people could play mini-golf or hang
out in the arcade afterward.

The organist changed tunes, and everyone turned en
masse to the back of the church as Jill walked forward,
holding a bouquet of flowers, gorgeous as always. A few
steps behind her, Kat followed, arm-in-arm with her father. Her dress was white but short with red trim. Ian
stood up straighter, his chin quivering slightly like he
might actually be holding back tears. Wade kicked the
back of his leg to snap him out of it.

"What," he whispered harshly over his shoulder.

"Try not to curse during your vows."

"Shut up." Ian grinned.

Thankfully they hadn't gone with a full mass. Jill read
a Bible verse and Father K. gave a short homily about the
sanctity of marriage before the vows. Ian finally relaxed
after that part. He kissed Kat for so long that Father K.
had to clear his throat to cut them off before announcing
the new Mr. and Mrs. Dakalski.

After waiting around forever for the photographer to
take pictures of every possible combination of relatives,
Wade's mom finally gave him the okay to go. Downstairs,
tables and chairs had been set up in the gymnasium
with a space left open at the front as a dance floor. He
scavenged some broken cracker pieces and the last few
slices of salami from the appetizer table as a black-clad

catering girl started clearing away the plates. She looked familiar, but it took him a few seconds to place her.

Oh shit.

He spun around, craning his neck to see over the shoulders of the group in front of him until he spotted Rob and Drew sitting at a table across the room. He weaved through the crowd and then plopped down beside them.

"Guys, Caitlin Jones is here."

"We know." Drew popped a grape into his mouth.

"You're cool with that?" Wade asked. Drew had once written a song about one of their many break-ups— something about strangling her with her own intestines and leaving the carcass to melt in the summer sun.

"Come on, that was high school."

Rob glanced over at Caitlin, pushing his glasses further up on his nose. "She got hot."

Drew shrugged. "Whatever. I fucked like three different girls this month, and they were all way hotter."

Wade smirked and caught Rob's eye. *He wishes.*

Jill peeked around a Greek column wrapped with plastic ivy. "Babe, the deejay needs us up front."

Wade shoved the rest of the crackers in his mouth and followed her to the head table as the deejay asked everyone to take their seats. He then played a slow but punky song as Ian and Kat made their way up to the front and started dancing. Ian whispered something in Kat's ear and she laughed and kissed him. Jill watched them, brow furrowed. She always looked so serious when she was deep in thought. It was adorable. Wade stuck out his tongue at her until she finally noticed and gave him a small grin. He climbed over the two seats between them and wrapped an arm around her shoulders, swaying lightly to the beat.

"What were you thinking about just now?"

She leaned into him. "I like how they kept everything simple. It's just two people declaring their love in front of all the people they care about." The family fun park idea was probably out, but it didn't really matter. They had the whole rest of their lives to drive go-karts.

When the song ended, Wade climbed back to his own chair to make room for Ian and Kat. The deejay then introduced Jill as the maid of honor and passed her the microphone.

"As soon as I met Kat, I knew she and Ian were going to wind up married. They both still look at each other like there's no one else in the room, and it's obvious they're not just in love but also genuinely like each other. They're wonderful people who have their priorities straight, and I know they're going to have a beautiful life together."

Everyone clapped as she passed the microphone to Wade. There was no way he could follow that, so he might as well not even try.

"So that was a great speech, huh? I probably should've asked to go first." He rested a hand against a Greek column that swayed with the weight and almost tipped over as he scrambled to catch it. Somewhere in the crowd, Rob snorted.

"Okay, so be careful with the columns, everyone. They're not as sturdy as they look."

Ian dropped his head into his hands, but Kat just laughed and draped an arm around him. *Bingo.* Wade pointed to them.

"See, this is why Kat's awesome. She keeps Ian from being too serious. And Ian is great too, because he could've killed me just now, but didn't. We've had our differences over the years, but I know he's got my back. Kat's lucky to have him, and he's even luckier to have her. I'm super excited for them. Congrats, guys."

Everyone stopped pretending to be formal once dinner was served and the alcohol started flowing. Ian got so drunk so fast, he talked the ear off anyone who would listen about how great love is and how he wished everyone he loved could be this in love too. Wade and Drew made a game out of it, following him around and taking a drink every time he said the word "love," but their glasses were soon drained.

"I gotta piss." Drew swayed as he stood up from the table and headed toward the bathrooms.

Wade leaned back in his chair, grinning as his father swung his mother around on the dance floor. It was a rare and goofy sight, but made them seem like normal people who'd once been young. Behind them, the door to the schoolyard was propped open and an awesome pink and orange sunset blazed across the sky above the swing set.

I have to do it now.

Butterflies in his stomach, he turned around looking for Jill, but instead locked eyes with his great uncle Rick, sitting alone at the table behind him. He must've lost at least 30 pounds since his wife's funeral last year, and looked like a skeleton with skin. Wade shifted in his seat. He should probably say something.

"Did you like the ceremony?"

"What?" Uncle Rick barked, raising a shaky hand to his ear. His breath smelled of cigarettes and vodka.

"The ceremony," Wade continued, wishing he hadn't said anything. "Did you like it?"

"I couldn't hear it." His voice was calmer, but still gruff. "Your mother's taking me to get ear surgery next month. I might lose my hearing."

"I'm sorry. I hope it goes well."

"You're lucky you're young. When you're old, every-thing falls apart. I can't hear, I can't walk, and everyone I love is dead. First my friends and brothers, and now my wife." He leaned in. "Death is easy—it's being left behind that's hard."

Wade nodded, trying to think of something support-ive to say. *I'm sorry it sucks being old* sounded harsh, even if it was true. He glanced back at the open door. The sunset was already fading. "I'll be right back."

He squeezed between the chairs and jogged over to the gift table where Jill was flipping through the well wishes book. "There's a really awesome sunset right now. Come on." He took her hand and led her outside into the cool evening air.

She sat on one of the swings, smoothing out the folds in her dress as he hung his arms over a trapeze bar. Behind them, the windows of the fourth grade classroom were dark. He had maybe two minutes of sunset left.

"Back when we were kids, if someone told me we'd meet again in college and start dating, I'd swear they were crazy."

She gave him a half smile as she peeled a strip of old paint from one of the swing set poles. If she wanted simple, he could do simple. Heart pounding, he disentangled his arms from the trapeze bar and then knelt in front of her, taking her hands.

"Jill, I love you with all my heart and wanna spend the rest of my life with you. Will you marry me?"

The muffled beats from the gym reverberated through the air as she stared at the fading sky, eyes welling up. A knot grew in the pit of his stomach. These didn't seem like happy tears.

"Jill?"

"I can't."

His mind reeled, unable to form a complete thought. "What?"

She stood up from the swing, wiping her face with the back of her hand. "We'll talk about it later, okay?"

Without waiting for an answer, she pushed past him and hurried down to the parking lot. He slumped to the ground, watching her go, the knot in his chest exploding like a grenade.

There had to be a reason she said no. Something he could fix. Clutching the swing's chain, he pulled himself up. The sound of shouting from across the yard snapped him out of his trance.

A side door flew open and two bodies spilled out. The larger man took a swing, but the shorter one ducked out of the way and laughed.

"Rob? Drew?"

Red in the face, Drew froze mid-punch, panting. Rob grinned, his hair disheveled and shirt untucked. Nothing about this night made any goddamn sense.

"Rot in hell." Drew spat at the ground and then straightened his tie as he stomped away.

Rob adjusted his glasses, sizing Wade up. "You look worse than I do. What happened?"

"I just asked Jill to marry me."

Rob laughed, slapping him on the back. "And I just fucked Caitlin Jones. Let's get out of here."

CHAPTER 2

Eleanor

Backpack slung over her shoulder, Eleanor crouched behind the railing at the top of the staircase. Down below, a group of scantily-clad undergrads were crammed onto the couches, their limbs draped over one another like some kind of grotesque tableau. They were supposed to be at a movie. She'd overheard two of them making plans in the kitchen earlier that week as she snuck one of the last boxes out to her car. But they were still there—along with their obnoxious friends—and it was almost midnight. The longer she waited, the more likely she'd need to nap in some dubious truck stop parking lot before arriving in Scranton. But if they saw her with the backpack they'd certainly ask questions.

She tiptoed back to her bedroom, shutting the door behind her. Moonlight streamed through the window and illuminated the bare wall where she'd taped her last rent check. Pushing up the wire screen, she stared at the grass roughly 12 feet below, her stomach lurching. If she hung out the window by her arms the drop would be cut in half, but the last thing she needed was to start her new life with a broken ankle—or worse.

A surge of laughter echoed up through the vent and her whole body tensed. Actually, the last thing she needed was to endure a barrage of questions from a bunch of people who didn't really care about her.

She tossed her backpack into the yard and it thumped lightly as it hit the ground. She swallowed hard, remembering what the visiting firefighter had taught them in grade school—bend your knees and roll to the side when you hit the ground.

You can do this.

Carefully, she climbed over the windowsill, her sweater catching against the rough brick exterior as she lowered herself along the side of the house. Palms clammy, she tried to check the distance to the ground but couldn't see past her shoulder. Her arm muscles burned as she stared at the brick less than an inch away from her face. She wasn't strong enough to climb back up.

She held her breath and let go.

A small scream escaped her mouth as she smacked into the ground, the whole left side of her body smarting. She rolled onto her back in the grass and clutched her aching hip. She'd probably have a couple of nice bruises but nothing felt broken. Above her, the window remained open. Oh well. Hopefully it wouldn't rain before they noticed she was gone.

Standing up slowly, she brushed the dirt from her corduroys and limped toward her backpack. A warm breeze played with her hair as she closed her eyes and lifted her face toward the sky. By tomorrow morning she'd be in the same city as Trent.

CHAPTER 3

Wade

Rain dribbled down the window glass, the sky a sheet of grey behind it. Slouched in the recliner, Wade stared at the screen with zombie eyes, mashing buttons on the X-Box controller. His brain throbbed from lack of sleep but he couldn't shut it off.

"We weren't even fighting."

Sprawled on the couch, Rob kept his eyes on the game. "If you haven't figured it out by now, you probably won't. You'll just have to wait until she tells you."

"How does it even work when a girl rejects your proposal—do you automatically break up, or do you stay together and pretend it didn't happen?"

"Which do you want?"

"I wanna figure out what I did wrong and make it right." The doorbell rang, freezing his insides. "Is that her?"

Rob peeked through the mini-blinds in the front window. "Yeah. She's got a box."

The shrapnel in his gut inflamed anew as he shut his eyes and dug his fingers into his forehead. It was over.

"You want me to go?" Rob asked.

"No." Wade peeled himself out of the chair, his legs numb from sitting so long. "I don't wanna be alone when she leaves."

Rob grabbed the bag of chips from the coffee table and plopped back down on the couch as Wade hobbled over to the door. Jill stood on the front stoop, cardboard box balanced against her hip and holding a jacket over her head. She smiled as if she hadn't shattered his heart less than 24 hours ago.

"Hey, let me in, it's awful out here." She pushed past him and set the box on the floor. It was folded closed, but the cover of a movie he'd lent her a few months back peeked through the slit at the top.

She noticed Rob and lowered her voice. "Can we go to your room?"

Wade shrugged and led the way across the apartment to his bedroom. She chose a spot on the bed with plenty of room beside her, but the closer he was to her, the more likely he might cry. He took the computer chair instead and she looked wounded. Picking up the corner of his blanket, she smoothed it between her fingers.

"I'm sorry about the way I acted last night." She forced a laugh, but then started talking faster. "But what was I supposed to do? You propose to me without a ring or a speech, like it's the least serious thing in the world..." She stared at the ceiling as tears pooled in her eyes.

Even when he was mad, he could never stand watching her cry. Holding back his own tears, he wheeled his chair over, rubbing her back as she wiped her eyes with the blanket.

"I'm sorry," he said. "I know you hate it when people buy you clothes because they're never your style, so I thought we could pick out the ring together so you'd be sure to get one you liked."

"This isn't some ordinary gift, Wade, it's an engagement ring. It's supposed to show how serious you are about building a life with me. If I didn't like it we could've exchanged it, but to not even get one at all?"

He wiped a tear from her cheek, praying the problem had an easy solution. "I'll buy a ring and ask again. Just tell me what you want, and I'll do it."

"It's not the same if I have to make you do it."

"You're not making me do anything. I want you to be happy."

"You wanted to move out of your parents' house too, but I was the one who had to find the apartment and practically sign the lease for you."

"You were gonna move in with me after your other lease was up. Same as the ring, I wanted to make sure you liked it before I dropped a ton of money on it."

"You can't even keep this place clean." She gestured toward the pile of laundry in front of the closet.

He shook his head. "I swear I'll clean up more often, especially once you move in."

"That's exactly what I mean. You're full of promises, but never follow through with any of them." She hugged the blanket. "Did you know that Kat and Ian split all the wedding responsibilities down the middle? He booked the church, she booked the caterer. He's writing thank you notes to his family, she's writing them to hers."

"Good for them," he said flatly.

"They worked as a team. She didn't have to run around making sure he did all the things he said he would. He just did them."

Wade rubbed his forehead. Jill was supposed to be the one person who didn't compare him to his brother. "Look. I'm sorry. I suck at planning, and can be a slob sometimes, but I promise I'll always love you and we'll always have fun. Isn't that more important?"

"I need someone who's responsible *and* fun." She sniffled. "And that's not you."

Rain dripped down on the awning, making a hollow echoing sound. He clenched his fist to keep from crying. "Is there someone else?"

"No. I never cheated on you."

That made him feel even worse. "So you'd rather be alone than with me?"

"You're a good guy, Wade."

He shook his head, tears forming at the corners of his eyes. "Don't say that."

"But you are. And we can still be friends—just nothing more than that."

He squeezed his eyes shut. "Can you think about it some more? Please?"

"I've been thinking about it for weeks," she said quietly.

He flashed back to the weekend before when they'd stayed up late playing *Beautiful Katamari* and fooling around in bed together. He felt like throwing up. He'd never know which memories were real and which were lies.

Back in the living room, he watched from the window as she got in her car and drove away. Rob leaned an elbow on his shoulder.

"I never liked that bitch."

"Don't start with that." Wade pushed Rob's elbow away and then collapsed facedown on the couch. "She wants to stay friends."

"They all wanna stay friends until someone better comes along." Rob sat on the edge of the couch. "It sucks balls, but you'll get over it as long as you're smart. Don't hang out with her, don't call her, and for the love of everything holy, don't fuck her."

Wade groaned. He rolled over onto his back, pressing his palms to his forehead. "I wanna hate her so badly, but I can't. She didn't even cheat on me."

"Why'd she dump you, then?"

"Because I don't take life seriously enough."

"Fuck that. She was a bully who tried to kill your spirit. If you ask me, you dodged a bullet."

"No, I'm pretty sure it's lodged in a vital organ. I'll probably bleed out before morning." He pictured himself hanging upside-down off the side of his bed, his tongue sticking out, crime scene tape barricading the doorway. A police officer consulted his notepad and declared Jill a murderer. At least if he died tonight he wouldn't have to go to work in the morning.

Rob punched his shoulder. "Get up. I'll buy you tacos."

Thunder rumbled in the distance as Wade awoke in his darkened bedroom, sheets twisted around his legs. Head aching, he squinted at the bedside clock. It'd only been two hours. He rolled over and tried to go back to sleep, but his arms felt empty and awkward. He'd never be able to wrap them around her again. He hugged his pillow as hard as he could, but his whole body ached from the inside out. Giving up on sleep, he turned on the smaller TV at the end of his bed and watched horror movies until a faint grey dawn seeped in through the blinds.

Traffic on I-81 was so backed up that his usual 10-minute drive from Dunmore into downtown Scranton took almost half an hour. Of course, it was exactly then that his exhausted body finally decided it wanted sleep. Stopped at a red light near his office building, he cranked up the volume on the car stereo and shook his head rapidly, trying to wake up.

A pretty girl holding a lime green umbrella crossed the intersection in front of him, standing out amongst the sea of black umbrellas. He'd been with Jill so long he'd forgotten the thrill of being free to pursue any girl who caught his eye. Still, it felt like leveling down. With every new date he'd be back at square one, buying expensive dinners and gauging how far the girl was willing to go, when all he wanted was someone familiar to relax with after a long day at work.

God, I'm just as boring as Ian.

He parked in the lot and hurried through the lobby, wishing he'd had time to grab an energy drink. When the elevator opened on the third floor, he made his way down the long row of cubicles to his desk where he was immediately greeted by a smiling photo of Jill.

Fuck my life.

He yanked the photo off the wall and shoved it into a drawer as he fired up his computer. Only two new help requests, but they were both mass data entry. If the universe had a heart it would've given him a nice slow day of surfing the web or even some absurdly complicated technical problem to puzzle out, but no, it had to be an evil bastard and give him drudge work so his bored mind would settle right back on her.

He opened the database and started working, but couldn't sit still. His shirt felt too tight across his chest and the empty space on the wall mocked him even more than Jill's face had. He needed to calm down. Carrying a manila folder to make it look like he was working, he took the elevator all the way down to the basement, which had the least frequented bathroom. He then locked himself in a stall and jerked off thinking about the girl with the lime green umbrella.

Less anxious but still tired, he trudged back to his cube and browsed one of his favorite gaming sites, determined not to think about Jill. An article about the new Torque video game engine caught his attention. He leaned back in his seat and almost managed a smile, remembering the hours spent with friends in high school creating custom levels in *Tomb Raider*. He didn't have any experience with legitimate game design programs, but it might be a fun way to keep his mind occupied for a few days.

His desk phone rang and Betsy's name appeared on the screen. She was a hefty dark-skinned lady who was always super nice. He'd once taught her how to copy and paste using keyboard shortcuts, and ever since then she called him directly instead of submitting requests through the system.

"Wade." She sighed dramatically. "I'm having trouble with my computer again. Are you busy?"

"Nope," he said, grateful for something to do. "Be right down."

The call center was abuzz with a dozen different conversations as he wheeled a chair from an empty cube over to her desk. "You know you don't have to break your computer every time you wanna see me, right?"

She laughed. "I don't do it on purpose! I just have no luck with this dang computer."

"What'd you do this time?"

"A box popped up and said I entered a bad code, but every time I click 'okay,' it pops right back up without giving me a chance to fix anything."

"This program's pretty buggy. Did you restart your computer?"

"I didn't want to lose the file."

"Alright, let's see what we can do." He reached for the mouse.

"Oh my goodness, your brother's wedding was this weekend, wasn't it?"

He cringed. Of all the things she could've chosen to talk about. "Yeah, it was."

"How was it?"

"Nice, I guess. Very traditional. They're down at some Caribbean resort for the week."

"Are you taking your girl anywhere special this summer?"

His hands froze at the keyboard. He had to get her talking about something else before he burst into tears in front of everyone. "I don't think so. What about you? Taking your grandson anywhere?"

Thankfully, it worked, and she spent the next few minutes showing him the latest batch of baby photos.

He spent the rest of the day seeking out as many obscure projects as possible. If he was stuck feeling miserable, at least he could try to get a raise out of it. By the time he stumbled back into his apartment he was so drained he didn't bother to get undressed before collapsing into a deep sleep.

He awoke in darkness to the lawnmower-like sound of his phone vibrating across the bedside table.

"Mom?" His voice was scratchy with sleep.

"Wade, honey, did I wake you?"

"It's fine. What's up?"

"Uncle Rick died last night."

He sat up, trying to process the news. The guy had seemed fine at the wedding—old and crabby, but not sick. "What happened?"

"Aunt Sally went to pick him up for a doctor's appointment this morning and got worried when he didn't answer the door. She called the police, and they found his body in the basement. They think he fell down the stairs sometime last night."

He wondered when one crossed the line from being regular old to so old that people automatically assumed you'd died if you didn't answer the door.

"Wade, honey, are you still there?"

"Yeah. That really sucks."

"We're planning the funeral for Saturday morning since Ian gets back Friday. I haven't called him yet, though."

"Mom, he's on his honeymoon. Don't call him."

"You'll go, right? I'm worried about the turnout since everyone was just here for the wedding."

"I'll go as long as you don't call Ian before Friday."

"Ha ha, very funny." She sounded at least partly amused. "I'll call you again once I know more."

Rolling over, he pulled the blanket up to his chin, but kept picturing his great uncle lying at the bottom of the basement stairs, broken and wishing for death. Sitting up, he turned on the lamp and reached for his laptop, grateful for the distraction of the game engine. As it was installing, he tapped his fingers on the nightstand, staring at his phone. If this wasn't a good enough excuse to call, then what was?

His heart beat so fast he worried he might have a heart attack. After four rings the line went to voice mail, and he choked back tears as her cheerful voice instructed him to leave a message.

"Hey Jill, it's me. I just found out my great uncle died, and could really use a friend right now. Call me back when you can."

He wiped his eyes, looking at the clock. It was only 9:15. Jill couldn't possibly be asleep yet, which meant she was avoiding him. He mentally kicked himself for calling so soon after the breakup. Even if she truly wanted to stay friends, he'd probably just fucked it up.

Promising himself he wouldn't call again for at least another week, he picked up his laptop and watched the game engine's installation progress bar inching across the screen like some kind of countdown until the end. He wished his mom had called with better news because now, on top of his heartbreak, he couldn't stop thinking about death. Was there really such a thing as passing away peacefully into the night? Because it seemed like most ends were essentially the same—you stopped breathing and then suffocated. Unless you shot yourself in the head. That was pretty immediate.

He froze, remembering Uncle Rick's words. *Death is easy. It's being left behind that's hard.*

CHAPTER 4

Ian

Ian tucked his shirt into his pants and checked his watch. The viewing was scheduled from 8 to 10, but he was aiming for 9:45 as it was the latest they could show up while still technically being on time. He dragged Kat's half-emptied suitcase out of the way of their shared closet and then browsed through the ties hanging from pegs on the back wall.

"Have you seen my grey tie?" he called out as he bent down, picking up a bunch of colorful bras and panties from the floor and tossing them into the laundry basket. He loved the shit out of her, but sometimes living with her felt like sharing a room with his younger brother all over again.

"What?" she called back, voice faint.

He strode across the upstairs hall and pushed open the partially closed bathroom door to find her sitting on the toilet with a magazine, her little black dress bunched up around her waist. He shielded his eyes and half pretended to be disgusted.

"Oh my God, just because we're married now doesn't mean I wanna see you shitting."

She laughed. "It's only pee, I swear."

"That doesn't make it better!" He ducked out of the room, feeling weirdly aroused. "My grey tie—have you seen it?"

Her voice echoed in the small bathroom. "It's in my suitcase. I brought it on the trip but never wore it."

"You were gonna wear my tie?" He was honored.

"Is that bad?"

"No, it's pretty fucking adorable."

He found the tie exactly where she said it'd be. Standing in front of the full-length mirror, he fumbled with the knot, unable to get it right. He swore under his breath as she walked up beside him, taking the tie into her hands.

"We don't have to go if you don't want to," she said.

"I'll never hear the end of it if we don't."

She finished with the tie and then slipped an arm around his waist, admiring their reflection in the mirror. "I'll be right beside you the whole time. If at any point you wanna leave, just say the word and we're gone."

He kissed her forehead, grateful for the reassurance. "Let's get this over with."

* * *

The somber legato of the pipe organ greeted them as they passed through the thick wooden doors of the church. In front of the altar, the casket lay open, and a group of people he didn't recognize took turns hugging his parents. His brother sat alone in a back pew, head bent over his lap.

"Go on ahead," he told Kat, seizing the opportunity to get out of seeing the body. "I'm gonna say hi to Wade."

She squeezed his hand before walking up front. He genuflected at the end of Wade's pew and then slid in to find his brother doodling a building with flames shooting out of the windows on the back of the funeral bulletin.

"As if today weren't morbid enough already."

Wade didn't look up. "Jill dumped me."

"Shit, I'm sorry." The two of them had been dating even longer than he and Kat and everyone expected them to get engaged any day now. "What happened?"

"I didn't magically turn into you."

Ian raised an eyebrow. "What's that supposed to mean?"

"Never mind."

"You can't say something like that and not explain it."

"I don't wanna talk about it."

"Whatever." Ian leaned back against the pew. Up at the altar, Kat was hugging everyone and talking to them as if they were her own family. She was so much better at these kinds of things. He turned back to Wade. "Did you go up yet?"

"Yeah."

"How does he look?"

"Dead."

"No shit, asshole."

Wade twirled the tiny church pencil in his fingers. "I think it was suicide."

Ian rolled his eyes. "Of course you do."

"He said stuff to me at the wedding about feeling lonely and left behind. I don't think it's a coincidence that he had a mysterious accident the very next day."

"Old people fall down. It's not that mysterious."

"Mom said she sees it all the time at the nursing home," Wade said, a faraway look in his eyes. "When one half of an elderly couple dies, the other usually isn't far behind. It's like they don't remember how to function without the other around."

"That doesn't mean they kill themselves. They're just more susceptible to diseases and accidents, like the one Uncle Rick had."

"Everyone he loves is dead."

"That's not even true. Mom and Aunt Sally visit him all the time."

"They take him to doctor's appointments. It's not the same thing."

Ian rubbed his forehead, wishing they were talking about anything else, but morbidly determined to prove Wade wrong. "If he wanted to die, he wouldn't do it by throwing himself down a flight of stairs. He'd probably just shoot himself in the head."

"Do you think he had a gun?"

"How the fuck should I know?" He responded louder than intended, and up at the front their father looked over before excusing himself from the other mourners.

"Because if he had a gun, he probably would've used that instead," Wade continued. "Unless he didn't want the family to know."

"Shut up. Dad's coming." Shoulders tense, Ian stood up as his father pointed to his watch.

"Cutting it a bit close, don't you think?"

"We were up late last night unpacking and doing laundry."

His father studied him from over the top of his wire-rimmed glasses, his grey hair slicked back. They were the same height and build—Ian had often been told it was like looking backward and forward in time when they were together.

"If you're going to pay your respects, do it now. Father K. wants to get started." He glanced over at Wade, who'd resumed drawing. "Put that away and go sit with your mother."

Wade met Ian's eyes as their father walked away. "Just close your eyes and pretend you're praying."

Ian scoffed. *Easy for an atheist to say.*

As he neared the casket, he locked his gaze on the strip of polished wood across the top of the open lid, keeping his great uncle's form out of focus at the far bottom of his periphery. It wasn't the bodies that bothered him as much as the fact that they would never move again.

He envied Wade's total disbelief. The finality of death would be so much easier to accept if he could only make up his mind one way or the other on the God question. But as much as he doubted there was some glorious picnic waiting on the other side, he still desperately needed to believe it.

He closed his eyes and counted slowly to 10 before blessing himself and then joining Kat in a pew near the front.

She rubbed his arm. "You okay?"

"Fine," he mumbled. If there was one thing that usually made him feel worse, it was people asking whether he was okay.

The organist played one more solitary drawn out note before Father K. ascended to the pulpit, arms raised in prayer. Ian bowed his head but tuned out the words, concentrating instead on his cousin Jeremy's one-year-old son JJ, who sat in the pew in front of him playing with an oversized felt book. He gave Ian a gummy smile as he stood up, his miniature hands gripping the back of the pew.

"If he starts bothering you, let me know," Jeremy whispered.

Ian mussed JJ's hair. "Nah. It's good to see someone smiling around here." The boy let go of the pew to reach for Jeremy's curly blonde ponytail, but slipped, slamming his bottom against the hard wooden pew. For a second he looked simply stunned, but then started wailing.

Jeremy sighed. "So much for smiling." He cradled JJ against his chest. "Come on buddy, let's go outside and find Mommy."

"Let me take him." Ian reached for the boy. "I could use some fresh air."

"Thanks, man. Much appreciated."

Outside, the sun's rays warmed Ian's face as he sat on the front steps, bouncing the child on his knee.

"Scream all you want, little guy. If it wasn't for you, I'd still be in there chanting 'Lord have mercy' while Father K. goes on and on about how death is a part of life, as if we don't all know that by now. For once, I wish someone would have the guts to say, 'You know what? Death sucks. Let's skip all this sad stuff and go out for pizza instead.'"

The boy stopped crying, pushing his head back so far he gave himself triple chins, as if he suddenly realized with horror that he had no idea who he was with.

"I'm impressed." Alicia trudged up the sidewalk, diaper bag slug over her shoulder, her long red hair blowing around her face. "It usually takes me at least twice as long to get him calmed down."

Sitting on the step, she produced a disheveled plush monkey from the bag. JJ promptly stuck one of its ears in his mouth and grinned as if nothing had ever been wrong.

Ian shook his head. "My God, they cycle through emotions fast."

"I know, right?" Alicia said, taking her son into her arms. "Are you and Kat planning to have kids any time soon?"

"We *just* got married." Ian laughed. "But yeah, eventually. Between the wedding, the honeymoon, and the house, we're pretty much broke right now."

"They don't cost as much as you think. At least not at this age. You can get almost everything secondhand, so mostly you're buying diapers and food. By the time they get older you'll have more saved."

She stroked JJ's hair, which was red like hers but curly like Jeremy's. He was a perfect mix of both of them, yet still his own person—a blank slate who could become anything at all. Ian had to admit the whole idea did have a certain appeal to it.

He scratched his head. "I don't know. It's still a huge responsibility. How did you know you were ready?"

"I didn't." She laughed. "You just have to jump in and do it or you never will."

After the service, he and Kat joined the line of mourners as they shuffled out of the church and into the parking lot. His father handed him a funeral procession flag.

"Make sure you catch up with your mother at some point. She's going to clean out your uncle's house and needs all the help she can get."

"Understood." Sorting through an old man's possessions sounded miserable. Maybe he could get away with just helping move the furniture once everything else was gone.

His eight-year-old cousin Greta bounded over and tugged on his sleeve. "Can I ride with you guys?"

"If it's okay with your mom."

"Mom!" Her voice pierced through the otherwise polite murmurs. "Can I ride with Ian?" Aunt Sally nodded and went back to her conversation.

As Ian started the car, Greta knelt in the space between the front seats, studying Kat. "You're pretty."

Kat smiled. "Thank you. So are you."

Ian extended his seatbelt over his chest and reminded Greta to do the same as he drove to the end of the procession. Kicking her feet against the bottom of the seat, she leaned back, staring out the rear window.

"Is Heaven really in the sky?"

Oh God, not right now.

He silently pleaded with Kat to take this one. She squeezed his shoulder and swiveled in her seat.

"Some people think so, but nobody knows for sure."

"Could we check if we flew on a plane?"

Kat rested a finger on her cheek and looked up, as if she were considering it. "That's a smart idea. You should try it sometime."

Greta scrunched up her face. "But if we put Uncle Rick in the ground, how does he get to the sky?"

Kat shrugged. "It's a secret trick. You only learn it when you're really old."

"Like my mom?"

Ian burst out laughing, and Kat smacked his arm. "No, not like your mom," she said. "Uncle Rick was much, much older."

Ian grinned. Not only was Kat smart and gorgeous, but she could gracefully answer tough kid questions that would've tripped up almost anyone else. He probably would've gone the logical route, giving concrete but conflicting answers that only confused and upset everyone. His kids would be lucky to have her for a mother, if only to make up for all the things he would inevitably suck at. As Greta chattered on about school and the funny things her cat did, he pretended she was their daughter and they were on their way down the shore for a family vacation.

At the cemetery, Greta ran on ahead, zigzagging between the headstones as they hiked up the hill, the damp smell of freshly turned earth wafting through the air. At the summit, the name *MURPHY* was engraved across a modest white stone, with his great aunt and uncle's names and dates beneath it.

Wade wandered over, craning his neck to gaze into the abyss of the open grave. "You can see Aunt Rita's casket."

"I didn't need to know that," Ian said. Part of him was curious, but his rational mind knew better than to look.

"Do you think husbands and wives are ever buried in the same casket if they die at the same time?"

Ian ran a hand through his hair, wanting to deck his brother. "I have no idea."

"Cause it's kind of sad that their bodies are gonna be so close together yet so far apart."

"Oh my God, please shut up." Closing his eyes, he pictured a cross-section of earth with two caskets, forever separated by a two-foot gulf of wood and dirt. He immediately wished he could un-see it, but knew he never could. *Fuck Wade and all this funeral bullshit.*

He whispered in Kat's ear, "I wanna go home."

Taking his hand, she led him back down the hill.

"Where are you going?" Wade called out.

"If Dad asks, tell him I wasn't feeling well." He stopped short. "Oh, and by the way, Mom needs help cleaning out Uncle Rick's house if you wanted to check for a gun."

"Oh, thanks. That's a good idea."

Idiot.

He thought he'd feel better once they were back in the car with Yellowcard playing on the stereo, but as he drove slowly toward the cemetery entrance, his chest felt so tight he could barely breathe. If he died right now, what would he leave behind? The school would easily fill his position, and Kat would probably marry some other guy. It would be like he was never there.

He took a sharp left and drove deeper into the cemetery.

Kat glanced at him. "Where are we going?"

He parked in the grass under a huge weeping willow and took her face in his hands, kissing her hard.

She slowly pulled back. "Are you okay?"

He shook his head. "I just love you so fucking much."

"I love you too." She stroked his cheek.

"I wanna make a baby with you." He didn't mean to put it so bluntly, but was glad to get it out there.

Her eyes grew wide. "Let's not get carried away."

"We always said we wanted kids—why not now?"

"Because we agreed we'd be closer to 30 before we even started *thinking* about it."

"I know it sounds crazy, but life is so goddamned short. I don't wanna miss a single thing." He sat up straighter. "It's true we don't have a lot saved up, but my parents had Wade and me while my dad was still in grad school and they were living in the apartment over my Babcia's house."

He wanted it so badly it hurt—and if she didn't agree right away, he'd probably use those exact same arguments to talk himself out of it by dinner. "No one's ever really ready. We just gotta jump in and do it."

Kat twisted the fabric of her dress between her fingers, brow furrowed. "If we did this, you'd split the responsibilities with me, right? I mean, to this day my dad brags about having never changed a diaper in his life. I don't wanna be the one doing all the dirty work."

Relief washed over him. "I swear I'll help. I watched Greta a few times when she was a baby, so I'm already way ahead of your dad on that one." He held her hands. "I don't wanna be one of those dads who acts like their kids aren't real people with thoughts and feelings of their own. I wanna teach them things and really get to know them. And I wanna do all of it with you. I can't believe how good you were with Greta today. Well actually, I can, because you're the most amazing person I've ever known."

She looked away, biting her lip. She didn't want to do it. His shoulders sunk. She was probably right—they weren't ready at all. He let go of her hands and turned to the wheel when she grinned and shook her head.

"Okay, then."

Holy fuck. He grabbed her face and kissed her. "For real?"

She shrugged. "Why not?"

He laughed and kissed her again. "Holy shit, I can't believe we're gonna do this." He unbuckled his belt, determined to try at least once before he lost his nerve.

"You wanna do it *here*?" She spun around, looking out the windows.

"It's okay. None of them are watching."

She groaned before sliding her panties out from underneath her dress and climbing onto his lap. "Oh my God, why am I having a baby with you? You're such a dork."

"And you're perfect."

CHAPTER 5

Kat

The automatic doors slid open before her as she strolled into the hotel lobby, wearing a blazer and pencil skirt combo and pulling a wheeled suitcase behind her. Two young men staffed the front desk. She approached the better-looking one.

"Hi, my name's Katherine Kerwin. I need to check into the conference as a vendor."

Looking up, he did a slight double take and then smiled. He was definitely into her. "You got it. What company?"

"Aberdeen Foods."

He entered the information into the computer and handed her a badge. "You're in booth 14. Have you been here before?"

She tilted her head to the side. "Nope. First time."

"I'll show you to the hall, then." Coming around the side of the desk, he reached for her suitcase. "Let me get that for you."

He was cute in the same high-functioning geeky way as Ian, with defined arm muscles she wished she could run her hands over. He led her down a nearby corridor. "Are you from Binghamton?" he asked.

"Scranton, actually."

"Nice place." He nodded. "I went on the coal mining tour once."

"What were you down for?"

"School field trip." They entered a modest conference hall where a dozen other vendors were already organizing tables and pinning up banners. He stopped in front of an empty booth. "How long are you in town?"

"Just today. I'm driving back after the conference."

"What? That's a two-hour drive. *And* it's Friday. I'll see if I can get the manager to comp you a room for the night."

She grinned. This one had guts. "Oh yeah?"

He dropped his voice to a playful whisper. "Between you and me, the food here isn't that great, but I can recommend a couple of nicer spots if you decide to stay."

She was supposed to meet Ian back in Scranton later that night for the Bayside concert, but might have time to lounge around the pool for an hour before conveniently missing dinner. Brushing a strand of hair behind her ear, she leaned in and matched his tone.

"Thank you. That's very thoughtful."

His posture suddenly stiffened. He was staring at her wedding ring.

Regaining his composure, he dropped into customer service autopilot mode. "If you need anything else, please don't hesitate to call the front desk." He made a beeline for the door.

Really? You're giving up that easily?

She loved Ian more than anything and would never *actually* cheat on him, but couldn't help feeling disappointed. Even on the eve of their wedding she'd been able to command the attention of their closest male friends as they played a round of pool after the rehearsal dinner. These guys knew for a fact she'd be off-limits starting the next day, yet had no problem flirting and watching intently as she bent over the table at an angle where they'd be sure to get a good view.

It was all harmless fun, but now she felt guilty. What was wrong with her that she wanted the attention of other men even now that she was married? Still, she couldn't deny the high she got whenever guys hit on her. Feeling like an asshole, she slipped the ring off her finger and tucked it into her blazer pocket. She'd put it back on as soon as she was done working, and if it helped get more leads, even better.

After the conference, she packed her work suitcase into the trunk of her car and grabbed the smaller duffel bag with her concert clothes in it. Sitting in the back seat, she dialed her boss's number and set the phone to speaker before pulling off her shoes and pantyhose.

"Kat. How'd we do today?"

"Thirty-seven new leads." She beamed as she changed into her favorite jeans. "Maybe half of them are legitimately interested."

"That's fantastic. I had my doubts about this one, but I'm impressed."

"Thank you."

She bent over to pull on her socks and suddenly felt dizzy. Leaning back, she rubbed her temples, trying to pay attention as her boss outlined a new conference opportunity. The world started tilting slowly to the left. Whenever she blinked, it would momentarily right itself before slipping off its axis again. Her stomach churned. *Oh God.* She fumbled with the door handle and threw up into the parking lot.

"Kat?"

Her mouth tasted like acid. "Sorry, gotta go. I'll submit the leads first thing Monday morning."

She hung up the phone and clutched her stomach. She should be screaming or jumping for joy, but felt only a vague sense of detached fascination, much like the first time she'd had sex.

She'd been in her dorm room at the University of Scranton with a guy she'd met during freshman orientation. They were watching a sex scene in some generic action movie when she decided she was tired of being a virgin. She'd expected to feel overwhelmed with love, pleasure, or even regret, but the reality was kind of boring. She didn't even bleed. Afterward, she went to class like any other day and no one looked at her any differently.

She finished getting changed and drove a mile down the road to the Target she'd passed on the way up. Inside, racks of tiny bikinis in all sorts of pretty colors and patterns greeted her. She smoothed the fabric of one top between her fingers. *Of course I'd get pregnant right before beach season.* Counting the months on her fingers, she estimated the baby would be born sometime around New Year's, so at least she'd have the weight off in plenty of time for next summer. That is, if there even *was* a baby. It might be food poisoning. That front desk guy did say the hotel food sucked.

In the pharmacy section, she scanned the shelves full of tests, aghast at the prices. Were women really dumb enough to pay that much for a glorified litmus strip? She grabbed a generic brand two-pack that was less than half the price of the others and got into the checkout lane. As she dug through her purse for her wallet, the elderly male clerk looked her up and down before shaking his head and scanning the box. She had a young face, and without her wedding ring or business attire, he probably assumed she was some irresponsible teenager. She fought back the urge to scream, *I'm 24 and married—I'm allowed to be pregnant, okay?*

With a gnawing feeling in the pit of her stomach, she locked herself in one of the public restroom stalls and sat on the toilet, reading the box. Two lines meant pregnant, one line meant not. In the movies, all you had to do was pee on the stick, but this test was more complicated. It came with a miniature eyedropper and a warning not to flood the test strip or it wouldn't work at all. Reaching between her legs, she managed to fill the eyedropper without making a mess. She carefully squeezed a single drop into the hole at the base.

Please be negative.

It was going to be hard telling Ian she'd changed her mind. Deep down she'd known the whole time she wasn't ready, but he was so excited. She thought she'd get there too once it actually happened, but now only felt more anxious. She held up the test as the liquid crept toward the clear lines, turning the first a dark purple, and the second a lighter shade of lavender. She was pregnant.

The fluorescent lights buzzed above her as she wrapped the test in toilet paper and stored it in her purse. Coming out of the stall, she caught her reflection in the long mirror over the row of sinks. Lifting her shirt, she turned sideways, admiring her mostly flat stomach. Maybe it wouldn't be so bad. Babies were only 6 or 7 pounds, not counting the extra padding and fluids. If she watched what she ate and exercised daily she might be able to keep the total gain to under 20 pounds. She pushed out her stomach as far as it would go, and used her arms to approximate the diameter of a basketball.

A high-pitched but distant wailing grew steadily louder as footsteps approached the door. She yanked down her shirt just as a young woman in sweatpants stormed into the bathroom, dragging a shrieking preschool aged boy behind her. His beet red face was scrunched up like a dried prune, and a glob of snot hung down from one nostril.

She shoved her hands under the faucet but kept watching in the mirror as the mother yanked the boy into a stall. As soon as she let go of his hand, he threw himself onto the tile and continuing screaming.

Holy Christ, what have I done?

The drive back to Scranton was a long stretch of interstate flanked by swaths of forest and tall rock walls where they'd blasted the mountains with dynamite to make room for the road. She'd grown up in the crowded bustle of Northeast Philadelphia, and the isolation of upstate Pennsylvania was still uncomfortable. If she ever became stranded away from a main road without a phone, she'd never be able to find her way home, and no one would hear her calls for help. She'd known nothing about the area when she chose a college here, only that the freedom of living two and a half hours away from home sounded glorious. She was grateful for that buffer again now. She'd have to tell her mom about the baby eventually, but at least she could take her time coming up with a plan first.

She'd avoided the torture of a micromanaged wedding by pretending she'd only gotten engaged two months prior when everything was already picked out and planned, but she couldn't fudge the dates with a baby—at least not by more than a few weeks. But she could worry about that later. Right now she had to figure out how to tell Ian, while pretending to be excited about it. She didn't want to make a big deal out of it, but casually mentioning it in conversation felt even weirder. *Hi honey, how was your day? Mine was good. The conference went well, and oh, by the way, I'm pregnant.*

She still hadn't figured it out by the time she arrived in the foyer of the small, grungy club. Mismatched guitar chords and drum beats echoed from the darkened stage where roadies were setting up instruments. Her hand shook as she held out her ID to the bouncer, who then wrapped a thick paper bracelet around her wrist and stepped aside so she could climb the stairs to the bar area. She wound her way through the sea of bodies smelling of sweat and pot until she spotted Ian at the bar, beer in hand.

Gripping her purse strap for courage, she squeezed in beside him and kissed him. "Did I miss much?"

"Only the first opener. They were decent, but nothing special." He held up his beer. "Want some?"

She couldn't have planned it better if she'd tried. "I don't think I should."

"Why n..." His eyes grew wide as his gaze darted toward her stomach. He ran a hand through his hair. "Holy shit."

She couldn't help but smile at his enthusiasm. Maybe this whole baby thing would grow on her faster than she thought. Until then, she'd have to fake it. "I took a test this afternoon."

He rubbed her stomach, still disbelieving. "There's a baby in there? *My* baby is in there?" She nodded. He laughed and turned to the bartender. "I'm gonna be a father!"

She stroked his cheek. "I hope it looks like you."

"Are you crazy? Who'd wanna be stuck with my face when they could have yours?"

"I love your face."

"I love *you*." He kissed her deeply until the laughing bartender interrupted with another beer for him, and a cola for her, on the house.

"First thing tomorrow, we'll call my mom and get a recommendation for a good doctor so we can get you checked out and started on vitamins."

She swirled the ice in her glass, biting her lip. "I don't know. I already have a doctor. Plus, I think it would be kind of romantic if we kept it a secret. At least for a little while."

He kissed her forehead. "Okay, but you still have to call the doctor on Monday."

The lights dimmed and the crowd cheered as the next band took the stage. She reached for his hand. "Come on, let's go!"

He stood still. "We'd better stay up here. I don't want you getting hurt in the pit."

Seriously? He was acting like he'd become *her* father. "I'll be fine. And the baby's the size of a dime—it's not gonna feel anything."

"I don't wanna take any chances." He led her toward the balcony railing. "We can see better from up here anyway."

If I wanted to see a concert from afar, I would've stayed at home and watched it on YouTube.

But the band was playing now, the volume making it impossible to have a conversation without screaming in each other's ears. She leaned her elbows on the railing and tried to enjoy the music, but a growing sense of dread gnawed at her. She would've expected to be treated like a frail flower by her mom or even well intentioned strangers, but Ian was her best friend. She couldn't shake the feeling that she'd just ruined the best thing that ever happened to her.

CHAPTER 6

Wade

The inside of the bedroom closet smelled of moth-balls and stale cigarettes, much like the rest of the house, only more condensed. Coughing, Wade reached up and tugged on the drawstring, the low-watt bulb illuminating yet another tightly packed collection of clothing and other probably useless things. Climbing onto the stepstool, he rummaged through the contents of the top shelf, but found only old tax returns, two bowling balls, and a plaque recognizing 30 years of service to a now defunct shoe company. Tapping his fingers against his legs, he glanced back at the already full cardboard boxes his mother had labelled "keep," "trash," and "good will." The sheer volume of stuff two people could accumulate over 60 years of marriage was staggering. Even if there were a gun, he was never going to find it.

Deciding he'd earned a break, he snuck past another bedroom where his mom and Aunt Sally were sorting through old photos and went down to the kitchen. For some reason, all the drinking glasses had a thin brown film lining the insides. Taking one to the sink to wash it, he spotted a door cracked open at the far end of the room and his heart skipped a beat.

On the other side of the door, steep wooden stairs led down to an unfinished basement, pale shafts of sunlight illuminating a dusty workbench at the bottom. He imagined his great uncle up late at night, drunk and missing his wife, and seeing the cracked door as an invitation. He probably stood in this very same spot, sizing up the fall to determine if it would kill him. Wade couldn't exactly blame him. If he felt this shitty losing his girlfriend of two years, he couldn't begin to imagine the devastation of losing the partner with whom you'd spent the majority of your life.

The warped steps creaked beneath his feet as he ventured into the gloom. At the bottom, he laid on the concrete floor to share what might've been Uncle Rick's last view. On one side was a folded up Ping-Pong table and a wicker chair set draped in cobwebs—on the other was a collection of vinyl records in a glass-fronted cabinet. It was sweet in a sad way. To anyone else, this stuff was junk, but Uncle Rick died among his memories.

"Wade," his mother called from somewhere upstairs.

Not wanting to have to explain himself, he scrambled to his feet and jumped the stairs two at a time, arriving in the kitchen right as she did. She brushed her fingers through his shaggy dark hair.

"What were you doing? You've got dirt all over you."

He pushed her hand away and rumpled his hair, pretending to be surprised at the debris that fell out. "I was looking for something to eat."

"Why don't you order a pizza? I've got cash in my purse."

"I have a job, Mom. I can afford pizza."

When the food came, they sat together in the dining room discussing the highlights of their finds. For the most part, Wade listened, debating whether it would be appropriate to ask for more details about the death. Eventually his curiosity won out.

"So how do they think it happened, anyway? Was he trying to go downstairs?"

Aunt Sally reached for another slice of pizza. "Well, it was the night before recycling day and there was a plastic shopping bag full of cans hanging right inside the door. They think he may have been reaching for it when he slipped and fell."

It was a plausible story, but the whole thing still seemed like too much of a coincidence. "Was he drunk?"

"Most likely." She took a bite of pizza, looking like she might cry.

Feeling bad, Wade changed the subject. "So I found a plaque from a shoe company. What did Uncle Rick used to do for a living?"

"That was Aunt Rita's." His mother dusted crumbs from her hands. "She was a secretary. Uncle Rick repaired power lines for the electric company."

"He climbed up telephone poles?" Wade could barely imagine Uncle Rick climbing the stairs.

"Yup. They both retired early, though, and traveled a lot. They have entire bookshelves full of photo albums upstairs. I have no idea where we're going to put them all."

"They used to take us everywhere when we were little," Aunt Sally chimed in. "We were like the children they never had."

"I even found photos from the time they took you boys to Nay Aug Park to see the Christmas lights," his mom said.

He had a flashbulb memory of sitting on a picnic bench in the snow and sharing a can of grape soda with Ian and Jeremy. He couldn't have been more than five years old. He wished he had clearer memories, but Aunt Rita's Alzheimer's had kicked in about that same time, and they slowly stopped coming around. All those adventures—at the end, did she remember any of them?

Losing his appetite, he stared at a framed black and white photo on the dining room wall. It looked like it was taken sometime in the 1940s when they were about the same age he was now. Uncle Rick looked like Dick Tracy in his fedora and trench coat and Aunt Rita's hair was pinned up in curls. They stood in front of a street corner café, smiling at each other like nothing else existed.

The photo haunted him the rest of the afternoon, even as he returned home and showered, scrubbing away the ashtray smell that clung to his skin and hair. They couldn't possibly have made it through 60 years of marriage without at least *occasionally* fighting or disappointing each other. Did they get through those hard times because they loved each other more than he and Jill did, or were they both merely too stubborn to give up?

Toweling off in his bedroom, he stared at his phone. Almost a month had gone by since he'd left Jill that voicemail and she hadn't called back. So much for staying friends.

He plopped down onto the bed in his underwear. He should've bought her a ring. At the time, it seemed like such a stupid thing to get upset over, but maybe the fact that he honestly thought it wouldn't matter only *proved* he didn't have what it took to be in a serious relationship. But he *wanted* to be in one. That had to count for something.

The line rang four times and went to voicemail again. He shut his eyes tight, holding back tears.

"Hey Jill, it's me. I did a lot of stupid things, and I'm sorry. I really need to talk to you." He hesitated, swallowing hard. "I miss you."

He hung up the phone and sobbed. Lying on the bed, he could almost see her there beside him, having dozed off as they watched a movie. Whenever she woke up, she'd swear she'd been awake the whole time. It was fucking adorable. And then there were the times she'd suddenly hug him so hard it hurt, but he loved it. He felt so important to her in those moments. But now she wouldn't even take his calls. How could everything she'd felt for him this whole time disappear like that?

Desperate for a distraction, he fired up his laptop and opened the game engine's character generator screen. He toggled through the options until he had a character who vaguely resembled himself—dark hair and light skin, but much taller, with a t-shirt, jeans, and sneakers ensemble. He then switched over to the terrain screen with its large, empty grid and dozens of customization tools. The technology would let him create just about anything he wanted, but he had zero idea what the game's goal should be. Staring at the empty screen, he felt the tears threaten to return.

He picked up his phone again and called Rob. "Let's go bowling."

The bustling alley energized him, and it felt good to be amongst the world of the living again. Leaning against a rack of colorful bowling balls, Wade checked his texts. Ian and Kat were busy and Drew refused to come because Rob was there. He pointed at the text on his phone screen. "Drew's still mad at you."

"Good." Rob bent over and laced up his bowling shoes.

Wade rolled his eyes. "Can't you apologize already?"

"Why would I apologize when I'm not sorry?"

"Because now I'm stuck in the middle of it. I can't invite the whole group out anymore without worrying about who's mad at who."

"Sure you can. If he doesn't wanna show up, that's his problem."

"No, it's mine. Because if I invite everyone, I'm effectively excluding *him*, but if I leave you out so he'll come, then I'm excluding *you*. Either way, I have to choose between friends and I don't like it."

Rob picked up a neon orange ball and tested it for weight. "I don't know what to tell you, Wade. I'm not gonna pretend to be sorry."

Wade threw his arms in the air. "Did you even *like* Caitlin?"

"She was mad cool. She hates Drew almost as much as I do."

"You don't really hate him."

Rob sized up his shot and sent the ball rolling down the lane. "I assure you, he hates me just as much. Maybe more."

"He does not."

"He just hides it better because he's so concerned with looking like the bigger person."

Scowling, Wade watched the family in the next lane. A young boy struggled to carry a ball to the edge of the lane and then dropped it to the floor with a thud. It inched about a quarter of the way down before coming to a stop alongside the bumper.

Wade picked up a ball and waited for the pins to re-set. Why did Rob always have to drag this shit out for so long? It wasn't like they were really going to throw away more than 10 years of friendship over some girl neither of them actually wanted to date. But then again, the idea of Rob fucking Jill made him livid. Ten years from now, he hoped he wouldn't care. But honestly, he probably still would.

"What did you mean when you said you never liked Jill?" Wade asked.

"Exactly what it sounds like."

"But *what* didn't you like? Specifically."

"She was always talking shit about you right in front of your face. Like that time she went on and on about your trip to New York and how she didn't get to see everything she wanted because you overslept and then got lost."

Wade rolled his ball down the lane, remembering how Jill had flipped out in the car and refused to talk to him again until they'd finally crossed the George Washington Bridge. She had a point about the oversleeping, but the road closures weren't his fault, and anyone would've gotten confused navigating those weird New Jersey detours.

"Why didn't you say anything before?"

"I did. Every few months or so."

"Name one time."

"Last year—right before Thanksgiving. We were playing Cranium at my place and she pitched a fit be-cause she was tired of always being your partner. She made us draw names from a hat, but got stuck with you anyway and sulked until I agreed to take you so she could have Kat. I said, 'It's pretty bad when your own girlfriend doesn't wanna be your partner.'"

"It doesn't count as a warning if you say it as a joke."

"Would you have listened if I'd straight up said, 'Dude, your girlfriend's a bitch and you should dump her?'"

Wade hesitated, as the return belt spit out the ball. "Probably not."

"Exactly."

He picked up the ball and bowled again, this time straight into the gutter. Over in the next lane, a gorgeous bowling attendant with fire engine red hair walked up the beam between the lanes and dislodged the little boy's stranded ball with a long pole.

"You gonna try and get some of that?"

Wade whirled around to see Rob smirking at him. "What? No! I'm nowhere near ready for that yet."

"Yeah, right. You haven't been single for more than a few weeks since middle school."

"This is different. I didn't think I was gonna marry any of them."

Rob crossed his arms, staring at him over the rims of his glasses. Wade's face grew warm.

"Okay, fine. I did. But that was a long time ago, and I had no idea what I was talking about. I actually proposed to this girl."

Rob slapped him on the shoulder. "No offense, but you have no idea how to be alone. Give it a few more weeks and you'll be up to your eyeballs in pussy again."

The redhead walked back to the counter, her khakis clinging to her perfectly round ass. If she said she wanted him he'd probably be down. It would be sexy and fun—but then what? If they kept seeing each other, they'd eventually fight about *something*, and then he'd have to learn to compromise in all new ways. Even the thought was exhausting.

Back in his apartment that night, the electric hum from the refrigerator made him feel even lonelier than before. It was all Jill's fault. She'd made him get the stupid place and then bailed. It only had one bedroom so he couldn't get a roommate, but he also couldn't afford to break the lease. Living with his parents could be a pain in the ass but at least he'd still felt connected to the rest of the world.

Collapsing onto the couch, he flipped through TV channels until he landed on a pool tournament, the announcers chatting in low, bored tones as middle aged men knocked balls into holes with sticks. He pictured himself as an 88-year-old man, sitting alone in front of the TV and drinking vodka out of a dirty glass while much younger men knocked balls into holes with sticks. It was a wonder Uncle Rick hadn't killed himself much sooner.

Rolling onto his back, he caught a glimpse of something bright moving in his darkened bedroom. It was the laptop's screen saver. He sat up suddenly. The idea seemed kind of silly at first, but might just work. He jogged over to the laptop where his video game hero waited patiently for an objective. Toggling to the character screen, he changed his hair from black to grey and named him *Rick*.

The crowd at the sports bar erupted into a roar, clinking their glasses together as Wade hurried toward the cracked leather booth. He slid in across from Ian and Kat, and next to Drew, who was on the phone.

"Sorry, Mom. I'm still at work. I'll probably be here a while. Why don't you call Uncle Bob instead?" Drew rolled his eyes as Wade bounced in his seat, motioning for him to hurry up. "Okay. Yeah, that's fine. See you later." Drew hung up the phone and then cocked his head to the side in a show of exaggerated attention. "Yes, Wade?"

Wade placed both hands palms-down on the table. "You guys are never gonna believe this." He paused for dramatic effect. "I've decided to make a video game." He smiled and sat back, waiting for the awed reactions, but they all just stared at him as if still waiting for the announcement. "Guys—I'm programming a *full-length video game*."

Kat broke the silence. "That sounds really cool."

"Thank you, Kat. It is indeed cool."

Ian raised his eyebrows in that obnoxious way that always made Wade feel like a complete idiot. "You're doing this by yourself?"

Wade narrowed his eyes. Why did Ian always have to shit on his parade? "Yes, by myself."

"I'm just saying, it's a lot of work." Ian leaned forward, affecting his know-it-all tone. "There's graphics, animation, sound effects—not to mention a shitload of coding and debugging. It takes professional companies *years* to finish a game. You really think you could stick with such a complicated project for that long?"

He wasn't sure at all, but would be damned if he let his brother think he got to him. "Yeah, I do."

Ian shrugged. "Okay, then." He folded his hands on the table. "Actually, the reason Kat and I invited you guys out tonight is because we have some news of our own. We're having a baby."

"Holy shit, congratulations!" Drew reached over the table and shook Ian's hand before getting up to hug Kat. Wade crossed his arms and leaned back in the booth. Where was even a fraction of this excitement a minute ago? Drew plopped back down, clearly in awe. "When's the due date?"

Ian beamed. "January 9th—same as Wade."

Wade forced a smile, but couldn't help feeling steamrolled. Even his birthday wouldn't be about him anymore. He picked apart the breading on an onion ring as Ian rattled off a bunch of pregnancy facts as if he hadn't just looked them all up on the Internet that morning.

Drew only fed the flames, leaning forward and asking all sorts of questions when he hadn't bothered to say a damn thing about the game. Wade shifted in his seat. "So I guess no one cares about what *I'm* doing." He hated how petty he sounded, but this was the one good thing he had going on right now.

Ian raised his eyebrows. "Seriously, Wade? We're having a baby. We can talk about your little game project later."

"You could've at least waited until I was done talking instead of interrupting me."

"I didn't realize you had more to say."

"I know a guy down in New York," Drew cut in, scrolling through the contact list in his phone. "He went to Pratt and has friends in the gaming industry. If you're serious, he could probably hook you up."

Wade sulked as Drew scribbled his friend's name and number onto the back of one of his own business cards. None of them thought he could do it. Maybe Jill was right—his past was littered with flashes of brilliance that never came to fruition. Everything he'd ever accomplished was the result of someone else caring enough to work out the details and push him forward.

Across the table, Kat looked as bored as he was while Ian went on about the differences between nurses and midwives.

Wade leaned toward her. "Wanna play pinball?"

She nodded enthusiastically.

Back near the bathrooms was an old pinball machine that played the first few notes of *Mary Had a Little Lamb* every time you hit the bonus coil. He fished in his pockets for quarters, and handed two to Kat.

"You don't seem excited about the baby."

She pressed the quarters into the slot and pulled back on the ball launcher. "I'm not even out of the first trimester yet. I guess I don't wanna get too attached in case I wind up miscarrying."

"That makes sense." It was still an odd thing for a girl to say, though. He tapped his fingers against the side of the machine. "Has Jill said anything about me since we broke up?"

"She hasn't spoken to me since the wedding. I tried calling when I heard what happened, but she never called back."

"What about before the wedding? Did she say anything about being mad at me?"

She shook her head. "Sorry. I liked her, but we weren't really that close."

"But she was your maid of honor."

Kat shrugged. "Most of my friends are guys."

"She said she wanted to stay friends, but hasn't returned my calls. Do you think she meant it?"

"She probably just said it to make herself feel less shitty about dumping you."

He sighed. "I was afraid of that." The ball fell past the flippers and the cabinet dimmed.

"Do you really wanna be friends with her, or just win her back?"

"Well, obviously I want her back, but I'll take what I can get." He laughed. "That sounds pathetic, doesn't it?"

"A little bit." She leaned on the machine. "Maybe you should stop calling."

"You're probably right."

"Do you want me to delete her number from your phone?"

He rubbed the back of his neck. That seemed so permanent. But then again, he wasn't doing himself any favors by acting desperate. He squeezed his eyes shut as he handed his phone over.

Lounging on the couch with his laptop later that night, Wade browsed through a website of royalty-free music. *Take that, Ian. I don't need musicians—I have the entire Internet!* As he clicked around, downloading songs that held promise for his game, a long forgotten but immediately familiar chirping noise sounded on the computer.

It couldn't be—she hadn't used instant messenger in over a year. But there was her screen name, bolded, right at the top of his friends' list. It was like she somehow *knew* he'd deleted her number and was rubbing his face in it. He didn't believe in signs, but wasn't above taking advantage of an opportunity.

He opened a chat window and started typing, but before he could hit send she went offline again.

Fuck my life.

His phone was lying on the coffee table. Sure, the contact name was gone, but her number would still be in the call history. He rubbed his face. *One last time. If she doesn't answer I'm done for good.* He held his breath as the line rang four times and went to voicemail, as it had every other time.

"Hey, it's Wade. Thought maybe if you didn't have plans tonight you could come over and watch a movie with me. Just as friends. Call me back. Or don't."

He cleared his phone history of all calls and texts and then removed her from instant messenger and all social media sites. She rarely used them, but he needed to be absolutely sure she wouldn't randomly pop up again.

He awoke some time later to his phone vibrating on his chest. He must've fallen asleep on the couch. The screen glowed with an unfamiliar number.

"Hello?"

"Hey. Sorry I didn't answer earlier. I was at a concert."

Holy fuck. Heart racing, he sat up like a bolt, clutching the phone to his ear with both hands. "It's okay. Who did you see?"

"Some metal band. My friend had an extra ticket."

"How was it?"

"It was alright." She paused. "Did you still wanna watch a movie?"

He glanced at the clock. It was after midnight. "Yeah, sure. Come on over."

He hurried around the apartment gathering trash, and then threw a bag of popcorn in the microwave before brushing his teeth and changing into a clean t-shirt and pajama pants. The doorbell rang as he kicked the pile of dirty laundry into the closet. He brushed his hair down with his hands as he approached the front door.

Jill stood on his doorstep wearing shorts, a tank top, and no bra. He didn't know whether to curse the universe or thank it. "I made popcorn," he said, trying not to stare.

"Awesome." She kicked off her flip flops and walked right past him into the bedroom.

His heart raced. Maybe she wasn't here for a movie at all. But if he had even the slightest chance of getting back with her, he'd need to be careful not to blow it by saying anything stupid or making a move too soon.

He dumped the popcorn into a bowl and followed her into the bedroom where she sat on his bed flipping through a wallet of movies as if nothing had changed. She hadn't turned on any lights, so the room was still dark except for the glow from the TV at the foot of the bed.

Remember, you're just friends unless she says otherwise.

He sat on the bed beside her, leaning back against the wall. "I heard Alkaline Trio has a new album coming out," he said, trying to keep it casual.

"I don't know if I'm gonna get it."

"Why not? I thought you loved them."

"I do. Or I did, anyway. I'm not sure if it's me or them, but I didn't feel anything when I heard the new single." She pulled *Monty Python's The Meaning of Life* from the wallet and crawled toward the PlayStation, making sure he got a full view of her ass along the way. He kept the popcorn bowl firmly in his lap as she crawled back and sat beside him, resting her head on his shoulder. It felt so good having her close again, even if this was all they could ever be. He played with her hair as the FBI warning appeared on the screen.

"Why do you think it might be you?"

"I don't know. Lately I don't feel much of anything. It's like I'm watching my life happen to someone else." She rubbed his thigh lightly, the way she used to when she wanted sex but didn't want to come out and say it.

Fuck it. I'm never gonna be able to be friends with her anyway.

He tilted her face up and kissed her, lightly at first, but as soon as she kissed back he ditched the popcorn bowl and rolled on top of her, kissing her neck and pushing down her shorts and underwear until his fingers reached the warm space between her thighs. She hugged his neck so tight he almost couldn't breathe until her whole body tensed and she let out a small moan. He kept at it until she came two more times and he could barely take it anymore. "Are you still on the pill?"

She nodded and he yanked his own pants down and plunged himself deep inside her. Holy lord he'd missed this. It wasn't long before he shuddered and then collapsed in a sweaty heap beside her. "I love you." The words slipped out before he knew what he was saying.

She pulled up her shorts. "This isn't a thing, okay?"

"Okay." He grinned, admiring her form as she tied her hair back in a messy bun. She never did like to admit when she was wrong, but if she wanted to fool around in the meantime, he wouldn't complain. He pulled her back down beside him, but she pushed his arm away.

"I can't stay. I'm going down the shore with my sister tomorrow morning."

"Tell her I said hi."

She smiled awkwardly as she stood up. "See you later."

He reached for his pants. "Hold on, I'll walk you out." But she was already halfway out the door.

"It's okay. I'll let myself out."

He turned off the movie and cracked open the window above his bed, a cool breeze blowing across his hot face. Crickets chirped in the bushes outside as he lay back down, smiling. It wasn't quite perfect, but he'd take it.

CHAPTER 7

Eleanor

The scanner hummed as the black and white image appeared on the screen, segment by segment. A family of five stood on the front steps of a modest A-frame church, the father in a ditto suit and bowler cap, the mother in a dark high-necked dress, and the three teenaged daughters in matching white frocks. Using the clone tool, Eleanor touched up a few minor scratches and age stains around the edges of the photo. This one was fairly clean, unlike the last, which required over two hours of work replicating the twists and turns of an intricate wrought iron fence across a two-inch tear.

Leaning back in her desk chair, she studied the family's faces, imagining what they'd been like. The father's lips were tightly drawn, but there was a softness around his eyes. He was probably only stern in public, or when one of the girls misbehaved. The youngest was probably in trouble the most. Despite the obligatory serious expression of the times, she had an unmistakable glint in her eye, unlike the middle daughter, whose large sunken eyes seemed inconsolably sad.

Eleanor glanced at the accompanying fact sheet. *Reverend Charles Fleischer and family, Resurrection Church of Scranton, 1897.*

Resting her chin in her palm, she studied the photo again. For every person history deemed worth remembering, there were countless more it unceremoniously forgot. Most of the time, it was nearly impossible to find out the identities of these anonymous strangers, but if this was a family from the area then their birth certificates might be on file upstairs.

The hardwood floors creaked lightly beneath her feet as she passed by a few solitary patrons, their spines bent over thick reference books. A printed copy of the photo in hand, she pulled open a shallow metal filing drawer, the delicious smell of decades-old typewriter ink greeting her as she scanned the neat grid of microfilm boxes inside. Finding the one labelled *Birth Certificates, 1878-1905, E-G*, she took it to the nearby reader and spooled the film through the machine. She always felt a strong and immediate sense of the infinite toggling through these faded sheets of parchment with their rigidly formal cursive handwriting. Relics of another time, they were older than any currently living person.

The first Fleischer on record was a girl, Anna, born in 1881 to Charles and Margaret. Beaming, Eleanor copied the information onto the back of the photo. A few slides further she found Clara, born in 1887, but that was it. No more Fleischers born to Charles or Margaret. She examined the image again and did the math. At ages 16 and 10, Anna and Clara were clearly the oldest and youngest, leaving only the middle daughter with the sad eyes unaccounted for.

Don't worry. I'll find out who you were.

She found the library manager, Carmen, in the main foyer redecorating the display cabinet with a summer theme.

"Where do we keep the physical copies of genealogy records?"

"They're in storage at City Hall. Why?"

"I need to find a birth certificate from the 1880s."

"Registering births and deaths wasn't required by law in Pennsylvania until 1906." Carmen stapled a construction paper sun to the wall. "Trust me, if it's not on microfilm, we don't have it."

"But both the older and younger children had them."

"Then it was probably lost." She said it so casually, as if losing the record of someone's existence was nothing to get upset over.

Eleanor scuffed the toe of her oxford against the hardwood floor. "Thanks anyway."

"While you're up, could you cover the circulation desk for an hour or so? Penny has a doctor's appointment."

Eleanor glanced over at the line that was five patrons deep and cringed. Of all the times she could've come upstairs. "Sure thing," she said, trying not to sound annoyed. It wasn't Penny's fault. She was 80 years old and suffered from a host of medical issues. It was still obnoxious having to cover for her, though, especially when the public was involved. Squaring her shoulders, Eleanor strode behind the desk. She cleared her throat to access that deeper, more guttural voice she'd refined over the years for situations such as these.

"I can help the next patron over here."

Once the line and Penny were both gone, she plopped onto the stool next to the returns bin and began stacking books according to section, the tension slowly draining from her shoulders. Maybe Charles and Margaret's middle daughter was an orphan they'd adopted and raised as their own—either a relative's child, or a girl from the congregation. There might even be a newspaper article about it.

"Howdy," a voice called out. A girl around her own age with short dark hair and a polka dot blouse balanced a plastic bin full of books against her hip. "I'm here with your daily adult book delivery."

Eleanor blinked, sure she'd misheard. "Excuse me?"

The girl laughed. "They're books from your library that got returned to the children's library next door. I call them adult books because Penny doesn't get it." She plopped the bin on the counter. "You must be the new librarian. Eleanor?"

Eleanor nodded, dumping the contents of the bin with the other returns.

"Nice. When I heard your name, I assumed you were Penny's age."

"Nope." Feeling awkward standing there, she started scanning a pile of books into the computer, trying to look busy, but the girl didn't get the hint.

"I'm Natalie, by the way." She stretched out a hand, and Eleanor reluctantly shook it.

"Nice to meet you." *Now will you please go away?* She dropped her hand and continued scanning books.

"Listen, I gotta get back for story time, but I'm free around one if you wanna grab lunch."

Grab lunch. That was exactly the kind of obnoxious thing her old housemates used to say.

"Oh, no thanks. I have someplace else to go on my break today." Really, she'd planned on eating lunch in her office, but it was nice out and she hadn't stopped by Trent's apartment at this time of day yet.

"Cool. Maybe another time, then."

"Sounds good." If she stayed pleasant and non-committal, Natalie would probably forget all about her the minute she walked out the door. Those fake nice types usually did.

Fine droplets of sweat oozed down the back of her neck as she ate her turkey sandwich. Without air conditioning, it was much hotter than she'd thought, but she didn't want to call attention to herself by keeping the car running. She tied her long brown hair back into a ponytail and cracked open the window. Further down the street, a couple of kids bopped a beach ball around on their lawn while the mailman trudged from house to house, sliding thin bundles into the boxes along the sidewalk.

She sighed. Writing a letter would probably be easier, but she needed to see him first—partly to prove he really existed, but mostly to see who he'd become. So much could change in 10 years. What if he had a serious girlfriend or was married? She crumpled up her sandwich wrapper and shoved it into the brown paper bag.

You're getting ahead of yourself again. He might not even remember you.

She thought back to that day in history class, the students chattering on as they hurried about, rearranging their seats. Peeking out from behind the curtain of her hair, she clutched her backpack strap as she approached a girl sitting alone near the front. But right as she was about to speak, another girl plopped her books down on the first girl's desk.

Hating herself for not acting sooner, Eleanor scanned the room for her default partner, but was the only one left alone. She ached to scream, run away, or simply keel over and die, but instead just stood there holding back tears. Teachers who didn't check the number of students before assigning group work ought to be fired. Stepping around carelessly tossed backpacks, she approached Mr. Tomaselli's desk.

"Excuse me," she said, her voice catching in her throat. "There's an odd number of students. Can I work by myself?"

"One group of three is fine."

She glanced over her shoulder at the sea of strangers, dreading having to intrude upon an already established pair.

"I don't mind working alone." She looked directly into his eyes, silently pleading with him to understand, but without even a hint of discretion he called out to a pair of girls sitting near the windows.

"Abby, Marissa—you're going to be a group of three."

Wishing death upon him, she kept her head down to avoid the inevitable stares as she took a seat. The girls barely looked at her before continuing their conversation. Relieved, she opened her text and started looking up the answer to the first question. If she were lucky, it would take the rest of the class period to complete the assignment, so she wouldn't have to sit around awkwardly doing nothing. Finding the answer, she copied it carefully into her notebook.

"Why are you so quiet?" one of the girls suddenly asked, wrinkling her nose.

Eleanor cringed. "I'm doing the assignment."

"Well, talk more. You're creeping me out."

You didn't even invite me to be part of the conversation, she wanted to say, but only mumbled an "okay" as she continued writing.

"Do you have a boyfriend?" the other asked. According to the glittery writing on her notebook, she was Abby.

"Yeah," Eleanor replied, hoping it would prove she was normal and they'd drop it.

"Who?"

She stayed as generic as possible. "His name is John."

"John who?"

"Smith." *Oh no, I didn't just say that out loud.*

Marissa snorted. "Like Pocahontas?"

Abby narrowed her eyes. "What school does he go to?"

Eleanor picked at the frayed edges of her textbook. She didn't dare say Dunmore, but didn't know the names of any of the neighboring schools.

"It's on the Army base," she finally said, praying they wouldn't know there *weren't* any schools on the base, which was why she was at Dunmore in the first place.

Abby studied her for a few more seconds before turning back to Marissa and talking about some music video.

Breathing a silent sigh of relief, Eleanor stared out the window at the empty football field and dense woods beyond, willing time to speed up. If it could fast forward three more years, even better. College would be full of smart people who were actually there to learn, not a bunch of stupid girls obsessed with boyfriends and music videos.

Looking up at the board for the next question, she accidently locked eyes with a boy dressed all in black with a collection of wallet chains hanging from his pants. Her stomach flipped and she jerked her head around, staring at her textbook and pretending to read. The last thing she needed was some scary guy's attention.

Abby waved a hand in her face. "I asked you a question." Both girls were staring at her.

"What?"

"Do you like Bush?"

She'd heard of the band, but wasn't familiar with their songs. "Yeah, they're cool."

"I knew it," Abby said as both girls giggled. Eleanor looked from one to the other, waiting for someone to explain what was so funny.

"What about The Wilted Flowers?" Marissa asked.

Eleanor hadn't heard of them at all. "Sure. They're cool too." The girls laughed even harder, and her whole body tensed. "What's so funny?"

"The Wilted Flowers don't exist. I made them up."

Tears welled up in her eyes. She bowed her head, letting her hair fall across her face to hide them, but it didn't work.

"Oh my God, are you crying?"

"No." She flipped through the pages of the text, the words growing blurry.

"She's totally crying."

At the front of the room, Mr. Tomaselli's back was turned as he helped another group of students. This might be her only chance. She dumped her books into her backpack and stood up.

"I have to go to the bathroom," she muttered.

Warm tears streamed down her face as she hurried through the locker-lined hallway, searching for the girls' room and despising every ounce of her being. She'd promised herself it would be different this time—that she'd talk to people and make friends—but when it came down to it, she simply didn't know how to be anything but herself.

Hearing voices on the other side of the bathroom door, she ducked into the empty auditorium instead and climbed up behind the heavy stage curtain. The area was cool and quiet, lit by pale light streaming through the windows of the double doors near the back. She plopped down on a musty couch, wiping her eyes with her sweater sleeve.

"Are you okay?"

She whirled around, knocking her backpack onto the floor. The boy in black leaned against a stack of cardboard boxes, his long dark hair in his eyes, looking like some kind of Goth Elvis.

"I'm fine." She stared at the wooden floorboards, willing him to go away, but the clinking of his wallet chains grew louder until his sneakers appeared beside her backpack. He picked it up and handed it to her as he took a seat at her side.

"Thanks," she whispered. His ice blue eyes seemed to pierce right through her. She looked away, clutching her backpack to her chest.

"What school did you transfer from?" he asked.

"You wouldn't know it. It's in the middle of nowhere, Kentucky."

"Why did you leave?"

She hesitated, wondering why he was asking all these questions, but figured the information was harmless enough. "My dad's in the Army."

"Did he ever kill anyone?"

"I don't know." It was such a strange thing to ask, but something she'd also wondered. "He went to Iraq for a few months during the Gulf War, but doesn't like to talk about it."

The boy laid an arm across the back of the couch, dangerously close to her neck. She felt like she might throw up.

"Don't worry about those girls. Abby's always been a bitch, and Marissa's trying to impress her because she's in love with her."

"How do you know that?"

"It's a small school." He paused. "You can sit with me next time if you want."

"Okay," she said quietly, not knowing whether she actually would.

He stood up, his height towering over her. "Come on, let's go to the computer lab or something."

"Won't we get in trouble for leaving class?" She was already worried about walking out of History. The last thing she needed was to be caught walking around school without a pass.

"I ditch Tomaselli's class all the time. He doesn't really care as long as you show up for tests."

"But what if another teacher sees us?"

He shrugged. "You just gotta act like you belong wherever you are. Then nobody questions it."

His advice ran through her head again as she got out of the car and walked casually across the street. *I'm simply coming home from work and getting my mail.* Inside the box were two junk fliers addressed to *Current Resident,* and an envelope from Budget Rent-A-Car's human resources department with his name in bold capital letters— *TRENT ZARELLA.* Her stomach lurched. This wasn't a daydream anymore. It was actually happening.

She shoved the mail back into the box and hurried to her car, her mind already racing with plans. She could easily pretend to need a rental. And she'd need to show a driver's license to get it, so even if he didn't recognize her face, her name might trigger his memory. It was perfect, really. She'd dodge the awkwardness of knocking at his door like some pathetic weirdo, and put all the responsibility of making the first move on him. And if for some reason he still didn't make the connection, she could pretend to recognize him at the last second—especially if he wore a name tag.

She blew air slowly out through her nose, trying to keep her heart rate down as she wandered through the airport's baggage claim area. Following the signs for rental cars, she mentally confirmed her story. *I need to rent a truck this Saturday. I'm helping a coworker move.* It was an expensive ruse. She'd probably be stuck eating peanut butter sandwiches and ramen noodles for the next month to make up for it, but it would be well worth it if it worked. Someday they might even laugh about it.

Reaching Budget's doorway, she craned her neck to check out the employees behind the counter—a woman, an older man, and a tall younger man with slick black hair. Her chest constricted so tight she could barely breathe. It might be him, but she was too far away to tell for sure.

Heart racing a mile ahead of her, she joined the line of suitcase-dragging patrons.

As she got closer, she squinted, trying to make out a further resemblance. His build was about right, but a thick beard obscured most of his face. She bit her lip. Over the years, she'd imagined hundreds of scenarios where they'd meet again, but never considered one in which *she* didn't recognize *him.*

"Hey Anthony," the female employee called out. "Do we still have that Chevy Tahoe?"

He turned around. "Nope. Gave it out a few minutes ago."

Anthony. Not Trent.

Fighting the urge to cry, she ducked under the rope barrier and hurried back to the parking lot. She yanked the car door closed and screamed, pounding the side of her fists against the steering wheel. The hot car air filled her lungs, and for a moment, she felt like she was suffocating. Coughing, she turned on the air conditioning and slumped back into the seat.

There were seven days in a week and at least two shifts per day, which meant coming back at least 14 times to cover all the bases—but that still wouldn't take into account vacation days, or a job other than the front office. She groaned.

Knock on his door and get it over with. If he's not at work, he might be home right now.

She imagined Trent—who now looked more like Anthony—standing in the doorway of his second floor duplex with a puzzled expression on his face. What would she even say?

I don't know if you remember me, but my name's Eleanor Brown. We went to high school together for less than a month, so I decided to move 12 hours away and show up randomly on your doorstep. Want to hang out?

At best it would be awkward. At worst he'd laugh and slam the door in her face. Stalking his workplace wasn't any less crazy, but at least it afforded her the dignity of pretending it was a chance encounter. She'd waited 10 years—she could wait another couple days.

CHAPTER 8

Ian

Ian looked up at the clock—only 11 minutes until the bell rang. Outside, a truck beeped as it backed up and a thin breeze carried the diesel fumes through the open windows, making the stuffy classroom even more unbearable. Near the back, two girls were passing notes and a total of four students had their heads down. One appeared to be genuinely asleep. Leaning his backside against the teacher's desk, Ian cleared his throat and shuffled through a thick folder of paper.

"By now most of you have taken the SAT at least once, but anyone who hasn't needs to do so by November at the latest. Does anyone need the form to sign up?" A few pairs of glazed-over eyes stared weakly back at him, the rest intently focused on their desks or out the windows. He couldn't blame them. In the history of the world, nothing of substance had ever gotten done during the last week of school, yet they were still required to show up and pretend to care until it was officially over. Hell, he was probably only asked to give this last minute presentation to the juniors so the English teacher could skip four of her own class periods.

"Okay, I promise this is the last thing you'll have to do today," he said, passing out forms from the stack in his folder. "It's a quick survey about what you're looking for in a college in case anything's changed since you filled it out last fall. Come September, we'll be meeting with each of you individually to go over the results and help put your application packages together."

As they started on the survey, he loosened his tie and sank into the teacher's chair, beads of sweat dribbling down his back. Eight more minutes until he could go back to the air-conditioned bliss of the counseling suite. A hulking boy with a full beard and untucked uniform shirt raised his hand. Ian checked the seating chart taped to the desk.

"Yes, Tim?"

"What if we don't know our major yet?" He had the deepest voice Ian had ever heard in a high school student.

"Pick two or three subjects that interest you the most. Over half of all college students change their majors at least once anyway. I was one of them."

Satisfied with the answer, Tim hunched over his too-small desk and returned to filling in bubbles. Despite his adult appearance, he was otherwise still so childlike in demeanor. Looking out at all these almost-adults, Ian became uncomfortably aware that they were all someone's child. Someone had given birth to them, raised them, and was now preparing to send them off into the world. How did Tim's parents feel about their woolly mammoth of a son who didn't have a clue what he wanted to do with the rest of his life—disappointed, proud, nonchalant?

He always sort of assumed his eventual children would be smart and well-behaved, but what if they turned out to be idiots or criminals? He might as well have picked a random name from the phone book and made a life-long commitment to that person. His head spun. In no other life situation did people routinely act so recklessly.

Closing his eyes, he pointed a finger at the seating chart. *Susan Owens.* She was one of the girls who'd been passing notes earlier—short, blonde, and a little on the chubby side, with her uniform skirt hiked up so high he could see her boxer shorts underneath. He remembered sitting in the orchestra pit with Drew during band and looking up the skirts of the glee club girls on stage. What if one of them had been his daughter?

Banishing the thought from his mind, he instructed the students to pass their surveys forward as he handed out another stack of papers.

"This last sheet is a series of five common essay prompts on college applications. They'll be your first major English assignments next year. You don't have to do anything now, but it won't hurt to start thinking about them this summer."

From the back of the room came a clear, point-blank voice. "That's not a fair assignment." Rob's younger sister Darryn had a pixie haircut, a collection of bracelets up each arm, and a reputation for getting into pointless debates with her teachers—very much like her brother did.

"Like I said, you don't have to do it if you don't want to."

"Not your assignment, the one for English class." She held up the paper with disdain. "Some of us might not have any of these questions on our applications, and none of us will have all of them. It seems like a lot of busywork with very little payoff."

He straightened the stack of surveys in his hands. "You have to write essays all year anyway, so I don't see the difference. They're all gonna help you become a better writer, but at least these will help you get to know yourself better in the process."

She scoffed. "I already know myself."

Thankfully, the bell rang, releasing him from any obligation to argue further. "Then take it up with your teacher next year."

Back in the counseling suite, he collapsed into his desk chair, regretting how he'd handled Darryn's defiance. Passing the buck at work where he was still the low man on the totem pole was one thing, but soon he and Kat would become the ultimate authorities on someone else's entire life. He didn't feel nearly prepared for it.

His supervisor, Amy, stuck her head out of her office. "Sister Augustine wants to see you before you leave today."

Ian's heart stalled. Even when you were on staff, it was still scary when the principal wanted to see you. "What does she want?"

"She didn't say."

Shit.

While walking down to the main office, he mentally ran down a list of things he might've done wrong, as well as the excuses he could give for each. She was probably upset about the low turnout for Career Day, but it wasn't his decision to hold it the Friday before Memorial Day when half the professionals he invited were going on vacation. Or maybe Tyrell's parents were still angry about the missed scholarship opportunity and took their complaint up the ladder—but what did they expect when their son didn't ask for the recommendation letter until the day before it was due?

On the bulletin board in front of the main office, he spotted a flyer for the annual end of year picnic, and his heart sank. It made sense. If she was letting someone go, this was the best time to do it. No need to find a replacement mid-year or make awkward announcements. Even if he hadn't royally fucked up, it was no secret that Catholic schools across the country were going broke. But no matter the reason, he'd still have to go home and explain to Kat that he'd managed to lose his job right as they were about to have a baby.

Maybe Keystone College would let him have his admissions mailroom job back. If not, he might be able to take on a few SAT tutoring gigs over the summer until he found something permanent.

Sister Augustine's door was open. Sitting at her thick mahogany desk, she glanced up from her computer, a large wooden crucifix mounted on the wall behind her. She dressed like a regular businesswoman aside from the habit that covered all of her hair except for a tuft of silver bangs.

"Close the door behind you."

That didn't sound promising. He took a seat in one of the leather chairs facing her desk, feeling like he was 15 again. He'd only gotten one detention in his entire school career and sat sweating in this very chair as Sister Augustine drilled him on why he thought it was okay to lie to a teacher. He'd copied down the wrong due date for an important paper and panicked as the teacher began collecting them. He told her he'd left it at home and she mercifully gave him a one-day extension. Everything would've been fine if she hadn't walked by his lunch table later that day and caught him bragging about it.

"You wanted to see me?"

Sister Augustine folded her hands on the desk. "I'd like to thank you for your hard work this year. You consistently go above and beyond, and the faculty and staff all sing your praises. Career Day was especially well-organized, and I'm told that was your doing." She paused and he waited for the catch. "As you may or may not know, Amy is expecting and has decided not to return next year. I'd like to offer you her position as head college counselor."

He stared at her dumbly. He *hadn't* known Amy was pregnant, and was he really just offered her job?

"Yes." He smiled wide, giddy with relief and excitement. "Yes, I'd love to take the job. Thank you!"

He whistled a Less Than Jake song as he hopped up the front steps to his house, mind already whizzing with ideas for next year. He usually beat Kat home by at least an hour, but she sat at the dining room table with her laptop open, dressed in a tank top and pajama pants with her cellphone wedged between her shoulder and ear. Behind her, the sliding glass door to the deck was open, filling the whole first floor with warm light. He dropped his wallet and keys on the table beside the door and hugged her from behind.

"Tell him I'm putting the packets together right now. They'll be on his desk tomorrow morning in plenty of time for the flight." Kat rolled her eyes and mouthed *blah, blah, blah* as she squeezed his arm with her free hand. "Yes, I know. That's fine. Okay, I have to go make the packets now."

She hung up the phone and leaned into him. "God, people are dumb."

"Did you have a half day or something?"

"I wish. I threw up twice and felt like my head was gonna burst so I went home sick. I still have a bunch of work due tomorrow, though." She pressed a button on her laptop and a printer hummed in the adjoining kitchen.

He massaged her shoulders. "Is there anything I can do?"

"Not unless you can make the baby stop hating me."

"The baby doesn't hate you." He pulled out a dining chair and sat backwards on it, grinning. "I have news that'll cheer you up, though—I got a promotion."

Her mouth dropped open as she punched his shoulder. "Get out. Doing what?"

"Amy's gonna train me throughout July so starting August 1st, I can officially take over as Head College Counselor."

She hugged him. "That's great! I'm so proud of you."

"The raise isn't much but every dollar counts. Especially now."

"Did Amy find a better job somewhere else?"

"She's actually pregnant too."

"Oh." Kat nodded, taken aback. "Good for her."

"I was thinking of throwing a party—sort of an all-in-one celebration of the baby, my promotion, and our birthdays."

She perked up. "We should have it at that new dance club down in Wilkes-Barre. One of my coworkers went the other day and had a great time."

Every dance club he'd ever been dragged to was expensive, full of weirdoes, and played shitty music. "I was thinking more along the lines of a backyard barbecue."

"Come on. We have our whole lives to throw house parties, but I've only got a few more weeks to get dressed up before I'm stuck wearing stretch pants for the rest of the year."

"How about we have the barbecue here, but I take you out to a classy dinner some other time?"

"Alright, but it better be soon because I'm already showing."

He scoffed. "You are not. Look." He pulled up her shirt to prove his point, but her belly was noticeably swollen. *When did that happen?* Not wanting to lie, he changed tactics. "All I see is my beautiful wife."

She smiled. She wasn't stupid—she knew exactly what he did but let him get away with it because she wasn't insecure like most other girls. He kissed her cheek.

"I'm gonna have some leftover meatloaf. You want any?"

She wrinkled her nose. "Just the thought is making me sick all over again. You go ahead. I'm gonna shower."

Eager to get started on his new senior class spreadsheet idea, he quickly heated up the meatloaf in the microwave and then carried his plate upstairs toward the spare bedroom where his computer was set up. Through the pounding of shower water he thought he heard a small sob. He knocked on the closed bathroom door.

"Kat? Are you okay?"

The water continued to beat down with no other sounds.

"I'm fine," she finally called out.

He hesitated. Maybe he'd only imagined it, but if something was wrong, he wanted to help. He reached for the door handle, but it was locked.

CHAPTER 9

Wade

Sliding his chest up against her back, Wade spooned Jill tightly, their skin still sweaty and sticking together. Moonlight cast an otherworldly glow over the room, which was quiet except for their breathing. He'd almost fallen asleep when she spoke.

"Do you ever worry you're missing out?"

"On what?" he asked, yawning.

"I don't even know. I just can't shake the feeling that time's running out. I try to make smart choices, but every time I open a door two more close behind me."

He brushed her hair behind her ear. "I think you know more about what you want than you give yourself credit for."

"I used to have plans, but now every morning I feel like a different person—smarter than I was yesterday but somehow more lost." She looked up at him, eyes wet. "I've never even been off the east coast."

"So we'll go," he said cheerfully, trying to make her see that none of this was the huge deal she was making it out to be. "We can drive up to Canada for a few days, or go for broke and fly to California."

She stared at the ceiling, a tear escaping one eye. "But what if we get there and it's not what we expected at all?"

"Then we'll come back home," he said, stroking her arm. "No matter where we go, we'll always be us." She covered her face and sobbed quietly. Nothing he said seemed to help at all. "Hey. Look at me." When she parted her fingers enough for one eye to peek through, he squished up his face and stuck out his tongue. Letting out a stifled laugh, she hugged him so hard it hurt.

He awoke some time later to sunlight burning his eyes. Squinting, he rolled over, Jill's naked form gently rising and falling beside him. He grinned stupidly. It was the first time she'd spent the whole night since they broke up, which was definitely a promising development. He kissed her neck, and she blinked up at him, smiling for a few seconds before her expression turned to dread.

"Oh shit. I'm late for work." She threw the blankets off but he caught her around the waist before she could get up.

"Call out. We'll get breakfast at the diner."

She wriggled out of his arms. "I can't. I need those days for when I'm really sick."

She searched frantically through the blankets, pulling on clothing as she found it. Kneeling on the bed, he pulled her close for another kiss. She kissed him back for maybe half a minute before cracking a smile and point-ing a finger at him.

"Don't make it so hard for me to leave."

Feeling good about life, Wade strutted off the elevator and into the office, but found every cube empty. Were they off for some reason? The 4ᵗʰ of July had already passed, and there wouldn't be another holiday until Labor Day. Plus, all the lights were on.

He dropped his laptop bag on his desk and checked the calendar. *All-Staff Meeting – 9am.* His shoulders drooped. Those things were painfully boring and never pertained to his job, but if he didn't go it might look bad.

At the front of the overcrowded conference room, one of the head honchos droned on about budgets and spends, occasionally referencing the chart of multi-million dollar amounts projected onto the whiteboard. Wade weaved through the crowd in the back of the room until he found an open spot between a filing cabinet and the window, barely large enough to squeeze into. Three stories below, people strolled down the sidewalk in the warm summer light, wearing sunglasses and shorts, and generally enjoying life.

God, I miss summer vacation.

Pretending to take notes, he sketched out a rough map of a beach area, surrounded by dunes and ferns, and complete with jetties, a lighthouse, and a narrow boardwalk that led up to town. The scene would look best empty, the way it did in winter when all the tourists were gone. Flipping the page, he jotted down a list of sound effects he'd need: ocean waves, seagulls, footsteps in sand, footsteps on wood, grass rustling.

He didn't even realize the meeting had ended until people began chatting and filing out of the room. Grinning, he pushed past them, excited to get back to his desk and start working on the new level.

The sun shone high in the sky as Wade and Rob followed the smell of barbecue around to the backyard where a bunch of Ian's college friends relaxed in a rough circle of lawn chairs. Up on the deck, Kat emptied a case of beer into a bucket of ice water. "Come get something to drink," she called out, shielding her eyes from the sun.

Rob hopped up the steps, but before Wade could follow, Ian grabbed his arm and spun him around.

"Why did you bring Rob?" he whispered harshly, wielding his spatula like a weapon. "I specifically told you I didn't invite him because Drew's coming."

Wade kept his voice low. "I thought maybe if they were in the same room they'd finally remember how much they care about each other. Especially if it was a party and everyone was having fun."

Ian pulled his phone from his shirt pocket.

"What are you doing?" Wade asked.

"Warning Drew."

Wade snatched the phone from his brother's hand. "This is stupid. We're all friends and they both need to get over it already."

"Give me my phone." Ian stretched out a hand, palm up.

"Not until you promise to stay out of it."

Ian raised his eyebrows. "I *am* the one staying out of it."

"No you're not, you're picking Drew."

"So what? This whole thing is Rob's fault, not his."

"I know," Wade said. "I've been trying to convince him to apologize, but he won't."

"All the more reason to stay out of it. Now give me my phone."

"No."

"Don't make me take it from you."

Wade narrowed his eyes. It'd been years since they'd physically fought, but he was at a significant height disadvantage, and Ian almost always won. He hurled the phone over the fence into the neighbor's yard. "Go get it."

"Oh, real mature, Wade."

"Bite me." He flipped his brother off before joining Rob and Kat on the deck.

"We wanna get a volleyball game going," Kat said. "The three of us versus three of those guys." She pointed to the group in the lawn chairs.

"I'm down," Wade said.

"Great! You guys set up the net while I round up our opponents."

Down in the yard, Wade and Rob found the net lying in the grass and each picked up a side pole. Rob walked to the edge of the yard and drove his pole into the ground. "How's the game? Can I see it yet?"

Wade hesitated. It was cool of Rob to ask, but if anyone criticized his messy unfinished levels even a little bit, he'd almost certainly give up and never go back. "I'm not showing anyone until it's done."

"Can you at least tell me what it's about?"

"It's a quest. But that's all I'm saying."

"Is it about Jill?"

"Damn it, Rob. Stop asking me questions." Wade walked backward until the volleyball net was pulled taut.

"So that's a yes."

"No. It's not about Jill. We're trying to be friends, though."

Rob smirked. "How's that working out?"

"Fine."

"I still say you're better off finding a girl who actually wants to suck your dick."

Wade stared at the pole as he drove it into the ground. "Oh shit. You fucked her, didn't you?"

Wade's face grew hot. "So what?"

Rob shrugged. "At least you're getting some."

Wade scowled as Kat led three other guys toward the net while tossing a Nerf ball back and forth between her hands. "You guys ready?"

Within minutes he was out of breath, his chest burning as he ran back and forth after the ball. He wasn't fat, but had definitely gained a few pounds since college. Back then, he used to battle the campus's steep hills between classes, but now sat in a cube all day, barely moving. He wondered if that factored into Jill's decision to break up with him.

From the looks of Rob, he was feeling equally out of shape, but Kat was cool as ice. She somehow always seemed to appear wherever the ball came down in plenty of time to spike it clear across the yard.

Up on the deck, Ian carried a plate of hamburgers out through the sliding glass doors. When he saw them playing his eyebrows shot up so high they practically flew off his forehead.

"Kat," he called out, putting down the plate and jogging into the yard.

"What?" She picked up the ball and got ready to serve again.

"I don't think you should be playing sports in your condition."

"I'm pregnant, not an invalid," she replied. Her flowy tank top hid her stomach so well that Wade had forgotten about the pregnancy. But looking carefully now, he could make out a small bump.

"She's kicking all of our asses," Rob said, bent over and panting. "I think she'll be fine."

Ian ignored him. "What if you get hit in the stomach?"

"It's a *Nerf* ball," she said, holding it up in his face.

"It's the force of the impact I'm worried about."

As they continued arguing, Wade edged closer to Rob, feeling like he was watching something he shouldn't. "I've never seen them fight before," he whispered.

"Me neither."

"Okay, it's four-one, our serve," Kat called out, turning her back on Ian and ending the conversation.

Later that night, as the sky grew dusky and everyone else had gone, Wade and Rob stayed behind with Ian, nursing beers in the dancing light from a citronella candle. Behind them, Kat walked around with a trash bag, collecting used paper plates and empty cans before going back inside the house without a word.

"What's going on with you two?" Rob asked.

Grateful someone else had brought it up, Wade turned to Ian, eager to hear the explanation.

Ian looked over his shoulder to make sure Kat was still gone. "I don't know—hormones maybe? She's been acting really weird lately."

"Like how?" Wade asked.

"Like a girl."

Rob snorted. "She *is* a girl."

"But she never used to act that way. She gets moody for no reason, and a few times I've even heard her crying when she thinks I'm not listening. I've tried asking her about it but she denies anything's wrong." Ian shook his head, a faraway look in his eyes. "Today was the worst yet. As we were getting ready for the party she threw a fit—like screaming and crying—because her favorite jeans didn't fit anymore. I reminded her that pregnant women are *supposed* to gain weight and she hasn't spoken to me since, aside from the volleyball thing."

"No offense, but you deserve whatever you got for that one," Rob said. "You should've told her she still looked good."

"I tell her that all the time, but she keeps harping on it." He ran a hand through his hair. "She hasn't even told her parents about the baby yet. I can understand if she's scared—I'm scared too—but she keeps acting like none of it's happening. I mean, the girl is supposed to be the one reassuring the guy that everything's gonna be okay, right?"

Wade thought back to what Kat said at the sports bar. "Maybe she doesn't wanna get too attached to the baby in case you lose it."

Ian sighed. "She did mention that in the beginning, but she's past the three-month mark now—statistically, we're very unlikely to lose it from this point on."

Rob leaned forward, elbows on his knees. "Look. You're both about to become parents, but she's the only one with a kid growing inside her. Cut her some slack, and stop trying to rationalize with her. It's clearly pissing her off."

Ian rubbed his face and leaned back in his chair. Rob stood up. "Come on Wade, let's get out of here so Ian can get started apologizing."

A streetlight flickered on as they walked back to Rob's car. Wade gazed up at the darkening sky. All that talk about Kat only made him more confused about Jill.

"Do you think girls cry on purpose to get attention, or that they really can't help it?"

Rob shrugged. "A mixture of both, I suppose. Why?"

"Jill cried the other night."

"Jesus, Wade, were you really that terrible?"

"Not during sex, asshole. Afterward. We were laying there talking, and she started crying out of nowhere."

"Did she used to do that a lot before?"

"Not really. I mean, every now and then she'd get bent out of shape about something stupid the way Kat did with her jeans, but never out of the blue like that."

"Did you ask why she was upset?"

Wade jammed his hands in his pockets. "I was too afraid she'd say it was because of me."

"Do you think it *was* you?"

"Maybe. But then she slept over, which she hasn't done since we broke up, so maybe it was a good thing?"

Rob unlocked the car door. "She sounds conflicted."

Wade rested his arms on the hood. "I think she might be scared of how much she still loves me."

"I suppose it's possible."

"You don't sound convinced."

Rob sighed. "I'm never convinced of anything when it comes to girls."

CHAPTER 10

Kat

Sweating despite the air conditioning, Kat fanned her face with her marriage certificate and adjusted her bra strap through her too-tight blouse. As disgusting as her stomach felt bulging out through her stretchy maternity pants, she'd at least expected to gain weight in that area, unlike the new layer of fat that now circled her thighs and upper arms. Every time she moved, the extra skin chafed against itself or the fabric of her clothes, driving her crazy.

She stared jealously at the pretty bank associate with her delicate bone structure and trendy size zero dress that clung perfectly to her figure without betraying a single roll. *At least my boobs are bigger.*

"How can I help you today, Ms. Kerwin?"

Kat handed over the marriage certificate and a pile of checks. "I was told I need to add my married name to my account before you'll cash my wedding checks."

"Congratulations." The associate smiled as she began typing on her computer. Even the soft clicking of her fingers on the keys sounded elegant.

Kat's stomach rumbled. The quicker she got out of here, the quicker she could go home, change, and have a relaxing dinner with Ian.

The associate pushed one of the checks forward. "I'm sorry. I can't cash this one because neither name matches." It was the one on which Ian's aunt had spelled *Katherine Dakalski* with a C instead of a K.

Kat rolled her eyes. "I know, there's about ten different ways to spell Katherine, but it's obviously meant for me. The memo even says 'wedding.'"

"I'm sorry, but if the last name's different, the first has to match exactly."

Glancing over at the pile of accepted checks, Kat spotted the pink one from her mother. "You'll take the one addressed to *Mr. and Mrs. Ian Dakalski,* but not the one that clearly has my name on it?"

"I'm sorry, but it's bank policy."

If this bitch said she was sorry one more time she was liable to get punched in the face. Kat forced a smile. "I'd like to speak with a manager, please."

The associate smiled daggers at her, and for a dreadful second Kat wondered if she *was* the manager until she turned and left the room. She felt bad about being so curt. None of her problems were this girl's fault, but she was taking them out on her, just like those entitled customers always did when she worked at the coffee shop. It was probably the hormones.

Only four and half months left. Then I'll see my baby and fall in love, and everything will be fine.

A few minutes later, the bank associate returned with a balding man in an ill-fitting suit.

"The best we can do is deposit the check in your account with a 14-day hold," he said.

"Thank you." Kat nodded, trying to seem more like a pleasant, reasonable person.

He handed her a sheet of paper. "Here's a little something to help you get started on the rest of the process." It was a social security name change form. Her insides tightened. How dare he assume she was going to take her husband's name?

She took the form, quietly seething while he deposited the rest of her checks. Not wanting to be the type of woman who got up-in-arms about changing her name, she'd agreed to take Kerwin as her middle name and Dakalski as her last, but still couldn't stand the idea of people forever assuming she was a blind sheep who took her husband's name because it was what society expected her to do.

Back in her car, she filled out the form to see what both names looked like in print: *Katherine Ann Kerwin. Katherine Kerwin Dakalski.*

She'd never been fond of the name Ann, but the new name felt alien, like it belonged to someone else. She was already feeling like a stranger in her own body. The least she could do was keep the rest of her identity intact until after the baby was born and she started feeling more like herself again. She shoved the form into her glove compartment. If Ian asked about it before then, she'd pretend it slipped her mind.

Before she even walked in the house, she heard Drew's booming laugh and cringed. All she wanted to do was have a nice quiet dinner with Ian and then maybe retire to the bedroom. She loved their friends, but their time as a twosome was ticking away, making every night they spent alone together precious. She didn't want to be a bitch about it though, so she put on her best "everything is fine" smile as she opened the front door.

They were in the living room, eating pizza and watching the Mets-Yankees game.

"Hey guys," she called out, dropping her purse on the table by the door.

Ian looked at his watch. "Did you have to work late?"

"Nah, just ran some errands on the way home." She kissed him and then leaned over the loveseat to give Drew a hug, making sure he got a clear view down the front of her shirt. As long as she'd known him he'd always looked, but it was especially reassuring now that she was fat. "What's the score?"

Ian sighed. "Mets are down two to nothing at the bottom of the first."

Drew shook his head. "Every year I try to talk sense into him, but he's a stubborn asshole."

"Fuck your big money team." Ian laughed, and then motioned toward the pizza box. "You hungry?"

"God yes, but I need to get out of these clothes first."

"That's what I'm talking about." Drew held up a hand and she high-fived it before heading upstairs to change into a stretchy top and her maternity jeans. When she returned, all the good cheer had fizzled and a vein stuck out in Drew's neck.

"Everything's a fucking joke to him. That's the part I can't get over—that he laughed about it."

"I told you," Ian said. "I have no idea what he was thinking. I was drunk as shit and busy talking to relatives. I didn't even realize anything happened."

Poor Ian. He'd been over the whole Rob situation with Drew a dozen times already and every conversation was the same as the last. She sat beside him, giving his arm a small squeeze before grabbing a slice of pizza.

"He probably doesn't even *have* a reason," Drew said. "He just likes shitting all over people for fun."

Rob could be blunt at times, but he'd always been nice to her, and she doubted he'd hurt anyone on purpose. "You dated this girl in high school, right?" she asked. "Maybe he honestly didn't think you'd care after so long."

"No, he knew. Caitlin wasn't some girl I hooked up with once or twice. We were on and off again for two years." Drew shook his head. "If anything, this was the one girl he *knew* was off-limits."

"I'm not saying it was right, but sometimes things happen. We can't help who we're attracted to."

"Yeah, but we can damn well help whether or not we act on it."

Ian rested a hand on her leg. "Trust me, Rob's completely in the wrong on this and he knows it. Plus he's had all summer to man up and apologize if he felt any remorse."

"He's always been a dick. I don't know why you're still friends with him." Drew flung his pizza crust into the open box. "You know what? Fuck that guy—I'm tired of talking about him. Did you play the new *Metal Gear* yet?"

She'd never seen Drew so visibly worked up about anything before. The pure hatred in his voice and eyes was unsettling, but even more so was how quickly he switched it off and began enthusing about *Metal Gear* as if all were right in the world again.

Never having much interest in the series, she tuned them out, grabbing another slice of pizza as she leaned back into the couch to watch the ballgame. A light rain fell onto the field, much like the day she'd met Ian.

It had been the first day of her period and she'd been crampy and bloated all afternoon, but the tickets were a gift to her department from one of the higher ups and she didn't want to make a bad impression so soon after being hired. When the cold, wet drops started landing on her head midway through the first inning, she thought luck was on her side, but the teams kept playing. As the rain fell more steadily, she draped her jacket over her head to cover her frizzing hair until one of her coworkers lent her his baseball cap. She felt hokey wearing it, but it was better than getting soaked.

Not long afterward, Ian and Drew squeezed through the row toward the empty seats beside her. Ian asked what they'd missed so far, and was impressed by her detailed recap, saying most girls would've only told him the score. He was even more impressed when she explained that she'd played shortstop for her schools' softball teams since grade school.

Throughout the rest of the game, he kept finding excuses to talk to her, and from time to time she'd steal a glance only to find him already looking at her. He was adorable in a nerdy sort of way, but had the lean muscled build of an athlete. And best of all, he looked at her like she was the most beautiful girl in the world even though she was a disheveled mess. When he asked for her number at the end of the night, she was more than happy to give it to him.

Overwhelmed by it all, she reached for another slice of pizza. So many random things had to happen in order for them to meet. She happened to be given a ticket to that particular game, and out of the tens of thousands of seats in the stadium, she happened to wind up sitting next to him.

Following the trail back further, it was a complete fluke that she'd even moved to Scranton in the first place. In high school, she'd been browsing an enormous stack of college brochures when she fell in love with a photo of students lounging around a dorm room. All smiles, they looked like they were having so much fun that she immediately wanted to go there. It was completely irrational. She didn't even know "there" was the University of Scranton until she checked the front cover. If that photo had never been taken, she could've easily wound up in another city, married to some other guy, and living an entirely different life.

She felt sick to her stomach, but realized it was probably all the pizza. Had she seriously eaten three slices? No wonder she was gaining so much weight.

Her doctor explained that eating for two was a myth and an extra piece of fruit a day was all she actually needed, but she was starving all the time and never felt full no matter how much food she shoved down her throat. The other night, she'd devoured the biggest steak on the menu, ate the leftover potatoes from Ian's plate, and then came home and finished off a bag of tortilla chips. It was nice that Ian had been so forgiving about her weight, but it made her complacent. She was way too heavy, and deep down he had to be as disgusted by it as she was.

Excusing herself from the living room, she went upstairs and knelt on the fuzzy rug in front of the toilet. She'd thrown up *unwillingly* so many times in the first few weeks that she was fairly confident she could mimic the process. Holding back her hair, she leaned over the bowl and held her breath, constricting her muscles and making quiet gagging sounds until an acidic burst of cheesy chunks slid up her throat.

Leaning back against the tub, she wrapped her arms around herself, more disgusted by her actions than the smell. She didn't want to be a bulimic mom who starved her baby to meet some arbitrary societal beauty standard. She needed to stop feeling sorry for herself and get it the fuck together.

The next morning, she woke up early and scrambled a few eggs, figuring they were low-calorie and the protein would keep her going until lunch. As she divvied the eggs between two plates Ian came up behind her, his chin resting on her shoulder as his arms circled her waist.

"What's all this for?"

She shrugged, handing him the much fuller plate. "Just felt like having something besides cereal or granola bars."

He followed her to the dining room table, looking skeptically at her tiny pile of eggs. "Is that all you're eating?"

"I'm not that hungry. Plus, I've gotta save room for our celebratory dinner tonight."

He checked his watch. "Only nine more hours until we find out whether I'm painting the nursery pink or blue."

She scrunched up her face. "You better paint it blue either way."

He laughed. "I'm just messing with you. I know you'd murder me if I painted anything in this house pink." He took a bite of eggs. "Are you gonna call your parents before or after dinner?"

She pushed her eggs around the plate with her fork. When she said she'd tell her parents at the halfway point, it'd still seemed so far away.

"I was thinking I might wait until we see them at Thanksgiving. That way I can show up pregnant and say I planned it as a surprise."

His eyes widened like he thought she was insane. Why did he have to make such a big deal out of it, anyway? They weren't *his* parents.

"You saw how my mom was with the wedding," she explained. "She'll start bombarding us with questions and advice like we're idiots, and I can't deal with that right now."

"I think it's weird, that's all."

She kissed his cheek. "That's because *your* mom is a sweet, reasonable person who knows when to step up and when to step off." She slid her plate into the dishwasher and pulled on her giant maternity blazer. "See you at the doctor's office."

The convention center was already abuzz with activity by the time she checked in and wheeled her suitcase down the hallway lined with colorful booths advertising various healthcare vendors and specialty drug companies. Interns had set up the Aberdeen booth the night before, but the logo banner that was supposed to stretch across the top hung limply to one side. Shaking her head, she dragged a metal folding chair out from behind the table and stood on top of it, reaching high above her head to tie the banner's cord back around the side pole.

"Let me help you with that," a deep voice called out.

Smiling, she turned around as a sharply dressed young man bypassed her table, heading straight for the one directly across the aisle where a bleached blonde in a low cut blouse was unloading a stack of metal catering trays.

Sure, help the Barbie doll but not the pregnant lady.

Feeling invisible, she yanked the banner cord into a hard knot, climbed down, and began setting up the table with brochures, flyers, and business cards.

It turned out the woman across the aisle was from Aberdeen's biggest local competitor and her trays were full of hot appetizers. Once the Sterno cans were lit, a delicious smell filled the whole area, making Kat's stomach growl. She looked longingly at her own spread of donuts and pastries. If she ate even one, she'd have to skip lunch just to save enough calories for dinner. Ignoring her hunger, she grabbed her purse and set out to find the room where she'd be giving her speech.

It was fairly cramped, with a dozen rows of chairs facing a microphone stand at the front. She introduced herself to the main presenter, a silver-haired woman in a yellow pantsuit, and then took a seat in the front row, looking over her speech cards as the rest of the chairs slowly filled up. Eventually, the woman in the yellow pantsuit stood at the mic and quieted the crowd.

"Welcome to the food services management session! Before we get started, we have a special guest from one of our sponsors, Aberdeen Foods. Let's give a warm round of applause for Katherine Kerwin."

Standing up, Kat felt immediately lightheaded, but forced herself up to the microphone. *It's only ten minutes. I can buy a sandwich as soon as I'm done.*

"Hello! How is everyone?" The audience gave a lukewarm rumble, but she kept her voice cheery. "I know it's early, but we've got a great program today. Plus, there are plenty of free breakfast samples at Aberdeen's table, so please feel free to stop by."

An older man near the front kept staring at her stomach instead of her face. She wanted to scream. It was bad enough when it happened in the grocery store or on the street, but this was a professional setting and she deserved more respect.

"Okay, so we all eat multiple times a day, every day. We know what we like and where to get it, and even if we have a bad meal every now and then it's not the end of the world because we can always get something different next time."

The room spun and her limbs felt weaker by the second. She gripped the microphone tighter.

"But what happens when you're in the hospital and suddenly have to eat all your meals from the same source, no matter whether they taste good or not? By a show of hands, how many of you have eaten the food served to your patients within the last six months?"

Black spots swam across her vision as a few hands went up.

"That's great. Testing your own product is the only sure way... the only way..."

I'm gonna fall.

The next thing she knew, she was sitting on the floor surrounded by a forest of legs, and the lady in the yellow pantsuit was shoving an open bottle of water in her face. "Are you okay, sweetie?"

"I'm fine." She took the bottle and sipped the water slowly, praying this story wouldn't make it back to the office.

Get up. The longer you stay down, the more they'll remember it.

Supporting her stomach with one hand, she used the other to push off the floor, but got dizzy all over again. A man standing nearby helped pull her up the rest of the way. She never felt so ridiculous and needy in her entire life.

"Thank you all so much." She forced a smile. "I'll be at the Aberdeen booth if you have any questions."

Still weak, she walked slowly back down the hall, sipping water. Barbie was away from her booth, so she took the opportunity to load up on mini-hot dogs, quiches, and black coffee, not caring how bad it might look that she was eating the competition's food. Within a few minutes, she felt much steadier.

A brunette in her mid-40s approached the table and Kat wiped her mouth with a napkin before standing up. "How are you enjoying the conference today?"

The woman gestured to Kat's coffee cup. "You shouldn't be drinking that. Caffeine is bad for the baby."

"It's decaf," she stammered, immediately wishing she hadn't justified her choices to a complete stranger.

The woman frowned. "Hot dogs and lunch meat are off-limits too. Didn't your doctor tell you that?"

Kat glanced down at her plate. She hadn't realized what she'd been eating. A few mini-hot dogs couldn't possibly give her kid brain damage, right? "She said it was fine as long as I didn't eat them all the time."

"I suppose so—if you want to risk it."

Her blood boiled, but she forced a smile as she changed the subject. "What type of company do you work for?"

"I'm with a birthing center in Hazleton. Do you have a birth plan yet?"

Oh God, she's pitching to me. "Thanks, but I already have a doctor and hospital lined up."

"Hospitals aren't the smartest choice these days. They rush you in and out and pump you full of drugs that prolong your labor and make it difficult to bond with your baby. I labored for 18 hours in a hospital with my first, and I could tell the staff was getting annoyed. They tried to hurry me up with an episiotomy but it didn't work and I wound up with a C-section anyway."

Kat didn't want to indulge her, but was morbidly curious at the same time. "What's an episiotomy?"

"It's when they cut a slit in the vaginal opening to make it wider."

The hot dogs threatened to come back up. That was a *thing*? How come no one ever warned her about this kind of stuff *before* she'd gotten pregnant?

The woman placed a hand on Kat's shoulder. "Don't worry—our bodies were designed to do this." She handed Kat a business card. "At our center, we stay away from invasive measures unless there's a legitimate emergency, and we never pressure you to accept epidurals or other drugs." She then leaned in as if they were friends. "We're not these weak things doctors insist we are, and we have the right to be fully present participants in our own experiences."

I'd rather not be fully present for labor pains, thank you very much.

By the time Kat arrived at the doctor's office and changed into a gaudy floral smock, she was beyond exhausted, unlike Ian, who paced the examining room with excitement, browsing through an illustrated pamphlet entitled *Stages of Fetal Development.*

He had no idea how much easier he had it. Not only was he exempt from bodily discomfort, but he could go about his day without strangers knowing his private business and inflicting their opinions on him. Even after the kid was born, those same strangers would probably continue to judge everything she did while considering him a saint just for being involved. The discrepancy was right there in the titles themselves—*mothering* meant providing ongoing love and care, while *fathering* referred to the one-time act of getting a woman pregnant. She wasn't supposed to have a sex preference, but couldn't help it. Everything about girls was so much more complicated. Half the time she didn't even understand herself. Sitting on the examining table, she played with the ties on the front of her smock.

"I know you were only joking about painting the nursery pink, but if we have a girl, you can't treat her any differently than you would a boy."

Ian looked up from the pamphlet. "Of course I won't."

"I'm serious. You have to roughhouse with her and teach her how to play sports, like my dad did with me. He always expected me to be as good as or better than the boys at everything I did."

He kissed her forehead. "I promise."

The doctor knocked on the door. "You guys ready?"

Ian smiled wide. "Let's do this!"

The doctor pulled up the front of Kat's smock and squeezed warm gel onto her stomach before moving the wand back and forth, stopping every few seconds to punch a button on the computer. She always looked so serious, as if she was trained not to show any emotion until certain of whether the news was good or bad. Thankfully, she finally smiled as she removed the wand and handed Kat a towel for her stomach.

"Everything looks great. Did you want to find out the sex today?"

Kat squeezed Ian's hand. "Yes, please."

"Congratulations, you're having a girl."

CHAPTER 11

Wade

It was muggier inside his parents' house than outside. This was going to suck. In the kitchen at the far end of the house, Wade's mother chatted animatedly on the phone as she repotted a plant, the phone cord wrapped around her waist. She noticed him and held a hand over the receiver. "Ian's upstairs already. I'm making lasagna after."

He grinned. Dinner would definitely lessen the suck factor. He climbed the stairs to the second floor, passing the gallery of framed family photos that lined the wall beside it. In his office at the top of the stairs, his father sat in front of an ancient desktop computer, surrounded by floor-to-ceiling bookshelves.

"Hey, Dad."

His father lowered his glasses and peered over the thin wire rims. "Make sure you completely empty that room. The painters are coming first thing Monday morning."

Hello to you too.

Wade ran his fingers across the raised wallpaper in the hall until he reached his old bedroom. Ian sat shirtless and cross-legged on the floor, surrounded by cardboard boxes and piles of old toys, clothes, and sports equipment. The ceiling fan whipped around above them, but sweat already dribbled down his back.

"I almost forgot how much summers here sucked," Wade said, pulling his own t-shirt over his head and dropping it in the doorway.

Ian leafed through a magazine. "You know Dad. If it's not a hundred degrees, it's not worth turning on the air."

"I've had mine on full blast all summer." Wade plopped onto the floor and pried the lid off a plastic bin of action figures. He held up a beat-up Starscream and did the voice. "Who disrupts my room cleaning?"

"I swear if you start playing with those, I'm gonna murder you."

Wade scrunched up his face. "Says the one reading a magazine."

"I'm not reading it, I'm—never mind." Ian tossed it onto the stack beside him and stretched his arms over his head. "I'm taking the stuff by the door. Everything I don't want is under the window."

Wade eyed the pile by the door, prepared to argue over anything unjustly claimed, but it was mostly their old baby gear. Meanwhile, the discard pile included a Lego pirate set and a stack of board games. "When did you get so boring?" He held up the *Aggravation* box. "Your kid could totally play with this, even if you suck now."

"Half the pieces are missing."

"They're marbles. You can buy a whole bag at the dollar store."

"Babies can't play with marbles. They'll choke."

"Fine. *I'm* taking it, then." Wade slid the box into an unoccupied corner of the room and then opened another bin full of plastic dinosaurs. "Come on, you don't even want *these*? They're too big to choke on."

Ian shook his head. "You're gonna take everything in this room, aren't you?"

Wade laughed. "Probably." Before today, he wouldn't have remembered half this stuff existed, but now couldn't bear to part with any of it. If only his apartment had more storage space. "I wish Mom would let us keep everything here."

Ian slid the pile of magazines under the window. "She wants to turn this into a guest room."

Wade added the dinosaurs to his pile and then focused on a stack of books. Most were college texts the bookstore wouldn't buy back—one was still wrapped in plastic. At least there were a few things that wouldn't be coming home with him.

Pushing the stack of books toward the discard pile, he spotted a long, thin paperback wedged between the pages of a much bulkier text. It was their children's illustrated version of H. G. Wells's *The Time Machine*. A smile spread across his face as he flipped to his favorite page featuring a gangly, smiling Morlock climbing up the inside of a well toward the hero. The thing looked more like a lackwit sidekick than a murderous monster. He laughed out loud.

Ian's whole body tensed as if he really was holding back murderous rage. "What now?" he demanded.

Wade held up the book. "Remember this?"

Ian laughed so hard he forgot to be angry "Oh God. I'd be trying to do my homework and suddenly that thing would appear over the side of the table and start talking to me."

Wade tried to remember the voice he'd used. It was higher pitched, half-nasal, half-sultry, and he'd draw out the vowels, especially in Ian's name.

"Iiii-an. Taaake the diii-nosauuurs, Iiii-an."

They both cracked up and spent the rest of the afternoon taking turns making the Morlock say silly things as they cleared out the room.

By the time Wade forced his car's trunk lid down over the boxes of stuff he'd rescued, the sun was setting behind the mountains, bathing the sky in pink and orange. Wiping the sweat from his forehead, he followed the smell of garlic and tomatoes into the kitchen as his mother pulled a baking dish from the oven. Leaning against the counter, he plucked a slice of garlic bread from the cutting board.

"Don't touch that." She rapped his hand with a wooden spoon. "Dinner's in five minutes."

He popped the bread in his mouth and folded his hands under his chin, trying to look cute. "Can we pleee-ase put the air on? Just for a little while?"

She studied him for a moment before pointing her spoon at him. "Keep it on low."

"Thank you!" He kissed her cheek and bounded toward the thermostat, almost mowing down Ian along the way.

"And put your shirts back on," she called out. "You both stink."

After washing up, he joined the rest of the family at the dining room table and scooped a heaping helping of lasagna onto his plate.

His mother turned to Ian. "Is there anything else you need for the baby?"

"Honestly, I didn't realize babies need half the stuff they do." He laughed. "I'll go through it all with Kat when I get home and let you know."

"If there's anything you don't need, bring it back, and I'll store it down the basement until Wade has kids."

"Who said I'm having kids?" He stuck out his tongue.

"You better. I want lots of grandbabies."

He imagined lying on the couch in his apartment with Jill and watching TV as a little kid played with his dinosaurs on the floor. It could be fun, but going on adventures like Uncle Rick and Aunt Rita did might be even more so.

"How's the new job, Ian?" his father asked. "Are you ready for next week?"

"I thought I was, but then Sister Augustine told me she's not hiring for my old position, which means I'll be doing to the work of two people, and I really wasn't prepared for that."

"Are you getting a bigger raise?"

Ian scoffed. "No. And she's also making me teach health class four times a week even though I'm not a certified teacher. I have no idea how I'm gonna find time for it all."

"You've always been a hard worker. I'm sure you can handle it." He turned to Wade. "How about you? Any closer to a promotion?"

His shoulders drooped. "The tech support department is just me and my boss, and I don't think he's leaving anytime soon." He'd explained this multiple times already, but his father never accepted it, which made no sense considering he made a lot more money than Ian.

"What about other departments?"

"I like my job," Wade said flatly.

His mother wiped her mouth with a napkin. "The boys put everything they didn't want in the garage. I figure I'll drive it over to Goodwill sometime next week."

Grateful for the reprieve, Wade helped himself to more garlic bread, using it to sop up the extra sauce from his plate. His phone vibrated in his jeans pocket. Sliding it out, he read the text from Jill. *Wanna watch a movie tonight?*

"It's getting worse with these kids and their phones." His father shook his head. "You try to give a lecture and half the class is staring into their laps."

Ignoring him, Wade texted back. *I'm having dinner with my parents. Come over in an hour.*

Back at his apartment, he took an extra-long shower, giving Jill plenty of time to show up and let herself in. Hoping to find her waiting naked in his bed, he wrapped the towel around his waist and struck a sexy pose outside the bedroom door, but she wasn't there. He turned around to find her sitting in the living room, fully clothed, and holding up a DVD boxed set of *Doctor Who*.

"Look what came in the mail."

"That's great." He tried not to sound frustrated. Hadn't they gotten past pretending?

"Go get dressed. I'll set up the DVD."

He trudged into his bedroom and pulled on a t-shirt and pajama pants. Was she really making him get dressed just to get undressed again? Maybe she was on her period and only wanted to hang out. That might bode well for their finally getting back together, but a knot still grew in the pit of his stomach.

He turned off the living room lights and joined her on the couch as she pressed play. Usually she cuddled up against him right away, but this time she relaxed into the couch, a pillow in her lap. Holding onto the faintest hope that the weirdness was all in his head, he leaned in, planting long slow kisses on the side of her neck. She let him do it for maybe half a minute before pausing the DVD.

"Be right back." She headed to the bathroom. A minute later she returned, taking a seat in the recliner instead of with him on the couch.

Fuck my life.

He took a deep silent breath. "What's going on?" he asked in the most non-accusatory way possible.

She smoothed out the wrinkles in her shirt. "Um, we're watching a show?"

Oh God, we're playing this *game.* "Why won't you sit with me?"

Her mouth tightened as she stared at the ceiling. "Because you're gonna try to kiss me again."

His heart deflated into an angry blob. "That didn't seem like a problem the last time you were here."

"I told you this wasn't a thing." She sat up straighter, a handful of recliner fabric in her fist. "If you couldn't handle it, you should've said so."

"I'm not an idiot. I know you felt something." He needed her to confirm it, but she shook her head.

"I knew this was a mistake." She ejected the DVD from the player. "You're clearly not capable of handling it like an adult."

He clenched his fist to keep from crying. "Right, because lying about your feelings is so mature."

"I never lied about anything." She shoved the DVD back in the case. "I *broke up* with you. What part of that did you not understand?"

"I don't know, maybe the part where we talked about the future and fell asleep in each other's arms."

"It's not my fault you thought that meant something it didn't."

He spoke low, trying to keep his voice from shaking. "If you changed your mind—fine, whatever—but at least have the guts to admit that some small part of this was real."

"It wasn't." She yanked the front door open. "Don't call me anymore."

He threw his arms in the air. *You're* the one who called *me!*"

The screen door slammed shut behind her. Forgetting he was barefoot, he kicked the cardboard box underneath the coffee table and stubbed his toe hard.

"Goddammit!"

He lugged the box outside and hurled it at the curb as her car sped away. It split open on impact, spilling its contents into the street. Right on top was the plush alligator wearing an "I love you" shirt that he'd bought for her last birthday. Scattered around it were photos and movie stubs. She hadn't been returning his possessions so much as purging his entire existence from her life.

He sobbed. *I'm a fucking idiot.*

CHAPTER 12

Eleanor

It'd been raining all morning and the cold water now pooled in the sunken patches of sidewalk leading up to the church. The basic shape of the building was still the same, but the trees huddled around the perimeter had been largely cut away and replaced with a row of pastel-sided houses that backed up against the cemetery fence. Clutching the framed photo to her chest, Eleanor followed the path around to a blocky addition near the back labeled "Church Office." A man looking like an out-of-costume Santa Claus greeted her from behind a table where he was stuffing flyers into envelopes.

She closed her umbrella. "Hi. I work at the Scranton Public Library, and was wondering if you could help identify this girl." She handed over the photo. "She might be the daughter of one of your former pastors, but I can't find any record of her."

The man squinted at the frame through his bifocals. "Oh my. How old is this?"

"It's from 1897."

He chuckled and handed it back. "Sorry. If it was taken sometime during the last few decades I could probably help, but this is before even *my* time."

She blushed. "Oh, I didn't think you would know her personally. I thought maybe you'd have records here that could help—parish lists or other photos, maybe?"

"I wish we did, but there was a fire back in the 70s and we lost everything."

"Oh." That was it, then. With no birth certificate, newspaper articles, or church records, she was at a dead end. "Thanks anyway."

"If you don't mind, could you send us copies of that photo and anything else you have about the church? We'd love to have them."

"Sure thing." She turned to go, but then stopped short, glimpsing rows of wet headstones through the window. They looked old. "Are the former pastors and their families buried here?"

"Most of the older ones are, anyway." He pointed to a thick oak standing sentry near the back fence. "Try that section over there."

Stepping carefully through the slick grass, she scanned the names on each stone she passed. So many faceless strangers, most of them dead for so long that no living person would remember them. That was when you were truly dead.

A few yards from the oak, she spotted a tall, thin stone with a cross engraved above the name. *Reverend Charles*

Fleischer. Her breath caught in her throat. Beside it were three smaller stones—his wife Margaret, and their two already accounted for daughters Clara and Anna—but no other Fleischers or girls with a different last name born around the same time.

Rain drops splattered against her umbrella like tiny drums as she bent down to further examine the stones. Ten-year-old Clara had died in 1897—the same year the photo was taken—and her sister Anna had lived to 75, but still had her father's last name.

75 years alone. That would be like living her entire life again, twice over.

Back in her car, Eleanor sat motionless as the wiper blades swooshed across the windshield. Every day felt a little less meaningful than the one before. She supposed she could go to Budget and look for Trent again, but after months of disappointment, it'd become mostly an expensive way to kill time. She might as well save the gas money and go home.

She parked her car in the alley behind the thrift store and climbed the fire escape stairs to the third floor landing. It was almost noon, but the sky was so gloomy that even the usually beautiful green mountains rising up behind the city more closely matched the dour brown color of the storefronts below.

Leaving her wet shoes by the door, she curled up on her futon with a cracked plastic photo album. Her mother bought it for her at the end of fourth grade, along with a fairly decent camera, so she could take pictures of her friends to remember them by. It was the first time she was old enough to feel the full sorrow of leaving a place behind and she cried for days.

Skimming the faces of those little girls, she remembered playing kickball with them behind the commissary and piling into the one girl's den to fight over whose turn it was to be Mario. Before leaving, she collected their addresses so they could become pen pals, but not a single one returned her letters. Looking back, it was probably silly to expect as much from a bunch of 9-year-olds, but at the time she'd been devastated.

At least back then all it took to make friends was a common interest in games or toys. In her next town, the girls didn't spend the summer splashing in pools pretending to be mermaids, but sunning themselves out on the deck and talking about boys, makeup, and other things she knew nothing about. Bored out of her mind, she once suggested they go to the playground and they looked at her like she had two heads. She didn't miss them at all when she moved again, yet pasted their photos in the album anyway in a lame attempt to convince herself she had friends.

Those girls probably grew up to be a lot like her old housemates. How long had it taken them to realize she was gone, anyway—a day, two days, a week? Once they realized the room was empty, they probably spent another day or two in mock concern, asking each other if they had any clue where she went before quickly moving on to the more exciting task of choosing a friend to take her place.

Turning another page in the album, she found the only photo of Trent she had. The lighting was dim, and his face was in profile. She stroked the page, thinking back to the afternoon she took the photo.

In the auditorium, she'd pushed the heavy stage curtain aside, clutching a similar photo album to her chest. Shoulders bent over a sketch pad, Trent sat on the floor, his jet black hair hanging in his face.

"What are you drawing?" She sat down, plopping her backpack between them.

"I'm thinking of getting it as a tattoo." He pushed up his t-shirt sleeve and held the drawing against his upper arm. It was a man's face from the eyes up with a huge bleeding gash across the forehead, but instead of muscle or bone there was green computer circuit board underneath. "What do you think?"

"It's really cool." Much cooler than her own art. She slid the album underneath her backpack, but not before he saw it.

"Are those your photos?"

"Oh. Yeah." Her face grew hot as he flipped through the album's pages. "They're nothing special. Just barns and nature and stuff."

"No, they're really good."

She rubbed the back of her neck, trying not to look too pleased. "You think so?"

"Definitely. Are there any stories behind them?"

"I go for walks sometimes and take pictures of things that speak to me." She pointed to an image of a plow with a cracked wheel, rusting in an overgrown field. "I felt bad for that plow. At one point it had a purpose, but now it just sits there, alone. I wanted to give it a new purpose."

His icy eyes met hers and she willed herself not to look away. "Do you have your camera with you right now?"

"Yeah. I take it everywhere, just in case."

He stood up and stretched out his hand. "Come on, I wanna show you something." His hand was so much bigger than hers and he didn't let go, even as he led her toward the double doors at the back of the stage.

"We're going outside?" The grounds around the football field were empty, but anyone might see them from the windows.

"Don't worry. It's not far, and I think you're really gonna like it."

They stuck close to the building before cutting across the field and entering the woods. Pale patches of sunlight streamed down through the leafy treetops as they walked in silence, still holding hands. Whenever she sensed him looking the other way, she stole glances up at him, wondering if any of this could possibly be real. It was the kind of thing that only happened to other people.

A row of gable-roofed houses stood at the end of the woods, one of which had fallen into disrepair with thick sheets of opaque plastic tacked over the windows.

"It's been empty for years," Trent said, holding down a branch so she could step into the overgrown yard.

The house was beautiful in its decay, a vast reservoir of secrets and stories. She framed it in her camera's viewfinder and snapped a photo.

"Check this out." He climbed the warped wooden porch steps and peeled back one of the plastic sheets to reveal a window without glass in it. He crouched, making his hands into a step. "Come on, I'll help you in."

Careful not to catch her hands or sweater on the jagged wooden sill, she eased herself down onto the cracked linoleum floor. Aside from the air's moldy tinge, the empty kitchen would've fit right into any one of the homes she'd moved into and out of over the years with its curtained windows and intact wooden cabinets.

"What happened to the people who lived here?"

"No idea." Trent climbed in after her. "I was out riding my bike a few years back when I noticed all the plastic."

It was strange they didn't use wood. Plastic was surely more expensive and seemed more like insulation, as if they were planning to come back, but never did.

Crouching in front of a countertop with her camera, she zoomed in on an upside-down fly carcass, its legs crossed over its chest like a mummy. In the next room, Trent peered into a closet. While he wasn't looking, she quickly snapped a photo of him before focusing back in on the fly.

"You think I could borrow some of your photos?" he called out. "I wanna try drawing them."

"Sure." Stepping over a tangle of disconnected telephone wire, she joined him in the living room. Scattered along the faded floral-printed walls were darker rectangular patches where photo frames had probably once hung. Her heart felt heavy. Whoever these people were, they must've lived here a long time for there to be that much discoloration.

Sitting on the floor at the base of the staircase, she angled her camera upward, adjusting the focus so the edges of the closest steps were clear while the details of the second floor landing remained fuzzy.

Trent sat down beside her, his body pressing firmly against hers. Feeling like she might throw up, she kept her eye firmly on the viewfinder, focusing and refocusing the shot without taking any pictures.

"Eleanor."

She almost jumped out of her skin. His icy eyes were so close that she forgot how to talk or even breathe. He pressed his lips against hers, sliding his warm tongue into her mouth. Shaking uncontrollably, she tried to mimic his movements, sure she was doing it all wrong, but he kept going for what seemed like forever. Finally, he pulled back, smiling.

Dumbfounded, she sat in silence as he scrawled their names on the wall with a permanent marker.

Trent and Eleanor were here.

Shutting the album, Eleanor lay back on the futon, closing her eyes and imagining he'd just come home from work. She unbuttoned the front of her pants and slid a hand inside, her free arm clutching a pillow tightly to her chest. Moving slowly, she concentrated on the sensation, imagining his weight on top of her. It would be different now that she knew how her body worked. As her muscles tensed, she moved gradually faster until her hips jerked forward and she let out a small scream. Breath ragged, she repeated the process again and again until her legs felt like rubbery dead weight.

Rolling onto her side, she surveyed the photographs she'd hung in frames on the walls, purposely leaving space in case Trent wanted to move in and display some of his own art. A tear escaped down her cheek. If only she'd had more time to think things through 10 years ago.

A few days after they'd visited the abandoned house, she'd come home from school to find her father assembling cardboard boxes and swearing under his breath. He'd been given emergency orders to a base out in Colorado and they were moving at the end of the week. She'd cried and pleaded to stay back with her mother until at least the end of the school year, but neither parent ever cared about her opinion. To them, she was only another object to pack up and ship off in a truck.

Knowing she'd cry all over again if she explained in person, she tried to write Trent a letter, but the more she thought about it, the more hopeless the situation seemed. He'd almost certainly kissed girls before. Maybe even a lot of them, the way it was so easy for him. She had no way of knowing whether she was anything special. Even if she was, it wouldn't matter. She was moving 2,000 miles away. Eventually he'd forget about her like everyone else did, or worse, he *would* keep in touch and she'd be forced to hear all about his new girlfriends.

So she didn't tell him. She spent those last few days soaking up the feeling of being with him and taking dozens of mental pictures, committing every detail to memory until that Friday afternoon when she hugged him goodbye as if she would see him again on Monday.

He was the best friend she ever had and she walked away. And for what—so she wouldn't get hurt? Well, she got hurt anyway. All these years she might've had a friend to lean on, no matter how far away. Someone she could actually talk to, who might've even helped her move back sooner so they could be together. But now he was a stranger, like everyone else in her album, and she was alone in Scranton without a single friend.

CHAPTER 13

Ian

Soft rock elevator bullshit played on the other end of the line as Ian bent over the file cabinet, looking for college brochures that matched the results of Darryn Fitzgerald's survey. He'd been on hold for so long that when a voice finally spoke, he momentarily blanked on the reason he called.

"Hi, I'm the college counselor at Holy Nativity Academy in Scranton. Could you check on a transcript for one of my students?" He reached for the sticky note where he'd scribbled the kid's name, social security number, and birthdate. "I sent it twice already but his mom called again this morning saying you still haven't received it."

There was a knock at the door. A tall boy with long bangs stood awkwardly in the doorway, holding a sheet of paper.

"Hold on a moment, please." Ian covered the receiver with his hand. "Yes?"

"I need a recommendation."

"I write one for every senior. They'll be done before Thanksgiving." He'd explained this in class at least a half dozen times already, but teenagers never gave a shit about anything until it personally affected them.

He recited the information from the sticky note to the admissions clerk and was promptly put on hold again. The boy lingered by the door.

"Did you need something else?" Ian asked.

"It's due next Friday. It's for a scholarship."

Bloody hell. "Give it to me. I'll see what I can do." He examined the form as the kid slunk off.

The recommendations he wrote were glorified form letters with a few blank spaces to insert whatever personal details he'd gleaned about the kid during class and individual meetings, but these instructions listed a series of painfully specific questions with minimum lengths for each answer. Who the hell did they think had time for that?

He was still on hold with the college when the bell rang, leaving him with yet another call to follow up on. He jammed the recommendation form inside his health text before trudging up to the second floor.

The kids were even more restless than usual and he had to shout to get their attention. "Okay, everyone break off into groups and answer the questions at the end of chapter four. Whatever you don't finish will be this week's homework, so get to it."

As they dragged their desks around, still laughing and chatting loudly, he plopped down at the teacher's desk. Taking out the recommendation form again, he realized he'd forgotten to bring the kid's file. He hadn't met with him yet this year, but seemed to recall he liked math and planned to major in engineering. He flipped to a clean sheet of paper, but then paused, pen hovering above the page. What was the kid's name—Adam? Alex? It definitely started with an A—or was that his last name?

Fuck.

Gripping a handful of hair, he looked out at the kids bent over their textbooks, doing a bullshit assignment from a guy who'd never taken a single teaching course and hadn't even read the chapter himself. He was no better than that bitch of an English teacher he'd written that song about. She'd assigned a huge group project worth a third of their final grade and then stuck him with a bunch of slackers, all but guaranteeing he'd have to do the whole thing himself. Already fraying at the seams from the workload in the rest of his classes, he begged to be switched into another group, but she told him to get used to it because college would be much harder. He tried to remember the lyrics.

Do you remember what it was like to try your hardest and still not succeed? / No! / Because your life's in order now / It won't happen to you anymore / You're at the top of the world, and you'll never have problems like ours again.

God, he was naïve. The most disillusioning part of growing up was learning how many adults were faking it. Now he was one of them.

There was a knock at the door, and the gym teacher beckoned him into the hall.

"I found Susan Owens crying in the locker room," she said. "Seems she didn't get into her first choice of college. I walked her to the counseling suite but was told you were here."

He gestured toward the class. "They're busy with an assignment. Could you keep an eye on them?"

He shuffled back downstairs, wondering why the gym teacher hadn't been tasked with teaching health in the first place. Probably because she was part-time and Sister Augustine would have to pay the difference, whereas he was salary and could be forced to do anything she needed without being offered an extra dime.

He found Susan sitting in his office, red-faced and wiping her eyes with her sleeve. He wheeled his chair around to the front of the desk. Leaning forward, he propped his elbows on his knees, folding his hands between them.

"Well, this sucks, doesn't it?"

She blinked, eyes glistening. "I didn't get into Syracuse."

"Did the letter say why not?"

"No." She sniffed.

"I'll call and find out if there's anything more we can do, but there might not be. Did you hear from any other schools yet?"

"I got accepted to Temple."

"That's great." He sat up. "No matter what happens, you'll have somewhere to go next year, and that's the important part."

Instead of the smile he was hoping for, she only buried her face in her hands and sobbed, her blonde ponytail bobbing up and down. He wished he could put his arm around her and tell her it was going to be okay. That we don't always get our first choices, but it doesn't mean we can't be happy.

He held out a box of tissues. "What about Syracuse did you like so much? If Temple doesn't have it, I'm sure we can find another school that does."

"Nikki and I applied to all the same schools but now she only wants Syracuse. She knew I didn't get in but paid her deposit anyway, and now she's rooming with Becca instead." She blew her nose into a tissue. "She's acting like I'm stupid for being upset about it. She said I need to grow up and get over it."

There was never a bubble for it on the surveys, but a good half of all students seemed to base their college decisions on where their friends or significant others were going, and it was usually the half that had no clue what they wanted to do with their lives. He would've done it himself if Heather hadn't gotten a scholarship to an insanely expensive school without a music program.

At first, she came home every weekend. They'd have band practice at Drew's house on Saturday afternoon and then go on a date later that night. But soon it became every other weekend, and then only once a month until that frozen February morning when she told him she'd met someone new. After one more awkward band practice, she quit that too and never spoke to him again.

Looking into Susan's swollen eyes, he wished he could reassure her that even though most friendships don't last, we always find new people to fill the holes. But what's easy to accept in hindsight is often too painful to consider in the moment.

"Do me a favor, Susan. Imagine Nikki changed her mind about Syracuse and said she'll go anywhere you want and be your roommate. Where do you think you'd go?"

She swallowed. "Marywood."

That was easy. "What do you like about Marywood?"

"We went there a few years ago to watch my cousin play basketball. After the game, she gave us a tour and showed us her dorm, and I just really liked it. I looked them up online last year and they have an Elementary Ed program and a bunch of clubs I like."

"Did you hear back from them yet?"

"I didn't apply."

"Why not?"

"Nikki said it was too close to home. She wants to go somewhere at least two hours away."

"But you don't mind being close to home?"

"I only agreed to go away because I thought she'd be with me."

Did Nikki have any idea how much power she held over this girl? Ian fished out a Marywood application from the file cabinet. "Fill this out and bring it back to me, and we'll see about getting you into your dream school."

She gave him a tiny half smile, and he swelled with pride. *Maybe I can do this father thing after all.*

He wrote her a late slip while she used the private counseling suite bathroom to rinse off her face. When she left, Darryn was already waiting outside on one of the couches. She was a top honors track student and could get into just about any college she wanted. With any luck, her meeting would be over in less than five minutes, and he could use the extra time to call back about that missing transcript.

He wheeled his chair back behind the desk as she took a seat, her many bracelets jangling against each other.

"Okay, I have your transcript and survey results here and everything looks good," he said. "Have you applied to any colleges yet?"

"I've decided not to."

He raised his eyebrows. So much for a short meeting. "Why's that?"

"It's a waste of money," she said.

"What are you gonna do instead? Do you have a plan?"

"Rob's friend is getting me a government office job."

Of course it was her brother's idea. The whole argument *did* seem too devoid of emotion for a high school senior. "And what does your mom think about that?"

Darryn rolled her eyes. "She doesn't care. She can't afford to send another kid to college anyway." That last part was probably true. Mrs. F. had been on disability for years, and the only reason they still had the house was because Rob paid the mortgage. But that's what grants and scholarships were for.

"Did your mom fill out the FAFSA yet?"

"No offense, but I'm tired of school. I've learned more on my own from books and the Internet than I ever did in class."

"That may be true, but you still need a degree to even get an interview in most fields. You're too smart to be satisfied in some menial office job for long."

She shrugged. "If I get bored, I'll go back and get a degree when I have more money."

"The older you get, the harder it is to start over." He couldn't imagine squeezing in classes at this stage of his life. "You'll have more commitments and maybe even a family to support."

"So it's better to be Rob and have a degree I'll never use, and a mountain of debt that won't be paid off until I'm 80?"

He rubbed his face. It kept coming back to Rob. The guy was like a brother to him, but he worked at Best Buy and sold questionably obtained computer parts online. "If this job is so great, why isn't *he* taking it?"

"I don't know, ask *him*."

His head throbbed. He wasn't going to win this one—at least not today—and he had a ton of work to finish before going over to help his father winterize the house. He plopped a pile of brochures on the desk in front of her.

"Do me a favor. At least take these home and look them over before you make your final decision."

"Fine." She jammed them into her backpack. "Can I go now?"

The sun hung low over the mountains but the sky was still bright as he closed his parents' front door, having changed into jeans and a faded grey long johns shirt. His father was already up on a ladder propped against the side of the house, a bucket dangling beside him. Spotting the old cooler they used as a toolbox, Ian dragged it toward the nearest basement window and sat on it.

"How's the new job going?"

Ian cringed. Of course that would be the first thing his father asked.

"I was excited to spend more one-on-one time with the students, but with all the extra duties I have, I'm seeing them even less than I did before." He chipped away at the old caulk with a screwdriver. "A girl came to me today with a problem, and I felt like I really made a difference, but then I realized it was sort of my fault to begin with. I met with her a few weeks ago and she assured me all her applications had been sent out, so I let her go. But if I wasn't in such a rush, I could've taken a few extra minutes to chat and found out she'd applied to all the wrong schools."

"Have you talked to Sister Augustine about this? It seems she should know her students aren't getting the best counsel."

As if he didn't feel shitty enough already. "Her only advice was to delegate, but I don't have anyone to delegate *to*. The other counselors are swamped with more intense issues like broken homes and suicide threats, but at least there are two of them. I still have to do all the administrative stuff myself."

"You need to schedule your time more efficiently. Break down your projects into smaller tasks and set up a master schedule to get them each done."

"That was the first thing I did." Ian threw the screwdriver to the ground, picked up a caulk gun, and started re-lining the window. "I've started looking for a new job, but most of the Catholic high schools around here have closed or merged. I'm thinking of trying colleges next. Maybe Keystone."

He'd actually already checked with his old boss and knew no admissions jobs were open, but maybe his father could pull some strings like he did last time. Never knowing whether he'd gotten that first job on his own merit always bothered him, but he wasn't in the position to be choosy right now.

His father wiped a rag across the top of his window. "I'd concentrate on looking for a solution instead of a way out. You have a child to provide for now."

"I know that." Ian gripped the gun so hard that caulk spurted all over the glass. He was 25 freaking years old— why couldn't they talk man to man without everything becoming a goddamned lecture? He worded his next sentence carefully, hoping to prove he wasn't a complete moron.

"I'm starting to wonder whether sometimes the solution *is* to find a way out."

His father was quiet for a minute. *Oh God, here it comes.*

"I'd wait until you've been there for at least five years before you even think about jumping ship. As you said, schools are closing everywhere. All the teachers who've been let go are vying for the same positions, and many of them have decades more experience than you. You don't want to wind up permanently unemployed."

"Obviously I wouldn't quit until I had something else lined up." He wished he hadn't said anything at all. He stood up and stretched. "I'm not really gonna leave my job. I only wish I'd found a way to make it better already."

His father climbed down the ladder and rested a hand on his shoulder. "You were always the one I didn't have to worry about. I'm confident you'll figure something out."

The house was dark when he got home since Kat wasn't back from her event in Bloomsburg yet. Muscles sore, he took a hot shower before changing into his pajamas and heading into the spare bedroom. Next to the computer desk was a walk-in closet full of various odds and ends they never got around to unpacking after the move. Pushing aside a few of Kat's garment bags, he found the top of his guitar case peeking out from behind a stack of boxes. He set it gently on the floor and flipped open the latches along the side.

The guitar was a low-end BC Rich he'd bought the summer between eighth and ninth grade using graduation money. Originally the body was white but over the years had been plastered with a colorful patchwork of band logo stickers. Between the frets he'd drawn color-coded stars to help him remember which notes were which.

Sitting cross-legged on the floor, he balanced the guitar on his thigh before fingering a G chord and giving the dusty strings a strum. It was disgustingly out of tune, but he grinned, following up with an A, an E, and finally another G, the way he always did to test the accuracy of the tuning. Without a piano or fresh batteries for the tuner, he settled for tuning the strings to themselves, humming the pitch from the first as a guide while he tightened the knob of the next to match it.

After playing a now harmonious G, A, E, G sequence, he took a deep breath as he prepared to play the song about his English teacher, but then froze in horror. He remembered how to play all the chords, but not which order to play them.

He cracked his neck and sat up straighter. *It's not as bad as it seems.* He remembered the melody and most of the lyrics, so all he needed to do was sing the song one note at a time until he figured out which chords matched. He cleared his throat and sang the first word of the song, drawing it out as he played every chord he remembered, but none of them sounded right.

Fuck.

He wanted to cry. He'd played the song hundreds of times before, burning the chord patterns into muscle memory until he could play the damn thing in his sleep. Somewhere in the closet was a folder stuffed with the lyrics sheets he'd obsessively transcribed, but now he wished he'd tried a little harder to do the same with the music instead of rebelling against his professor's unfair standards.

He'd stood in front of her desk in an otherwise empty classroom, beaming at having played his song perfectly when she delivered the blow.

"D."

He didn't understand. "It might not be the best song I've written, but I didn't make any mistakes."

"That's the only reason it wasn't an F." She handed his sheet music back to him. "The piece didn't meet the technical requirements of the assignment, and wasn't performed as written."

He ran a hand through his hair and looked down past his guitar at the floor. College was supposed to be where you *learned* things, yet every music program in the country required you to be an expert before they even let you in. If he couldn't pass the remedial class, there was no way he'd be accepted into the full program next year.

He raised his voice to keep from crying. "I can write and play my own songs. Why does it matter if I can't figure out the damn sheet music?"

She pursed her lips before speaking. "People pay musicians for two reasons—to perform sheet music or to teach *others* to perform sheet music. Whatever talent you think you have is worth squat if you can't apply it to either of those things." Reaching for her briefcase, she gave him one final piece of advice before walking out. "If you want to be a rock star, I suggest declaring a business major and starting a band."

But his band was dead. Shortly after Heather quit, Drew and Greg got bored with practicing, opting instead to spend their free time on various college campuses, drinking and going to parties. At the end of freshman year he finally admitted defeat and transferred to Keystone as a Psychology major, much to the delight of his father, who wasn't shy about saying "I told you so."

He never meant to stop playing forever, only to take a break until it was fun again. But the years flew by, and now there he was, unable to play a single song, with fingers too sore to keep trying.

CHAPTER 14

Wade

The Pomeranian desk ornament's head bobbed ever so slightly, a goofy smile on its face. Beside it sat a framed photo of Alan's wife standing atop a ski slope, bundled up in a parka and clutching a pole in each hand.

What was the question again? Oh yeah, the database.

Wade scrunched up his eyebrows and tried to remember if he'd run the update last week, but everything outside the game world was a blur. How far were they into the current week, anyway? He'd come to work yesterday, so it wasn't Monday, and it probably wasn't Friday either or he'd be more excited about the weekend. Maybe it was Tuesday or Wednesday? He looked down into his lap.

"I'm sorry. I think I forgot to do it."

"That's two weeks in a row." Alan shuffled the papers on his desk. "I also got a message from the call center manager this morning complaining that his team has been waiting over a week for a simple software upgrade that shouldn't take more than five minutes per computer.

I checked the help queue to see what was going on and it's overflowing."

Wade slumped further into the chair. He'd meant to get to that as soon as he finished the carnival level, but it was taking longer than expected and he was on too much of a roll to abandon it for even a few hours. He tried to think of a believable excuse, but his mind felt like molasses.

The lines on Alan's balding forehead became more pronounced. "You're usually a great worker, but you seem distracted lately. Is something wrong?"

I'm lonely as fuck, and I don't give a shit about this company or anyone too dumb to install their own damn software.

Maybe he should say it out loud and get fired. That way he could spend the next few months at home working on his game in peace. But if he didn't finish by the time the unemployment checks ran out, he'd have to move back in with his parents and listen to his dad's lectures every day.

"I'll do both things today and make sure it doesn't happen again."

Back in his cube, he jotted down the words *ski lodge level + dogs* on a sticky note before trudging off toward the elevator with the software disc.

He spent the rest of the afternoon bouncing from desk to desk, doing more work than the last few weeks combined. Just the sight of him in the call center seemed to remind everyone about all the other stupid issues they were having with their computers. He fixed what he could and told the rest of them to log official requests, hoping they'd forget, but when he checked the queue at the end of the day the number of jobs had actually gone up instead of down.

Head pounding, he staggered through his apartment door, leaving the mail on the floor as he changed into a t-shirt and pajama pants and collapsed into bed.

He awoke in darkness to a knock on the window. Groaning, he pulled up the blinds to find Rob flipping him off. Whatever this was, he wasn't in the mood. He opened the window and a blast of cold air smacked him in the face.

"What the fuck, Rob?"

"Let me in, it's cold out." Rob jogged around the side of the apartment before Wade could ask any more questions. Shivering, he closed the window and pulled on his black hoodie as he took his time getting to the front door.

"I'm not feeling well. Why didn't you call first?"

"I did." Rob rubbed his foggy glasses against his jacket sleeve. "I called three times but you didn't answer."

"And you didn't conclude I was busy?"

Rob took a clean cup from the drain board and filled it from the tap. "Close. I concluded you were ignoring me to work on your game, so I came here to force you to take a break."

Wade closed his eyes and held onto the back of a dining chair. "Normally I wouldn't mind, but I had a really shitty day and all I wanna do is go back to sleep."

"You'd be doing us both a favor. *You* need to get out of the house and *I* need help picking up some computers from work."

"So this is really about you?"

"Pretty much. But I promise to buy you tacos when we're done."

Wade's stomach rumbled. "Fine, but you're driving."

As Rob cruised up I-81, Wade's breath formed little clouds in front of his face. Shivering, he pulled his hood strings tight around his chin and was just about to close his eyes when they passed the Dickson City exit. This couldn't be good.

"Where are we going?"

"I'm taking you on an adventure."

"Are you fucking serious?" Wade rubbed his face. "I told you I didn't feel good."

"You don't feel good because you haven't left your apartment in weeks."

"I go to work every day."

"You know that doesn't count."

"What about the computers?" Wade asked.

"There really are computers we could pick up if you wanna be a pussy, but I promise you'll be much happier if we go out and have a good time instead."

Wade closed his eyes, almost afraid to ask. "How far away is this adventure?"

"Clark's Summit."

"Clark's Sum—?" He desperately wanted to point out that heading a few towns over hardly qualified as an adventure, but kept his mouth shut in case Rob agreed and then dragged him all the way to New York. "Fine. Wake me when we get there." He reclined the passenger seat all the way back and curled up into a ball.

He awoke to florescent lights and Rob calling out an order at the Taco Bell drive-thru. Squinting, he adjusted his seat back to the normal position.

"I got you five tacos, an order of nachos, and an orange soda," Rob said. "Is that cool?"

Wade rubbed his face and nodded as Rob paid for the food and passed the bag over.

"Don't open anything yet. We're almost there."

"Fuck you, I'm hungry." Wade tore open a taco wrapper and took a huge, defiant bite. He was halfway through eating it when Rob pulled into the bowling alley parking lot. "You dragged me out of bed to go *bowling*? This couldn't have waited until the weekend?"

"Nope." Rob put the car in park. "Because Amber's working *tonight*."

"Who the fuck is Amber?"

"That redhead you were checking out the last time we were here."

He vaguely remembered the girl having a really nice ass. "How do you know her name or when she's working?"

"One, they wear name tags, and two, there was a schedule on the counter when I was here the other day. I brought you tonight so you could ask her out."

Wade felt a stir of excitement until he looked down at his hoodie and pajama pants ensemble.

"You couldn't have at least told me to put on real pants?"

"Right, because it wouldn't have been suspicious if I suddenly cared about your clothes."

Wade flashed back to the time he'd picked up Jill to have dinner with her grandparents, and she'd made him go home and change first because his shirt wasn't nice enough.

He held his head high. "You know what? I'm glad I'm dressed like this. If she doesn't like it, then fuck her."

The alley was mostly empty except for a few groups scattered across the lanes. Amber leaned against a pillar behind the counter reading a magazine, her flame red hair tied back in short pigtails. Feeling suddenly shy, Wade grabbed the food bag from Rob and started walking away.

"I'll meet you at the lane."

"You don't even know which one we're on yet," Rob called after him.

Ignoring him, Wade sat at a random table, facing away from the counter. He pretended to take a phone call until Rob plopped a pair of shoes in front of him.

"I thought about getting them too small so you'd have to ask for a bigger size."

"I'm glad you didn't."

Rob changed his shoes. "The longer you wait, the harder it's gonna be."

"I haven't done this in years, okay? You didn't give me a lot of time to prepare."

"If I told you any sooner you would've talked yourself out of it."

"I still might." He followed Rob to their lane and opened another taco wrapper.

"I know I gave you shit for never being single, but that was before I knew what happens when you are. You're so depressed you're making *me* depressed."

Wade snuck a peek at the counter, admiring Amber's hourglass figure. She really was sexy.

"So are you going to ask her out or what?"

"On the way out."

"No, do it now."

"Why?"

"Because I'm tired of hearing you bitch and sulk. Go ask her out, and then you can come back and eat your tacos."

"Stop telling me what to do." Wade took another big bite of his taco before standing up.

Jill had been roughly his own height, but Amber was even taller, with at least an inch on him. He hoped that wouldn't turn her off.

She looked up from her magazine as he approached the counter. "Can I help you?"

"I hope so." Resting his elbows on the counter, he leaned forward, heart pounding. He always had the best luck when he laid it out straight.

"I couldn't help but notice how gorgeous you are. Would you let me take you out to dinner this Saturday?"

Her eyes sparkled as she sized him up. Relief flooded his system. He was in.

"My suitemates and I are throwing a party Saturday night over at Keystone," she said. "You should stop by." She had a confident air about her that was so much different than Jill.

"I'd love to." He grinned.

"It's starting around 8." She tore off a strip of receipt paper and wrote her number on it. "Text me when you get to campus."

"Awesome. See you then."

She winked. "Can't wait."

He practically floated back to the lane, grinning like a fool.

Rob smirked. "I'm assuming it went well."

"We're hanging out Saturday."

Rob punched his arm. "And you wanted to stay home and sleep."

Wade whirled around, afraid Amber might be embarrassed by Rob's childish gesture—God knows Jill would've been—but she just laughed. Wade shrugged at her and then pretended to slap Rob on the side of the head.

Rob cupped his hands around his mouth and called out, "Hi, Amber!" She struck a glamour pose and blew a kiss at them. "She's a good sport. If you fuck it up, I might ask her out myself."

"Stay away from my woman," Wade half-joked as he picked up a bowling ball.

"Oh, so now she's your woman? A few minutes ago, you didn't wanna talk to her."

"Fuck you." Wade laughed as he rolled his ball up the lane, missing half the pins.

"Excuse me? Don't you mean *thank* you?"

"Yes. *Thank* you, Rob. You're always right, and I'm always wrong. How can I possibly repay you?"

"You can help me pick up those computers later."

"I hate you so much." Wade shook his head, grinning.

Nestled in the woods, Keystone's campus was quiet except for the faint thumping of bass beats from one of the dorms. Hands in his coat pockets, Wade strolled up the path toward Amber's building as early-season snow danced through the air and landed in a thin blanket on the ground. He'd once dated another girl from this building who screamed so loud her RA banged on the door and warned them to keep it down. He grinned. If there was one thing he missed about school, it was being surrounded by pretty girls his own age. If one didn't like him there were always more who would.

Up ahead, Amber pushed through the front door wearing a little black skirt and a bright red pea coat that matched her hair. She skipped toward him.

"Hey! Glad you could make it." She tucked a lock of hair behind her ear. "Okay, so this is totally tacky of me to ask, but are you over 21?"

"Yes, ma'am."

"Sweet! Would you mind buying beer? I'll totally pay for it."

"No problem."

"Yay! My car's in that lot over there." She led him to a brand new Volkswagen Beetle that already had a huge dent in the passenger side door. Opening it, he found a biology textbook on the seat.

"Bio major?"

"Pre-Physical Therapy."

"Dr. Amber, huh? Need someone to practice on?"

She laughed. "Oh my God, you're so fucking cute!"

He couldn't tell if she was serious or making fun of him. His face grew warm. "I'm all right."

She drove onto the highway. "Are you still in school?"

"Nope. I work in tech support at an insurance company."

"Sounds boring."

"Well, it's kind of supposed to be, considering it's a front for my real job as a superhero."

She glanced over at him before looking back at the road. "What are your super powers?"

"Oh, you'll find out soon enough." He grinned.

At the state store, she picked out a case of Corona and he carried it to the counter. She swiped his ID before he had a chance to put it away.

"Aww, your hair used to be so much longer."

"Give me that," he reached for the card but she danced away, still staring at it. Her eyes suddenly grew wide.

"Are you related to Professor Dakalski?"

He rolled his eyes as he finished paying for the beer. He could never seem to meet anyone at Keystone without getting that same reaction.

"He's my father."

"No way." She squinted at the card as if looking for a resemblance. Thankfully, he'd always looked more like his mother. "I had him for bioethics last year. He was kind of an ass."

"Try living with him."

"No thanks." She laughed as she slid the ID into his front jeans pocket and patted it. Holy shit, this girl didn't waste any time.

She held the door for him and then skipped ahead to open the trunk of her car. As he leaned over to put the case inside, something smacked him in the side of the head and he jerked upward, smashing his head into the trunk hatch.

"Oh my God, I'm so sorry! Are you okay?" She rushed to his side.

Reaching in his hood, he felt the cold wet remains of a snowball. He leaned back against the car, pretending to be dazed.

"I might have a concussion. You should probably take me to the hospital."

He tried to suppress his smile, but she must've seen it because she gave him a strange look. Before she could react any further, he closed his hand around the snow and smeared it on the side of her face. She screamed and ran behind another car, laughing.

Crouching behind her car, he gathered up more snow from the ground as another snowball whizzed by his head. Popping up for a second, he hurled the misshapen mound, barely missing her. He couldn't stop smiling.

Making sure she saw him, he ran around the side of the building and flattened his body against the bricks, heart pounding. *Come on. Come find me.* When she finally peeked her head around the corner, he pulled her toward him, kissing her. Kissing him back, she jumped into his arms and wrapped her legs around his torso. Afraid they might both topple over, he quickly steadied her weight against the side of building. All the blood rushed from his head and pooled farther below, leaving him light-headed, but more alive than ever. He'd forgotten what a thrill it was to kiss someone new. It was like a live wire direct to his soul.

She pulled back, eyes sparkling. "Let's go back to my place and get drunk!"

Swept away by her enthusiasm, he probably would've agreed to rob a bank if she'd suggested it.

Her suite's common room was lit by strings of multi-colored Christmas lights draped around the perimeter of the ceiling. Four girls and a guy sat in a circle on the floor, listening to high-speed pop music and playing some kind of card game. One of them cheered when she saw the beer. Amber unbuttoned her coat to reveal a black t-shirt so thin that her leopard-print bra showed through.

"This is Wade, the guy I met at the bowling alley."

He swelled with pride knowing she'd talked about him.

Her friends widened the circle to make room for them as Amber passed around the beers. The game turned out to be a weird combination of Slapjack and Bullshit. Even after he got the hang of it he played dumb because every time he messed up, Amber would pull him close and whisper instructions in his ear.

They were all pre-med majors, and their conversations revolved mostly around various tests and papers. As much as he missed the steady social scene of college, he had zero desire to ever go back and do homework again.

Amber bopped her head along to the music, seeming slightly tipsy even though she'd only had one beer. "So what do you do when you're not hacking computers or saving the world?"

"I'm programming my own video game."

"Oh my God, that's so cool! What's it about?"

He hadn't revealed the premise to a single soul, but she was hanging on his every word and probably didn't know enough about gaming to criticize him.

"It's about a scientist whose wife is dying. He's going back and visiting places that were special to them while trying to develop a cure."

"That's so sweet. How does it end?"

He poked her side. "I can't tell you *that*. It ruins the surprise."

"Come on. I promise I won't tell anyone." She rubbed his leg.

"Well, he saves her." Saying it out loud for the first time made him uncomfortably aware of how cliché it sounded, but thankfully Amber kept smiling.

"Aww, yay!" She clinked her beer bottle against his.

They played another few rounds of cards until she suddenly turned to him, eyes wide. "Do you like oranges?"

He raised an eyebrow. "That's a strange question."

"Do you, though?"

"They're okay, I guess."

"Come here." She took his hands, pulling him off the floor and into a messy bedroom plastered with movie posters and lit with even more Christmas lights. He doubted very much that any of this had to do with fruit.

She hopped over a bean bag chair and grabbed an orange out of a basket on the mini-fridge. "Think fast!" Her aim was off, but he caught it right before it would've slammed into her computer monitor. This was definitely the strangest ploy a girl had ever used to get him in her room.

He shook his head. "You're such a weirdo."

"You love it."

"I can't dispute that."

Locking eyes with her, he playfully pushed her onto the bed. She looked up at him with big coy eyes and he almost couldn't breathe. Climbing on top of her, he kissed her again, this time more tenderly. He slid a hand under her shirt and felt rock hard abs.

"Holy shit, your body's amazing."

"Thanks." Her voice shook slightly.

He slid two fingers along the inside of her waistband and realized she wasn't wearing underwear. Grinning, he pushed up her skirt and buried his head between her legs. She arched her back and let out a stream of barely intelligible profanities as the music played on outside the door.

The next morning, he awoke with a crick in his spine from sleeping pressed up against the wall in the twin-sized bed, but smiled when he saw the mop of ruby hair splayed out on the pillow beside him. He draped an arm around her waist and kissed her neck.

She blinked up at him. "Hey, handsome."

"God, I could spend all day here with you."

"Well, you can't." She stretched. "I have to go home for my dad's birthday."

He traced the crease at her elbow. "When can I see you again?"

"I'm free next Saturday if you wanna catch a movie."

"Sounds perfect." He climbed on top of her and kissed her again.

His phone beeped and a photo of a little red dress appeared on the screen. *Can't wait to see you tonight.*

Is that what you're wearing? he texted back.

Not right now :-P

What are you wearing now?

Not much. Just got out of the shower

Okay, I'm leaving RIGHT NOW

Keep your pants on, cowboy... At least until tonight ;)

Leaning back in his computer chair, Wade stared guiltily out his bedroom window. He'd spent more time that afternoon texting Amber and taking snack breaks than actually working on his game.

Fuck it. He hadn't been able to concentrate all week. What was another day? He closed the laptop and pulled down his pajama pants, thinking about Amber.

Afterward, he stared at the ceiling, still bothered by what she'd said—or rather, *hadn't* said—about his game's ending. She'd thought it was sweet, but not much else.

Old school games barely had endings at all, but they made up for it with intense final boss music followed by a victorious anthem that made you feel like the king of the world. But you couldn't really get away with that anymore. These days, games had to have epic plots and twist endings. He needed something else—something that would stick with players long after they turned off the game.

Dumping out his wallet, he found the business card with Drew's game industry friend's number on the back.

"Hi, is this Thom?"

"Yeah. Who's this?"

"I'm friends with Drew Shafer. He said I could call for advice about making video games."

"Sorry buddy, that job was filled months ago."

"Oh, no, I don't need a job. I'm designing a game and the ending is kind of bland. I was hoping you could give me a few tips on how to make it better."

"What kind of game is it?"

"It's sort of like *Myst*. You explore areas and find clues."

"What's your target audience?"

Wade picked up a pen and started clicking it. "I don't know. I haven't really thought about it."

"Wait. Who commissioned this thing without doing the research?"

"No one. It's just a game I'm making."

Thom's tone soured. "Listen buddy, I know indie games have been getting good press lately, but most of those developers have been in the industry for years. You're one of Drew's Scranton friends, right?"

"Yeah," he answered tentatively, wondering what that had to do with anything.

"This might sound harsh, but trust me, nothing is happening in Scranton, Pennsylvania. If you're serious about breaking into the scene, you need to move out to New York or LA and get a job as a beta tester. Learn the ropes, network with the pros, and get involved with as much as they'll let you."

Wade scowled. Was this the advice Drew really had in mind, or did Thom misunderstand? "Look, I appreciate the advice, but is there anything you can suggest for someone like me who mainly wants to make sure their personal project doesn't fall flat?"

Thom sighed. "What are you trying to say with the game—is there a moral or a theme?"

Wade scanned the potato chip bags, empty soda bottles, and pages upon pages of maps and notes littering his desk. "I never really had a plan. The girl I wanted to marry dumped me and this is the only thing that's kept me from going insane. But now it's more than that. I don't really know why, but I think I will once I finish. And I *have* to finish, or else it's all been for nothing."

"Sorry, buddy. That's rough." The line went silent and Wade almost hung up, thinking that was all the prick had to say, but then Thom continued in a slightly more sympathetic tone. "Maybe go to the library—read up on the art of storytelling and figure out what you're trying to say. You'll probably have to scrap a lot of what you've already done, but at least the end product will be more coherent."

His head hurt. He thanked Thom as graciously as he could before hanging up and checking his bedside clock. It was almost 6 now, and he wasn't meeting Amber at the theater until 8. That was plenty of time for a short nap. He set the alarm for 7 and lay down, pulling the covers over his head.

Rolling over, he became aware of the soft blanket around him. His mouth tasted foul, as if he'd awoken from a particularly deep sleep. *Oh shit.* He jerked around, checking the clock. It was 10:54.

"No, no, no, fuck!" He grabbed the alarm clock. It was set for 7 *am* instead of *pm.*

God, I'm a fucking moron.

He had multiple texts and missed calls from Amber. Without bothering to check them, he called right back.

"What the fuck do *you* want?" Her voice wavered as if she'd been crying.

"Amber, I'm so incredibly sorry. I took a nap and overslept."

"Are you fucking kidding me? You leave me hanging for three hours and that's the best you come up with?"

"I know you're mad. I'd be mad at me too, but it's the honest to God truth, I swear. Let me make it up to you. I can come over right now."

"Oh sure, you wanna come over *now* when it's too late to see a movie and the only thing left to do is stay in and fuck."

What the hell? "That's not what I meant at all."

"Were you with another girl?"

"God, no. Why would you even think that?"

She sobbed. "I thought you were a nice guy, but you're no different than all the other assholes."

"Please let me come over. We don't even have to do anything."

The line went dead. He called back, but it went straight to voicemail. "Amber, I really like you, and I swear to God I never meant to hurt you. Please call me back." He jammed his feet into his sneakers and sprinted toward the door.

The freezing air ripped through his hoodie and thin pajama pants, but he didn't bother to go back for a coat, just hopped in his car and sped toward the highway. He mentally replayed the events of their date, trying to remember if he'd said or done anything that would make her jump to such awful conclusions about him.

Stopped at a red light, he scrolled through the texts she'd sent throughout the night. They started off flirty and friendly, asking if he was there yet, then transitioned to worried as if something bad had happened to him, then finally became bitter and angry as she described in detail why and how he could go to hell.

He'd put up with a lot of illogical shit from Jill toward the end, but she'd been so laid back in the beginning. It was one of the things that made him like her in the first place. If Amber was this crazy this early on, he was probably better off walking away.

When the light changed, he turned around and drove to Rob's place instead. The whole house was dark except for the basement windows. *God bless the insomniacs.*

Rob opened the basement door, looking him up and down. "What happened to you?"

Shivering, Wade bounced in place, trying to keep warm. "Would it be totally gay if I said I needed a hug?"

Rob enveloped him in a bear hug, almost knocking him over. "If there was anyone I'd be gay for, it would definitely be you." He let go. "Now get inside before we freeze our balls off."

Greeted by blessed warmth and the scent of fresh laundry, Wade ducked under a row of shirts drying on the clothesline and went into Rob's room. He collapsed on the unmade bed as Rob sat at his workbench, fiddling with the guts of a disassembled computer.

"So, what happened with Amber?" It was embarrassing yet somehow comforting that Rob always seemed to know what was wrong.

"She's insane—and not in a good way." He told the whole story, starting with their date the week before and ending at that very moment. "Promise you won't let me date anyone else until my game's done."

Rob screwed something into the computer's CPU. "That's a little extreme, don't you think?"

"I'm serious. I can't handle it."

"It sucks this one turned out to be bat-shit, but you can't deny you were happier for a few days."

"But now I feel worse than I did before. And I couldn't concentrate on my game all week."

"I say this with all the love in the world, Wade, but maybe you need to take a break from your game, not real life. I've seen you get together and break up with a lot of girls over the years, but even when you were really bummed, you always bounced back quickly. I know this shit with Jill is different, but you're drowning in your own sorrow and it's not like you at all."

"This isn't about Jill anymore. I don't even want her back."

"I believe you believe that."

Wade rolled his eyes. "Look, I admit I'm kind of down right now, but if I stop working on my game even for a little while, I don't think I'll be able to start again. It'll be yet another great idea that I never saw all the way through, and I'll hate myself for it."

Rob hurled an X-Box controller at him, hitting him square in the shoulder.

"What the fuck? That hurt."

"When was the last time you *played* a game—for *fun?*"

Rubbing his shoulder, Wade tried to think back but his memory was fuzzy. Was *his* game fun?

Rob held up the cases of *Dead Rising* and *Halo 3*. "What do you feel like killing tonight—zombies or aliens?"

As they played into the early hours of the morning, he had to admit there was something cathartic about creating makeshift weapons out of items at the mall and then using them to smash through hordes of the undead.

He slept late the next morning before driving to the library downtown. Thom was an asshole, but he had a point. Without a good story he couldn't have a good ending.

He hadn't been to this library since high school, but the musty air smelled immediately familiar. An elderly woman with a long white ponytail stood over a book cart near the front desk.

"Excuse me." He kept his voice low. "I'm looking for books about storytelling."

"Wonderful." She smiled brightly, beckoning him down a narrow corridor with floor-to-ceiling bookshelves on either side. "Are you writing a novel?"

It might be a little hard to explain, especially to some-one so old. "It's more of a short story."

She motioned to a shelf near the end of the row. "This is where we keep general information on literature and writing. Did you need anything more specific?"

"Nope, this is fine. Thank you."

As she walked away, he scanned the titles until he found one called *The Basics of Storytelling*. Sitting on a footstool, he skimmed through the pages and couldn't help but laugh. After a lifetime of constant media expo-sure, most of the advice sounded like common sense, yet he'd made almost every mistake listed.

A pretty girl with long brown hair walked past the aisle, holding a stack of papers to her chest. She looked strangely familiar, but he couldn't place her. Craning his neck, he peered through an empty space between the shelves, trying to sneak a better look.

His phone rang, echoing obnoxiously through the peaceful library chamber. Feeling like a jerk for not si-lencing it, he answered quickly without checking the caller ID.

"Hello," he whispered.

"Hey, it's Amber." Her voice was sweet and calm. "I'm sorry about last night. I was just mad because I thought you stood me up."

"It's okay." It really wasn't, but he didn't know what else to say.

"Do you wanna come over tonight? I promise I'll make it up to you."

Oh God, don't do this to me. He balled his hand into a fist and held it tightly against his forehead. It was guaranteed sex—but it would be with a crazy person. He'd also never hear the end of it after how much he'd gone on to Rob about needing a break from girls. *I can't believe I'm about to say this.*

"I don't think that's a good idea."

"What about tomorrow? My last class ends at four."

"No, I mean this isn't working out—you and me."

"I said I was sorry." Her tone sharpened.

"I accept your apology. But I don't think we should see each other anymore."

"Why? Do you think I'm some kind of whore? That you can sleep with me once and throw me away?"

Oh God, this is exactly why I'm not doing this. "No, I just don't think it's working out."

"Fine. I hope your next fuck gives you AIDS." She hung up.

He sat there, stunned. No girl had ever said such awful things to him, and he'd known her for less than 24 hours total.

He took the storytelling book up to the front counter, looking around for the familiar girl as he went, but she was nowhere to be found. At the desk, he met the elderly librarian again.

"Can I check this out? I don't have a card."

"I'll make you one. Can I see your ID?"

He handed over his license and then browsed the titles on the return cart while she typed his information into the computer. Finding the full version of H.G. Wells's *The Time Machine,* he pulled it out and flipped through the pages. It was almost as short as the children's version, *and* it was a classic. Maybe reading an actual novel could help him with this whole story thing. He slid it across the counter. "This too, please."

CHAPTER 15

Kat

S tanding in front of the mirror in the foyer, Kat zipped up her new winter coat and stared at her reflection in horror. With her top and bottom narrow and her middle so overstuffed, she looked like a Russian stacking doll. *Six more weeks, and I'll never have to look like this again.* At least it would make telling her parents easier—she wouldn't need to say a single word.

Picking up her purse from the foyer table, she glimpsed an envelope addressed to *Katherine Ann Dakalski* from the Social Security Office. Inside was a new card with that same name on it. *What the hell?*

Hands shaking, she stormed out into the crisp afternoon air as Ian loaded their suitcases into the trunk of his car.

"How dare you change my name without consulting me?"

Eyes wide, he raised both hands and took a step back. "The form was already signed when I found it. I thought I was helping."

She slapped the paperwork against his chest. "Then why is my middle name still Ann instead of Kerwin?"

"It must've been a mistake. I swear I didn't change anything." He examined the paperwork. "Look, there's a number here. You can call from the car and get it straightened out."

After being bounced from clerk to clerk, none of whom had any idea what might've gone wrong or how to fix it, they were halfway to Philadelphia before she was finally connected with a well-spoken man with a fancy title. She'd explained the situation so many times it rolled off her tongue like a rehearsed speech.

"It's part of the Patriot Act," he explained. "We can't change middle names anymore without a court order."

You've gotta be fucking kidding me. "How do I get one of those?"

"You'll need to file a petition with the court to be seen in front of a judge. If the judge grants the order, you'll have to advertise your new name in at least two local papers and submit notarized copies of all the documents to our office. All in all, it'll probably cost you a few hundred dollars."

Tears brewed in her eyes. There was no way she could justify spending that much on a name change. Not with a mortgage and a baby on the way. Even if they *could* afford it, it wasn't fair. Women had been taking their last names as middle names for hundreds of years without hassle. Did the government really think this was going to stop terrorists hell-bent on blowing up the country?

"There has to be another way."

The man on the phone sounded unconcerned. "You can hyphenate, or have two last names, or even change your first name. The middle name is the only one we can't legally touch."

The tears broke free and she sniffled through her words. "Why didn't anyone bother to call and tell me any of this? You didn't even give me a choice."

"I'm sorry, ma'am. The only other thing we can do is change it back to the way it was."

"How do I do that?"

"Fill out another name change form."

But in the meantime she'd be stuck with a name she hated. She threw her phone at the car floor and vented the whole ridiculous situation to Ian.

"It's not really that bad, is it?" he asked, staring ahead at the highway. "Either way, you're Katherine Dakalski. No one really uses their middle names anyway."

"That's not the point—it's still bullshit. I'm allowed to name our child *Mickey Mouse* or *Banana Sundae*, but not choose my own fucking middle name?"

"They had to come up with something to keep the country safe."

She wanted to slap him. "You're seriously agreeing with them?"

"I'm saying there was probably a well-researched reason behind the law. I'm sorry it means you can't have the
middle name you want, but it's the last name that counts,
right?"

"Easy for you to say. You get to keep your whole name
intact."

"I thought you *wanted* to change it."

"I did." She twisted her fingers above her bulging
stomach, trying to figure out why it bothered her so
much. "I know it's stupid and shouldn't matter, but I feel
like I lost a huge part of who I am. I never liked the name
Ann, but Kerwin was everything."

"So hyphenate it," he said, like it was really that
simple.

"That's even worse. Whenever people see hyphenated
names, all they think is, 'oh, she must be married.' They
make all these crazy assumptions about you before they
even meet you."

He gripped the steering wheel tighter. "Fine. Do what
you want."

Thanks for the permission.

She stared out at the rolling farmland. This was exactly why she didn't want to tell him she was having second thoughts. It was all his fault, too. He shouldn't have
mailed the form without saying anything—and what was
he doing in her glove compartment, anyway? Still, she
felt terrible for upsetting him.

"I'm sorry I flipped out." That much at least was true.

"It's fine," he mumbled, staring straight ahead. But it obviously wasn't. She kept waiting for him to say something else or reach for her hand, but he kept both hands firmly on the wheel, anger practically radiating from his stiff posture.

They'd had a few disagreements here and there, but he'd always been more frustrated than angry. The only time it came close to an actual fight was when she said she wanted to get married in a park or on the beach, and he insisted upon the church even though he barely set foot in the place. She knew how to talk him down when he was upset with other people, but not when he was mad at her.

They rode the rest of the way in silence, the sick feeling in the pit of her stomach growing as they left the Turnpike and drove down Roosevelt Boulevard, the sprawling shopping complexes and brick row homes counting down the minutes to the inevitable.

When they reached her parents' narrow one-way street, Ian pulled up beside the pair of weather-beaten patio chairs left to reserve their parking spot. Kat eased herself out of the car and carried the chairs up the steps to the gated patio where her bald and burly father sat, beer in hand, watching a basketball game on the tiny TV from her old bedroom.

"Hey Kat," he said good-naturedly, obviously having had a few beers before this one. "How was the drive?"

"It was okay." She was glad he was alone. Telling him first would be easier. "I have a surprise for you." She put down the chairs and opened the front of her coat. He did a double take before wrapping her in a big bear hug.

"Congratulations, Kat. That's great."

"Thanks, Dad." She breathed easier, knowing no matter what came next she'd have him on her side.

The gate creaked open behind them as Ian appeared with the suitcases. Her father shook his hand and slapped him on the back. "Makes you feel like a man, doesn't it?"

"It's pretty amazing." Ian smiled for the first time since that morning. Hopefully he wouldn't be mad for too much longer.

Her dad opened the cooler next to the TV and passed a beer to Ian. "Here you go, daddy." He patted Kat on the head. "Don't worry, you'll get yours as soon as you pop that kid out."

A shrill voice interrupted the little party. "You're *pregnant?*"

Her mother stood behind the screen door, blouse tucked into her khakis, short brown hair blown out and pinned back on both sides.

Kat cringed. "Surprise!"

Frowning, her mother turned on her heel and slammed the door behind her.

"Don't mind her, she's still pissed about the new TV." Her father rolled his eyes. "Said it was too big and disrupted the flow of the living room or some bullshit." He elbowed Ian, dropping his voice to a whisper. "I told her I was tired of watching porn in standard definition. Let's just say she was not amused." He chuckled. "But I guess she still won because the TV's going back to the store, and I'm stuck out here with this ancient piece of shit."

If Kat didn't go inside now, it was liable to be ten times worse later.

In the living room, the offending flat screen TV had been re-packed into a box almost as long as she was tall and propped against the glass display cabinet full of her various trophies, ribbons, and certificates. Slipping off her shoes, she draped her coat over the back of an antique armchair before venturing into the kitchen where her mother was emptying the dishwasher in the most needlessly dramatic way possible.

"When did you tell Ian's parents?"

Kat leaned on the counter next to a warm crock-pot full of meatballs. "I wanted to wait, but he told them early on."

"What about your friends?"

"He told most of them, too."

"Did he tell your workplace as well?"

Kat's hands shook, and she held her stomach for support. "I had to tell them about two months in, okay? I was going home sick so often they would've thought I was lying otherwise."

"So the entire world knew before your own mother." She slammed a cabinet door. "How far are you along, anyway? You're as big as a house."

Gee, thanks, Mom. "Seven months." It was really almost eight, but rounding down seemed safer.

"Seven months!" She threw her arms across her chest. "Do you have any idea how this is going to look to the rest of the family? To my friends?" She shook her head. "It was bad enough you wouldn't let me help plan the wedding, or even go dress shopping with you, but to hide a pregnancy from me for *seven months,"* she trailed off. "I'm disappointed, Katherine."

Her blood pressure skyrocketed. "I didn't wanna make a big deal out of it, okay?"

"You're having a *baby.* In what world is that not a big deal?"

"I'm perfectly aware that having a baby's a big deal. I just didn't want people fawning all over me or babbling on about babies as if that's all I could possibly care about now."

"Am I even going to be allowed to see it once it's born, or is it only going to have one set of grandparents?"

"Oh my God, Mom. For once, can you not make this about you? You haven't even congratulated me."

"I thought you didn't want to make a big deal out of it."

"I don't!" The baby kicked her hard in the ribs, as if even *she* was fed up with all the fighting.

"Are you finished?" her mother asked coldly.

Feeling like a scolded child, Kat breathed slowly through her nose, her temples throbbing. "I need to lie down. It was a long drive, and I'm tired. Excuse me."

Back aching, she climbed the stairs to her old bedroom where the hammocks full of stuffed animals and lacy purple curtains of her childhood still coexisted with the No Doubt posters and piles of cheap makeup from her teenage years.

Easing herself onto the twin bed, she reached for the plush spider her father had won for her out of a supermarket claw machine when she was little. Hugging it to her chest, she scanned the photos taped to the wall—old friends from school and various sports teams, and a prom photo with her high school ex.

She'd wanted to go all the way that night, but couldn't get her mother's voice out of her head. *Only stupid girls have sex.* She'd once threatened to drag her to the abortion clinic if she ever got pregnant so she wouldn't be doomed to flip burgers for the rest of her life. It was unbelievable. What her mother once deemed the worst fate imaginable was now the very thing she couldn't wait to brag to her friends about.

Kat massaged her stomach. "If you want your room to be pink, I'll paint it pink. I'll even paint it neon yellow with turquoise polka dots if that's what you want."

After a short nap, Kat washed her face and ventured back downstairs, still clutching the plush spider. Everyone was in the dining room, eating without her. She set the spider on the table and helped herself to spaghetti and meatballs.

Her mother wrinkled her nose at the spider. "Why is that here?"

"I'm giving it to the baby."

"Ian tells me it's a girl. Why don't you give her something nicer, like one of your teddy bears?"

"Because I'm giving her this."

Her mother sighed. "Well, get it off the table. We're eating."

Kat poured a glass of iced tea, ignoring the request.

"I'm thinking about the Radisson for the shower," her mother continued, twirling spaghetti around her fork. "They have that lovely little room with the mirrors and walk out courtyard. Marie's daughter threw her a retirement party there this summer and it was absolutely perfect."

"I don't want a shower." Kat cringed at the thought of middle-aged women feeling her up and forcing her to play baby-themed games.

"Why not? Did Ian's mother already throw you one?"

"No. I just don't want one."

"Honestly, Katherine. Everyone does it. I don't know why you have to be so difficult." She stabbed a meatball with her fork. "Who's going to be in the delivery room with you?"

"Only Ian. Everyone else can visit after we're home from the hospital."

She pursed her lips, but thankfully didn't press the issue. "Are you still working?"

"All the way until I go into labor. That way I can take advantage of the full three months of leave afterward."

"You're going back so soon? Who's going to take care of the baby?"

"We found a daycare near the high school so Ian can drop her off every morning."

Her mother frowned. "Can't you afford to live off Ian's salary? Donna McKinley put her son in daycare, but it's so expensive that her entire salary goes toward paying for it. She might as well have saved the money and spent more quality time with him. You can't get those years back, you know."

This coming from the woman who'd drilled it into her head that education and career were everything.

"*You* worked."

"I gave my two weeks the day I found out I was pregnant and didn't go back until you were in first grade. I would've stayed home longer, but we needed the extra money to send you to all those good schools."

"I don't get it. Why was my education such a big deal if your greatest ambition for me this whole time was apparently to become a stay at home mom?"

"Everyone needs a backup plan. What if you'd never gotten married, or Heaven forbid Ian becomes disabled or passes away?"

Kat's hands shook so much she had to put her fork down. Growing up, her parents and teachers had assured her that she was smart and talented and would go on to do great things, and she worked her ass off to prove them right. But for what? No one gave a shit about her GPA or any of those ridiculous awards in the living room.

Because in real life none of it mattered unless it had a direct effect on the bottom line. And now she was having a baby, which was statistically the *most* common and therefore *least* interesting way a woman could contribute to the world. She might as well wear a badge that said "failure."

Feeling like she might cry all over again, she stayed quiet as her mother babbled on about what her friends and their children were doing for the holidays. Meanwhile, Ian slowly sipped his beer and refused to make eye contact, making her feel even worse. After dinner, she pulled him aside.

"Can we please go to my room and talk?"

Wordlessly, he followed her upstairs. He sat on the bed beside her but left an awkward foot of space between them.

"I'm sorry," she said. "I should've told you I was having second thoughts about changing my name. I couldn't make up my mind and didn't wanna disappoint you until I knew for sure."

He ran a hand through his hair, taking a few moments to answer. "Well, honestly I *am* disappointed. First you don't want anyone to know you're pregnant, and now you don't even want them to know we're married," he trailed off. "I don't know, Kat, what am I supposed to think?"

"That's not what I meant at all." Tears streamed down her cheeks anew, and she wished she could take back everything she'd said in the car. None of it was worth permanently damaging their relationship over. "I love you, and I love our life together. And you're right—it doesn't really matter what my middle name is. I was just caught off guard this morning."

She waited for him to say it was okay or that he understood, but he only sat there, staring at the floor. "I just... I don't know," she continued. "So much is happening so fast. I used to feel like I knew exactly who I was, but now everything's getting blurry like I don't know who I am anymore."

"You're still the same person," he said quietly. "You're just overthinking it."

"But that's the thing. I wasn't thinking about it *enough* before." She searched for the right words. "It's like I'm not sure where other people end and I begin. Like, when I was younger, did I ever do anything because I really wanted to, or was I always just trying to impress or defy my parents?"

"All kids do that, Kat. It's part of growing up."

But it wasn't only her parents. There'd always been *someone* she was adapting for, whether it was friends, boyfriends, or some amorphous concept of society. She rarely stopped to ask what *she* wanted to do. And now she was doing it with Ian. Forget changing her name, she'd agreed to *have a baby* mainly to avoid disappointing him. She'd ignored that uneasy feeling in the pit of her stomach because she didn't understand why it was there. It hadn't occurred to her that she didn't owe him a logical explanation—that simply "not wanting to" was a valid enough reason to say no.

But there was no way to undo that now. Her only option was to be much more mindful about this kind of thing going forward.

"You're right. I probably *am* overthinking it." She sighed, hoping that agreeing with him would smooth things over one last time. "I'm just so tired of being pregnant. Everything hurts, and I'm always in some kind of mood. I think once she's out, I'll finally start feeling like myself again."

She inched closer and hugged him. He sat motionless for a few seconds before hugging her back so tightly it hurt. But she didn't mind the pain—it meant he still loved her.

CHAPTER 16

Eleanor

Stretching her arms above her head, Eleanor bent backward as far as she could, her muscles sore from hunching over her computer all morning. On her desk sat the culprit, a file of handwritten legal correspondence dating back to the 1870's. Halfway through transcribing a 4-page tome on the settlement of a disputed property line, she could no longer see individual words or phrases, only an impenetrable block of narrowly-spaced curlicues. She reached for her coat. If she didn't take a break now she'd go insane.

Outside the library, she sat on the low concrete wall that separated the sidewalk from the yard, the bitter wind coaxing her back to life. Across the street, a construction worker in a crane basket was re-painting the fourth floor windowsills of a castle-like building with turrets.

Downtown Scranton was a photographer's paradise, with beautifully eclectic architecture lining every street and wide swaths of ivy climbing even the plainest buildings. Not everyone got to work in a library modeled after a French chateau monastery. Some days it was the only thing that made life bearable.

Behind her, a group of college girls pushed through the library's main door, bundled up in hats and scarves and laughing way louder than could possibly be necessary. Shivering, Eleanor hugged her arms to her chest. She should've moved back sooner. With a college practically around every corner, she could've done her grad work here while taking advantage of the college scene. She might've even met Trent at school or through mutual friends.

But now she was too old for the college scene and too young for everyone else. Most of her coworkers were at least twice her age and busy raising families. It seemed like most students retreated to their hometowns after graduation, and anyone left behind immediately got married and started having kids. There was hardly anyone in between. Except Natalie.

She bit her lip. The last thing she needed was an obligation to make small talk at regular intervals with yet another fake friend. But if she didn't make a connection soon she might die of loneliness.

Ignoring the hollow fear in the pit of her stomach, she went back inside for the bin of returned children's books and then carried them next door. The rubber soles of her shoes squeaked against the tile floor, announcing her arrival to the woman behind the desk.

"Hi," Eleanor said, her voice high-pitched and small. Embarrassed, she reached for her lower register before continuing. "I'm here from next door to return your books."

"Thank you," the librarian said, reaching for the bin.

In the main room, a mother and two young children milled around a picture book display, but no one else was in sight.

Eleanor shifted her weight. "Is Natalie here?" she asked, half-hoping the answer was no.

"She's in the reading room doing story time."

Eleanor nodded, palms clammy. "Thanks."

She wandered through the stacks until she heard voices. In a side room, Natalie was surrounded by a semi-circle of preschoolers and their parents sitting in beanbag chairs or directly on the colorful alphabet carpet. Dressed in a bright green skirt and striped tights, Natalie matched the room's décor in an oddly endearing way that made her seem almost a part of it. Each time she finished reading a page, she'd flip the book around so the kids could see the picture. Maybe she wasn't so bad after all.

Eleanor hung back outside the door, mentally rehearsing what she'd say until story time was over and patrons began shuffling out. She walked up to Natalie, hands shoved in her coat pockets.

"Hey."

Natalie did a double take, but then smiled. "Hey! Eleanor, right?"

"Yeah." She blurted out the rest quickly, wanting to get it over with. "I was here returning books and wondered if you'd maybe want to go to lunch with me." She held her breath, waiting for Natalie to laugh or make some excuse, but she simply nodded and smiled.

"Sounds good!"

Sitting across the table from Natalie, Eleanor unwrapped the tinfoil around her bagel sandwich, trying to think of something else to say. On the short walk over from the library, they'd exhausted the easier topics like the weather and how much they both loved the sandwiches at the coffee shop. She'd recently read that the best way to keep a conversation going was to ask the other person questions, so *they'd* keep talking—except she wasn't so great at thinking up questions either.

"So, what do you do at the library?" she asked, hoping the question wasn't too dull or obvious.

Natalie shrugged. "A little of everything—help people find things, organize programs, scrape boogers off books."

Eleanor wrinkled her nose, secretly relieved that she had a similar story to share. "Someone once returned a book covered in sticky pink slime."

"Yeah, people are gross, and kids are worse." Natalie took a gulp of water. "Funny story. One time I found a picture book stuffed behind a shelving unit. When I pull it out, I see it's got macaroni noodles glued all over the cover. That was the last time we let kids bring books into the craft room."

Eleanor laughed, relaxing a bit. Natalie was actually kind of funny and didn't seem to be judging her at all. "How long have you worked there?"

"Almost a year. I started college wanting to be a teacher, but got placed in the library for work study and found out that was more my speed. Instead of teaching the same stuff to the same grade level every year, I get to help kids of all ages with tons of different projects. It's something new every day."

"I kind of always liked libraries because they *don't* change." Eleanor took a bite of her sandwich, weighing how much to divulge. "My family moved a lot when I was growing up and libraries were one of the few places that were the same everywhere. I always knew how to find exactly what I needed."

Natalie laughed. "That sounds fun, getting to move all the time. I grew up in Dunmore with the same hundred or so kids from kindergarten through high school."

Eleanor's heart raced. "What year did you graduate?" she asked, trying to sound only generally curious.

"2000."

She almost choked on her sandwich. They'd been in the same class. It was such a small school—she had to at least *know* Trent, even if they weren't friends. She hesitated to say anything in case Natalie suddenly remembered embarrassing stories about the awkward transfer student and spread them to the rest of the library staff, but she was out of ideas.

"I was in your class sophomore year, but only for a month."

Natalie's jaw dropped, the gears almost visibly turning in her head. "Get out, that was you?"

She didn't know whether to be elated or terrified. "You remember me?"

"Well, kind of. I remember a new girl showing up and then leaving again, but not really anything else. Who did you have class with?"

Her face grew hot. She didn't want to seem obsessed by bringing up Trent right away. "I had Mr. Tomaselli for History."

Natalie dropped her hands to the table. "He's in jail."

"What? Why?"

"Insurance fraud. He paid some guy to wreck his truck, but they got caught."

"That's crazy."

"I know. It was all over the news for weeks." She sipped her water. "But who did you hang out with, student-wise?"

Eleanor played with the edges of her sandwich wrapper. "Mostly this one guy. I think his name was Trent."

Her eyes grew wide. "Trent *Zarella*?"

Why did she say it like that? *Oh no, please don't let him be in jail or worse.* "Yeah, I think that was it."

"Last I heard he was still in the area, but he hasn't talked to anyone in years."

"Why not?"

"No one knows. People would see him around and try to say hi, but he'd start walking the other way like he didn't see them." Natalie shrugged. "He was always a little... out there."

She could barely sit still—that might as well have been a description of *her*. With everything they had in common, she surely still had a chance with him.

Natalie sat up. "My brother and I are having a bonfire this Saturday with some high school friends. You should come by. I'll ask around and see if anyone has Trent's number."

She felt sick. She wanted to see Trent more than anything, but the thought of a mini-class reunion filled her with dread. What if he rejected her in front of everyone? She didn't have much choice, though. It was either this party, or nothing.

She swallowed. "Sure. Why not?"

Shivering, Eleanor shoved her gloved hands in her coat pockets as she hung back behind a naked maple tree. About two dozen people mulled around the yard, mostly in a circle near a small brick fire pit. Squinting, she looked for Trent, but with everyone bundled up in coats, hats, and scarves, it was hard to distinguish one guy from another. Finally, she recognized Natalie as she emerged from the back door, holding a tray of miniature hoagies. She took a deep breath and sidled up beside her.

"Hey."

Natalie jumped. "Shit, you scared me." She set the tray on a folding table with other snacks and drinks. "Help yourself. The bathroom's at the end of the upstairs hall if you need it."

"Thanks." She wasn't thirsty but chose a can of ginger ale just to have something to hold. "So, who's all here?"

"Come on, I'll introduce you." Heart thumping frantically, she followed Natalie to the group around the fire pit, the flames painting dancing Rorschach shapes on their faces.

"This is Eleanor," Natalie said, "the girl I was telling you about. She went to Dunmore with us for about a month."

A friendly chorus of greetings followed. They seemed nice enough but were all staring at her and she had no idea what to say. She hugged her arms to her chest.

"Hey."

"What year were you?" a guy asked.

"2000." She rocked backward on her heels.

"I'm trying to think, but I can't remember. I probably didn't have class with you."

Another girl spoke up. "Yeah, you did. She was in Geometry with us but was really quiet and sat way in the back."

"Ohhhh yeah."

Eleanor wanted to cry. Being remembered as the quiet, unremarkable one was worse than not being remembered at all.

"Why were you only there for a month?" another guy asked.

"My dad's in the Army. He got emergency orders soon after we moved here."

"I thought all the Army kids went to Gouldsboro." He stared at her, waiting for an explanation like she had any idea how the system worked.

She shrugged. "I don't really know."

"No, they went to Dunmore sometimes," another girl added. "Remember Davey Horvath?"

"Oh my God, he was hilarious!" The mood in the crowd suddenly perked up as everyone agreed.

"Remember when we did *42nd Street* and he'd dance around backstage wearing the fur stoll?"

"I had such a crush on him."

"Wasn't he gay?"

"I don't think so. He was completely in love with Beth."

"*Everyone* was in love with Beth."

Eleanor kicked at the ground as they went on and on about how wonderful Davey the Army brat was, forgetting about her all over again. She turned to Natalie, keeping her voice low.

"Did you happen to talk to Trent?"

"I asked around but no one has his number. He's not on Facebook or anything either, so I couldn't invite him."

"Oh, that's okay." If she'd known ahead of time she wouldn't have bothered coming. Her chest felt so hollow she feared it might collapse. She took another sip of ginger ale. She should probably fake an illness and go home.

"Did you guys hook up or something?"

Eleanor almost choked on her drink. She wasn't even entirely sure what that phrase meant. "What? Oh, no. We were just friends."

"Did you wanna be more?"

She stared at the ground, wishing she were anywhere else. "I don't know. I never really thought about it."

Natalie nodded toward a guy across the yard. "There's the guy *I* like."

"Who is he?" Eleanor asked, relieved at the change of subject.

"My brother's friend, Nick. We've liked each other for years, but haven't been single at the same time until now. I'm totally hooking up with him tonight."

"How do you know he likes you? Did he tell you?"

"He didn't have to. No matter how many people are in the room, he's always paying attention to me. Sometimes we'll lock eyes for a second, and there's this unspoken understanding that we'd be all over each other if we weren't already dating other people."

"If you liked him so much, why didn't you break up with your boyfriend?"

"Because I loved him too much to risk losing him over a crush that might not pan out." Natalie shrugged. "But it turns out my boyfriend didn't *mind* being a cheating prick, so I dumped his ass and now get to have Nick with a clear conscience. Be right back. I'm gonna say hi."

As soon as Nick saw Natalie, he smiled and picked her up off the ground, giving her a big hug. If Eleanor didn't know better she would've sworn they were already together. It must be nice to feel so unafraid.

Abandoned in the circle, she pretended to sip from her now empty ginger ale can, willing Natalie to come back, but Natalie went in the house with Nick instead. She thought about following them and asking to be introduced, but with all these people around, she couldn't expect Natalie to stick to her side all night.

Instead, she tried to smile and laugh along with the group as they continued reminiscing about drama club, but there were so many inside jokes and non-sequiturs that she always lagged a beat behind and wound up feeling even more out of place.

The fire seemed to grow warmer with every passing minute. Sweating inside her thick coat, she felt like she was suffocating

Just ask someone a question. They won't kill you. They probably won't even think you're stupid or strange.

The girl beside her wasn't talking either, only laughing at what everyone else said. Trying to channel her work persona, Eleanor squared her shoulders and deepened her voice, asking one of her pre-prepared questions.

"So how long have you known Natalie?"

"Since kindergarten."

Eleanor hadn't known anyone but her parents for more than three years at a time, let alone 20. Everyone else sort of existed in these static bubbles of what it might mean to be 6, 12, or 18 years old, without any past or future.

"What's it like to know someone for that long?" she asked. "Do they change a lot, or mostly stay the same?"

The girl gave her a strange look. "Um, that's kind of a tough question." She laughed, and pondered it for a moment. "I think if you know someone long enough, you can usually sort of guess what they're gonna say or do next. But then sometimes they change so much so fast that you wonder if you ever knew them at all."

Before she could think of a reply, a big drunk guy let out a guttural yell from somewhere behind them. Rushing the circle, he threw his arms around the girl she'd been talking to, knocking half the crowd off balance. Flailing, Eleanor reached for the snack table, but missed, her palms scraping along the ground.

Clutching her aching hands, she looked up to find the circle had shifted and tightened, leaving her stranded behind a laughing wall of coats. They didn't notice she was gone—not even the girl she'd *just* been talking to.

Her lip trembled as tears pooled in her eyes. Pulling her hair across her face, she strode up and into the house, locking herself in the bathroom at the end of the upstairs hall. Doubling over, she squeezed her eyes shut and held her mouth wide open, screaming without sound. Why couldn't she be a normal human being like everyone else?

She paced the small room, holding her breath for 10 seconds and then letting it out in a slow, focused stream until her lungs were empty.

These are all perfectly nice people. They simply don't know you enough to care.

The panic ebbing a bit, she sat on the floor in front of the heating vent, leaning against the wall.

You're going to be okay. Take a few minutes to calm down, then go find someone else who's alone and ask them questions. You might even make a friend.

A muffled scream echoed through the vent. Brow furrowed, she leaned closer.

"Just a little slower. Oh my God, that feels amazing." It was Natalie.

Glued in place, she couldn't stop listening. How was that even possible? A half hour ago they'd hadn't even said they liked each other, and now they were having sex?

Her insides coiled into an angry ball. It wasn't fair. Why did everyone else get to have easy love and companionship while she was always stuck behind, watching and waiting?

Shaking, she stood up. None of them had his number, but she knew exactly where he lived.

The front windows of his apartment were dark, but a light shone like a beacon from a window near the back. Shivering uncontrollably with nerves and the cold, she climbed the steps to the second floor landing and knocked on his front door. She still had no idea what to say, but maybe it didn't matter. If this was supposed to work out, it would.

Cars whizzed by on the main road as she waited. Maybe he was in the bathroom. She knocked again, louder this time, but knew in her bones he wasn't there.

He was never there.

She slumped against the cold concrete wall, the last of her courage draining away. How many more times would she need to come back before he finally answered? She thought back to all those soul-crushing trips to Budget. She couldn't go through that again. One way or another, this had to end tonight.

Fumbling with her purse, she pulled out a small notepad and started writing.

Hey Trent—I don't know if you remember me, but we went to high school together for about a month back in sophomore year. I'm living in Scranton now and would love to hear from you.

She signed it with her name and number, and re-read it a few times to make sure it didn't sound too desperate. Sliding it into the mail slot, she felt an immediate wave of relief. She'd done all she could do. Everything was on him now.

CHAPTER 17

Wade

The smell of kielbasa and baked ham hung in the air as Wade kicked the snow off his sneakers in his parents' doorway. In the living room, Ian and Jeremy lounged on the couch watching TV. At the sound of the door his cousin Greta ran into the room and gave him a hug.

"You wanna see what I made?"

"You bet I do."

Taking his hand, she dragged him toward the Christmas tree, which was significantly smaller than the ones they used to get. She pointed to a heart-shaped construction paper ornament.

"I made them at school. There's one on my tree at home, and I gave one to Jeremy."

"Where's mine?"

"You have to share with your mom and dad."

"Whaaaat?" He rumpled her hair, and she ran away, laughing.

"What's up, little cuz?" Jeremy called from the couch, his blonde ponytail longer than it'd ever been. "Ian told me you're making a video game?"

"Yeah, I am," he answered, wondering what kind of shitty things Ian had said about it.

"What's it about?"

He gave a few details about the genre and style. "I'm done with four levels. I'll probably make one or two more."

"No shit." Jeremy nodded. "So it's like a real game, huh?"

Wade supposed that was a compliment.

"Um, yeah. I'm not sure about the ending, though. I've been trying to figure it out for the past couple weeks but haven't come up with anything good yet."

Ian assumed his obnoxious teacher voice. "When students tell me they have unsolvable problems, I tell them to think of at least three different solutions. The first is usually a cop out that requires everyone else to change while they stay the same, but by the time they get to number three or four, they start getting more creative. Plus, they're more likely to try a plan they thought up themselves rather than anything I suggest."

Wade expected a haughty put down, but Ian seemed to be taking him seriously. "That's... pretty decent advice."

Their mother interrupted, wielding her wooden spoon like an air traffic controller. "Jeremy, we need you in the kitchen slicing ham. Ian, you can start setting the table. And Wade, go upstairs and gather everyone else for dinner."

He found his father in his office, showing off a new all-in-one printer-copier-scanner-fax machine to Uncle Edward and Kat, who looked impossibly huge and miserable. Being pregnant must suck ass. He considered making a joke to cheer her up but decided it might wind up getting him killed instead.

"Mom said dinner's almost ready."

His father waved him away. "We'll be down in a few minutes."

Wade heard a squeal from his old bedroom. He pushed open the door and his jaw dropped. The walls had been painted pink, white lacy curtains hung from the windows, and a floral comforter was spread across a queen-sized bed where Alicia was changing JJ's diaper.

"Wow. My mom couldn't *wait* to flush out whatever testosterone was left in this room."

Alicia laughed. "At least you still *have* a room. My parents sold my childhood home and bought an RV as soon as I moved out."

"It's just... weird," he said, opening the closet door, a whiff of potpourri overpowering him. Coughing, he closed the door. "Obviously our parents weren't always parents, but it's so hard to picture it. Like, seriously— my mom and dad *dated*."

"I know, right?" Alicia balanced JJ against her hip. "And they had sex too."

"Oh God, now you went too far." Wade laughed, dropping his face in his hands and trying desperately to think of anything else. "How weird is it that one day JJ's gonna grow up and think the same thing about you and Jeremy?"

"It might be fun. When he's a teenager, we can threaten to have loud sex in the next room if he misbehaves."

"You're so mean."

"I know, right?" She grinned.

They went down to the dining room where the family was packed like sardines around the table. He squeezed into an empty seat as Alicia maneuvered JJ into his high chair.

Uncle Edward uncorked a bottle of wine. "If you kids keep having babies, we're going to run out of room at the table."

"We'll *make* room," his mother called from the kitchen as she carried in the platter of sliced ham. "So by all means, keep having babies."

"Not until this guy's at least potty trained." Jeremy winked.

Wade glanced around the room. Aside from Greta and JJ, he was the only one who wasn't married with kids. He felt more alone than ever. It would've been nice to at least have a girlfriend to hold hands with under the table.

His father raised his glass. "A toast—to the continued health and happiness of everyone here, especially to Sally's clean bill of health."

"Here, here." Everyone clinked glasses and set about to eating.

"What happened to your mom?" Wade asked Jeremy, keeping his voice low.

"She found a lump in her breast, but the biopsy was negative."

"What?" Wade almost dropped his fork. "When?"

"Early November."

"No one told me." He turned to Ian. "Did you know?"

"Dad told me."

"When?"

"I don't know—a few weeks ago?"

"Relax, dude." Jeremy shrugged. "It was benign."

Sulking, Wade shoved a forkful of potato salad into his mouth. He'd seen his parents on Thanksgiving and neither had mentioned it, yet they'd told Ian.

After dinner, he swiped a half-emptied bottle of wine and snuck into the basement. Whenever his parents bought a new sofa or TV, the old ones would be re-homed downstairs as a playroom for Ian and him. Kicking a deflated soccer ball out of his path, he scanned the collection of VHS tapes stored along one of the exposed wall beams, looking for something funny. He spotted a tape marked *Letterman Performance*, and a smile spread across his face as he slid it out of the case and into the VCR.

"My name is Ian Dakalski. On my left is Drew Shafer, on my right is Heather Ladczyk, and that crazy man behind the drums is Greg Fisher. We are Black Ice, and this next song is called 'Hate You.'"

They were set up in Rob's basement, an old blanket tacked up on the wall as a backdrop. Ian was still a scrawny beanpole and Drew's gut sagged over the front of his jeans—neither one had started working out yet. The camera panned back and forth, zooming in and out erratically. They'd hoped it would look like an MTV music video, but really it just made everyone dizzy.

Ian stepped up to the mic, violently strumming his guitar. *"Stars are burning bright and casting light upon my knife. I swear that this will be your last time."*

Wade cracked up. Drew's angry poetry sounded so silly in Ian's soothing voice, especially since he always stood up straight, looking so damned serious. Meanwhile, Drew thrashed around, occasionally kicking out a leg or jumping off the amps, while Heather stared at the floor like she didn't want to be there.

At the end of the song, Ian thanked his invisible audience and the camera panned to a metal-mouthed Rob sitting at a desk and wearing an oversized tweed jacket in a poor imitation of David Letterman. He clapped and gestured to the band as they took seats in folding chairs beside him.

"Give it up for our special guests, Black Ice! The band has graciously agreed to stay on and be interviewed about their early days and current success."

Ian and Drew took turns going on about how they met in middle school and decided to buy guitars one summer for the sole purpose of starting a band. Ian was giving a particularly pompous answer about his musical influences when the interview abruptly cut off. It was replaced by grainy video of the Sideling Hill Tunnel entrance along an abandoned stretch of the Pennsylvania Turnpike.

His heart stopped. He knew he should turn the video off, but couldn't seem to move a muscle. His own voice spoke off-camera.

"Ladies and gentlemen, we're just about ready to embark on a fantastic journey back to a long-gone era! Our tour guide tonight will be none other than my girlfriend, the lovely Jill!"

She sat on a fallen tree trunk wearing an Alkaline Trio t-shirt, pink streaks in her long brown hair. She giggled and covered her face as he zoomed in closer. She was so goddamned cute his heart ripped in two all over again. He felt like sobbing, and took a gulp of wine to keep it down.

"What do you want me to say?" she asked.

"Just talk about what we're doing like when you told me about the idea."

"Okay, okay." She waved at the camera like a goofball and tried to imitate his tone. *"Tonight we'll be exploring an old tunnel and looking for ghosts!"*

"Wooooooo!"

"Is that supposed to be a ghost?"

"It's a ghost call. It lets them know we're here so they get ready to show themselves."

She scoffed. *"They probably all flew away because of how stupid it sounded."*

"Whaaat?" He rushed toward her, and she screamed as he tackled her off the tree trunk.

The basement door creaked open and he fumbled with the remote control.

"Wade, honey, are you down there?" his mother called out.

"Yes," he replied, hoping she'd leave him alone, but knowing she wouldn't. She walked down far enough to clear the ceiling beams.

"What are you doing?"

"Watching movies."

"Well, we have guests, so you need to come back upstairs."

"*You* have guests," he snapped, not entirely sure why. It might've been the wine.

"Excuse me?"

"*I* don't live here anymore. So technically they're *your* guests, not mine."

"Don't be fresh with me."

"Why didn't you tell me about Aunt Sally?"

"What about her?"

"That she might've had fucking cancer!" He didn't mean to curse, or yell, but was glad he did. Maybe now she'd take him seriously.

She crossed her arms. "You know I don't like that kind of language."

"And I don't like when you keep things from me."

"No one was keeping anything from you."

"Then how come you told Ian and not me?"

"I didn't tell Ian—Dad did."

Now who's being fresh? "And how come you never took us to see Uncle Rick and Aunt Rita? I didn't even get a chance to know them."

"She had Alzheimer's, Wade. You know that."

"What about Uncle Rick? He was all alone every day taking care of her. He must've been lonely as fuck."

She gripped the railing, her knuckles turning white. "Do you have any idea what it's like to spend your childhood watching a relative waste away and die? No, you don't. And do you know *why* you don't? Because I do, and I spared you from it."

He felt awful, but didn't know what to say.

She let go of the railing to wipe a tear from her eye, her voice turning to quiet steel. "It's never the things you think you did wrong. It's the things you swore you did right or don't remember doing at all." She pointed at him. "Remember that."

She stamped up the stairs and shut the door behind her. He knew he should follow and apologize but didn't feel like it. No one ever cared when they were upsetting *him.*

Leaning back on the couch, he stared at the paused image of Jill on the screen. He missed her so much his whole body ached. It was Christmas. She was probably at home with her parents right now.

* * *

All the lights were on in Jill's parents' house as he trudged through the snow to the front porch. Her father answered the door, clearly taken aback.

"Jill didn't say she was expecting you."

"I just need to talk to her for a few minutes."

"Wait here." He closed the door.

Wade blew hot air into his hands and rubbed them together, his breath fogging in front of his face. A minute later, Jill stepped outside, buttoning up her coat.

"What are you doing here?" she whispered. "My whole family's inside."

"I swear I won't make a scene. I just need to ask you something and then I'll go."

She sighed. "What?"

"When we first got together, you were this carefree girl with pink streaks in her hair who wanted to explore tunnels and hunt for ghosts, but then you started wanting to wear fancy clothes and go wine tasting, and you wouldn't laugh at my jokes anymore. I wanna know what changed. And please don't tell me it's because you grew up. There has to be more to it."

She folded her arms across her chest, looking at him with a mixture of weariness and pity. "Because it was cute to be carefree in college. But after we graduated, I needed more out of life than playing video games and dyeing my hair. I wanted to start saving for a house and a family, but you were content to carry on exactly as before. I thought I could give you the push you needed by finding the apartment, but it made me resent you even more for making me feel like the naggy girlfriend."

"But even if we got married, bought a house, and had a kid, what then?" He shook his head. "We'd still be people, not robots that only pay bills and do chores. If we have to stop being silly and having fun, what's the point of the rest of it?" He didn't expect to change her mind, but wanted some kind of reassurance that he wasn't a hopeless cause—that her change of heart was the result of something specific, not the inevitable conclusion of all women.

The door creaked open and a basketball-player-tall young man in a sweater vest placed a hand on the small of Jill's back. "Is everything okay?" he asked.

Wade narrowed his eyes. *Who the fuck are you?*

"Everything's fine. We're pretty much done here," Jill said, resting a hand on the guy's chest. "Wade, this is Sam, my fiancé."

The word felt like a punch to the gut.

"Nice to meet you," Wade said through clenched teeth before turning back to Jill. "Can we have a few more minutes please?"

She stood on tiptoes and kissed Sam's cheek. "I'll be inside soon, babe."

Wade dug his hands into his pockets, clenching his fists to keep from crying as Sam went back inside. "You said there wasn't anyone else."

"There wasn't. I met him over the summer, the night before I broke it off with you for good."

His heart felt like it was dissolving in acid. "And after only four months, you knew he was the one?"

"I knew after the very first date." She shrugged. "I know it doesn't make sense—God knows my parents think I'm rushing—but once you know what doesn't work for you it's so much easier to recognize what does."

I'm what didn't work. He clenched his fists tighter. "Okay, then."

For a moment it seemed like she might hug him, but she reached for the doorknob instead. "Maybe I'll see you around sometime." After everything they'd been through, that was seriously all she could say?

"Yeah. See you."

CHAPTER 18

Ian

Ian sat at the edge of his chair as Sister Augustine silently scanned the report, her brow furrowed under the tuft of silver bangs. The median PSAT score was down 40 points from last year despite the mandatory in-class coaching sessions he'd run for both the sophomores and juniors. Either these kids weren't as smart as the last bunch or they simply cared less, but either way, it wasn't his fault. He'd done his job.

"They almost always do better on the SAT," he said, wringing his hands in his lap. "Plus, if you leave out the highest and lowest 10 percent, the median actually goes up 20 points."

"Run a remedial session for anyone who scored below the 50th percentile. Make it mandatory." She handed the report back to him. "How are we on college acceptances?"

"Most of the seniors have been accepted into at least one school, and those who haven't are mostly waiting on decisions that haven't been sent out yet. There's a few who've been consistently denied, but I'm working on getting them enrolled in community. And there's one girl going directly into the workforce."

"Whether she's getting a job is irrelevant—has she been accepted to college?"

"Well, no." He shifted in his seat. "She hasn't applied to any."

"What do you mean she hasn't applied?" Sister Augustine demanded, as if it were a grave oversight on his part. But he didn't have any more control over Darryn than he did the PSAT scores.

"I tried to convince her to reconsider but she's adamant. I even called her mother, but she fully supports the decision."

Sister Augustine's dark beady eyes pierced right through him. "Who is this student?"

"Darryn Fitzgerald."

She folded her hands on top of the desk. "The only reason Holy Nativity has stayed afloat these past few years is because of our reputation of academic excellence, which includes our widely advertised 100 percent college acceptance rate. If we allow parents to question whether the extra thousands of dollars a year are worth it, we may as well load their children into buses and drive them to Bishop O'Hara ourselves."

His heart beat faster. "Kids get denied all the time, but we don't count it against them as long as they eventually wind up *somewhere*. If Darryn doesn't apply, then technically she shouldn't count against the rate either."

"We're not in the business of technicalities, Mr. Dakalski."

His nostrils flared. *Everything* with her was a technicality. He sat up straighter. "Darryn's more of an exception than a technicality, anyway. She's extremely bright but money's tight for her family right now. Her brother already has the job lined up and it's office work, not retail or food service. I know she'll be fine."

He blinked, suddenly realizing he believed everything he'd said.

Sister Augustine's face remained hard. "The full list of acceptances is published in the graduation program each year. A blank space next to her name would jeopardize the livelihoods of our entire faculty and staff. I don't care if she's working for the President of the United States—get her accepted to college, or *else.*"

His blood ran cold. Did she just threaten to fire him? "Yes, sister," he mumbled, collecting his files.

He stopped by the main office to check Darryn's schedule before heading up to the third floor science labs, getting angrier with every step. Sister Augustine was a bully, plain and simple—no better than Harvey Mathis, the kid he'd once thrown up against these very same lockers for picking on Wade.

It was the beginning of Wade's freshman year and Harvey singled him out at least once a day for being almost a whole head shorter than the other boys. Taking the bait, Wade would grow red-faced and throw a fit right in the middle of the hallway. It was embarrassing to watch, and Ian hated the kid for taking advantage of such an easy target.

Thankfully, Harvey backed down without a true fight, and Ian spent the rest of the day with his head held high, proud of having come to his brother's rescue. But as soon as the school bus dropped them off that afternoon, Wade slammed his heavy backpack into Ian's side.

"What the fuck did you say to Harvey Mathis?"

Ian rubbed his side. "I told him to leave you alone. You should be thanking me."

"Yeah? Well, thanks a lot, because now he's telling people I'm a baby who gets my brother to fight my battles."

"What?" Ian felt legitimately bad for not foreseeing that possibility.

"I could deal with him saying I'm short, because I am, but now everyone thinks I'm a wuss."

"Right, because throwing a tantrum like a five-year-old is a perfectly legitimate way of dealing with it."

"What else was I supposed to do? I'm too small to fight him, but I can't just stand there and do nothing while he says shit about me."

A strange thought struck him. "That's exactly what you should do."

"Bullshit. Then everyone will *really* think I'm a wuss."

"Hear me out." Ian tried to grasp the idea before it floated away. "Why do you think Harvey started saying shit about you in the first place?"

Wade scoffed. "Because he's an asshole?"

"Yeah, but he's an asshole who's not much bigger than you." Honestly, that was probably the only reason he'd been brave enough to threaten the kid in the first place. "Maybe he was hoping if he singled you out as the short one, no one would notice that he's short too. Right now you look like an idiot for getting upset about it, but if you walk away and pretend it doesn't bother you, then *you'll* look confident while *he* looks like the idiot." Ian nodded to himself. "It'll probably take a few tries, but as long as you don't give him the reaction he's looking for, I bet he gets bored and moves on to someone else."

And his advice worked. By the end of the second week, Harvey seemed to forget Wade even existed. Sometimes the only way to fight bullies was to simply stop fighting them.

He knocked on the Chem Lab door and called Darryn into the hall. "I changed my mind. I think it's fantastic that you have such a clear idea of what you want out of life. I wish I had the same presence of mind at your age."

"Thank you?" She wrinkled her brow, waiting for the catch, making him feel worse about what he had to say next.

"However, Sister Augustine still wants you to apply to community even though you know you won't go. It's so she can keep advertising the school's 100 percent college acceptance rate."

"That's bullshit."

"Trust me, I know. But we all have to do things we don't like sometimes."

She crossed her arms. "Maybe *you* do."

He ran a hand through his hair. "Look, I know this must sound stupid to you, but there's a lot going on that you don't know about. It won't cost you a thing to humor her this one time."

"You're right. That does sound stupid."

He grit his teeth. If she were his child, he might slap her across the face for being so smugly obnoxious. But it was pointless. Even if she did promise to fill out an application, there was no guarantee she'd actually do it. Then he'd wind up back in Sister Augustine's office next month with no news of progress and his job possibly on the line for real. Fuck both of them—he could end this by himself right now.

Back in his office, he filled out an application to community with Darryn's information, but using Wade's home address so she never had to know. It was completely unethical, but would give both women the illusion of getting what they wanted while hurting no one.

His cell phone vibrated as he was printing out a copy of Darryn's transcript.

"Hey Kat, is everything okay?"

Her voice wavered on the other end. "My water broke."

CHAPTER 19

Kat

Screaming, Kat doubled over, pressing down hard on her stomach.

"Breathe, sweetie. You're doing so great," the nurse said, a hand on her shoulder. It was the same thing she'd been saying all night, but it was clearly a lie. If she was doing great the baby would've been there hours ago.

As the pain subsided, Kat collapsed against the propped up mattress, every muscle aching as if she'd been run over by a truck.

The nurse rubbed her back. "Try to stop pressing on your stomach. It's not good for you."

Fuck you. It's the only thing that makes me feel less like I'm dying.

"I'm going to check your blood pressure. Try to relax, okay?"

Used to the drill, Kat held out her arm for the blood pressure cuff. The nurse then pulled out a latex glove. *Oh fuck. Not again.*

"I need you to spread your knees so I can check your cervix."

Squeezing Ian's hand, she screamed again as the nurse inserted two fingers, sending a white-hot bolt of pain through her entire body. With all the machines she was wired to, it was bullshit that they couldn't measure her progress some other way. She held her breath, hoping for good news.

"You're still only dilated three out of ten centimeters."

Kat whimpered, covering her face. Aside from the pain and exhaustion, layers of dried sweat coated her skin and sticky residue clung to the insides of her thighs. Forget the baby, all she really wanted was a shower.

The nurse rubbed her back again. "Are you sure you don't want an epidural? It could still be awhile, and you're going to need your strength when it's time to start pushing."

"I'm fine."

Ian looked at the nurse, brow furrowed. "Do you recommend it?"

"I said, *no!*" It came out harsher than she intended but she didn't care. She was the one going through this, not them.

"There's no need to be worried yet. Last week I saw a woman go from three to baby in less than half an hour." She rubbed Kat's shoulder. "You're doing great. I'll check on you again in a little bit."

No sooner was the nurse out the door than another contraction came on. Shaking, Kat clutched the bed's side rail and moaned into her pillow. After thousands of years of human evolution, you'd think biology would've found an easier way to do this.

After a minute, her muscles relaxed, and she looked up at Ian. "I hate this so much."

He brushed a stray hair behind her ear, the lines across his forehead deep as ravines. "I don't understand why you won't get the epidural. This is a hospital. They wouldn't give you something that's not safe."

"It's not that... it's just... I've never felt as helpless in my whole life as I have during these last nine months." A warm tear slid down her cheek. "I need at least this one thing I can be proud of."

He kissed her forehead. "You have nothing to feel ashamed of. You're amazing and perfect in every way."

She choked out a laugh. "But I'm not. I'm a complete wreck—I've just gotten really good at hiding it."

"Come on. If *you're* a wreck, what does that make *me?*" He took her hand. "If our roles were reversed, would you wanna stand by and watch me suffer, or would you tell me to take the drugs?"

"But that's different."

"Why is it different?"

Because no one expects more from you.

That sounded so arrogant, like she thought he was trash and she was so much better—exactly like that judgmental lady from the conference who'd made her feel bad about taking drugs in the first place. Was that really all this came down to, winning some kind of female pissing contest? That wasn't the example she wanted to set for her daughter.

"I guess it's not different."

She took aspirin all the time for much lesser pains without feeling remotely guilty about it, but that was probably due to being raised by parents who freely used medication.

Oh my God, why is it so hard to figure out my own damn mind? She closed her eyes and tried to think. *What do I want more than anything right now?*

Her insides seized up again. She grit her teeth and grasped Ian's hand. "Call the nurse."

She awoke to dim grey light outside her window and the soft clicking of the IV monitor. Ian dozed in the reclining chair beside the bed. Squinting up at the clock on the wall, she did the math—it'd been roughly 20 hours. She tried to roll over, but her lower body was frozen in place. Even though it meant the pain was gone, it was still freaky, and she wished the whole damn thing was over already.

She pressed the call button. A few minutes later, the nurse arrived and checked her cervix again. At least this time it didn't hurt.

"Please tell me it's time to start pushing."

"I'm sorry, honey. You're still only at three."

Kat let out a half-laugh, half-sob. "How is that even possible?"

"It's called 'failure to progress.' It has nothing to do with anything you did or didn't do. It just happens sometimes."

As if she didn't already feel like a failure. "Isn't there something else you can do?"

"We could start you on Pitocin to try to speed things along, but you're coming up on a full day since your water broke, and you haven't dilated any further since you were admitted. I'll consult with your doctor, but she's most likely going to recommend a C-section."

Her heart stopped. She'd never even broken a bone before, let alone needed surgery. She imagined knives slicing through her skin and a hideous Frankenstein stitching across her stomach. She squeezed her eyes shut and tried not to cry.

"It's not as bad as it sounds," the nurse said, taking a seat on the edge of the bed. "The surgeon on duty today is excellent. He's been doing this every day for 20 years. And the scar isn't bad, either—it's a horizontal line right above the pubic area, so no one will see it, even if you're wearing a bikini."

But I'll see it. And so will Ian. She looked over at him, his chest rising and falling peacefully.

"Do you want me to wake your husband so you can talk about it?"

"No." She needed to figure this out by herself. And to do that she needed facts, not emotions. "What happens if I don't get the surgery?"

"Like I said, we'll start you on Pitocin to try to kick start the dilation."

"And what if that doesn't work?"

"At the 24-hour mark, we'll recommend surgery again. You can still opt out, but the longer you wait, the higher the risk of infection for you and the baby. And if there's an emergency you'll be rushed to surgery anyway, but under more dangerous conditions."

She breathed slowly, trying to take it all in. The surgery seemed inevitable. The best she could do was choose it while it was still a choice.

The next hour saw a flurry of activity as doctors and nurses came in and out of her room, taking her vitals, explaining the procedure, and giving her forms to sign. An attendant then wheeled her bed down a long corridor that stank of urine and bleach. Maneuvering the bed into a freight-sized elevator, he pressed the B2 button. Her heart skipped a beat. There was something fundamentally unsettling about being operated on in a basement. Weren't morgues on that level?

The doors opened into a dimly lit hallway lined with puke green tile that even *looked* like a morgue. It all felt strangely appropriate. After all, she'd failed to do the one thing her body was designed to do, and that untold billions of women had done throughout history. If she'd lived in any other time period, she'd be dying in agony.

The newspaper notice would read, *Katherine Dakalski, 25, died in childbirth.*

In the pre-op room, a young man named Mike introduced himself as the anesthesiologist as he fitted an oxygen tube under her nose. "I'll be standing next to you during the procedure and monitoring your levels. If you start feeling strange or sick in any way, let me know."

"Can you please just put me to sleep?" she asked. "I really don't wanna be awake while they're cutting me open." That was by far the scariest part.

"It's actually much safer being awake." He held back her hair and fitted a shower cap around her head. "Plus, this way you'll get to meet your baby right away."

During all the commotion, she kept forgetting the whole point of this was to have a baby.

Mike wheeled her bed into a cold, brightly lit room full of machines. Five or six staff members dressed in matching green scrubs, facemasks, and shower caps bustled around the large table in the center. Two of them helped Mike lift her onto it, and then hung a thick green sheet from a rod above her, so that she couldn't see past her neck. She didn't want to watch them cutting her stomach open, but from behind the sheet she couldn't see anything except Mike, the sheet, and the ceiling. She felt left out.

"Where's Ian?"

"As soon as we're done prepping you, he'll be allowed in," Mike said.

She heard a different voice from the other side of the sheet. "Can you feel this?"

"Is he talking to me?"

"Yup. Do you feel anything?"

"Is he touching me right now?"

"We're good back here," Mike called out, resting a cool hand on her forehead. "Can someone get her husband?"

She almost didn't recognize Ian, dressed in the same scrubs and face gear as the rest of the staff. He sat in a chair beside her and held her hand.

"You're almost done. Only a few more minutes, and we'll finally get to meet Lili."

"That's a beautiful name," Mike said. "What made you choose it?"

Ian laughed. "Well, originally I suggested Lilka, after a character in one of my favorite video games, but Kat said *Lilka Dakalski* sounded like an old woman in a kerchief straight off the boat from Poland, so we shortened it to Lili."

"I thought it sounded graceful and strong at the same time," Kat added.

"Is this your first baby?"

"Yup."

She couldn't see Ian's mouth, but knew he was grinning underneath his facemask.

"Congratulations," Mike said. "So should I expect to see you back here in another few years, or has all this turned you off to the whole birthing thing?"

Kat shook her head. "God, no. I'm never doing this again."

Ian looked a little taken aback, but Mike laughed. "That's what they all say. But they also say you forget the worst of the pain once it's over."

Sure. And I'm the Queen of England.

Listening to the murmurs on the other side of the sheet, Kat grew restless.

"When are they gonna start?"

"They already did."

The beeping of her heart monitor sped up. "What? They're cutting into me right now?"

"Yup. And you're doing great."

I'm not doing anything at all.

Ian craned his neck around the side of the sheet and immediately turned white, covering his mouth. "Oh God."

"What does it look like?" she asked, suddenly more intrigued than scared.

He shut his eyes. "Bloody."

She looked up at Mike. "Is there a monitor? Can I watch the rest?"

"Nope, but if you really want to, you can watch videos on YouTube when you get home."

After a few more minutes she heard the disembodied voice again. "We're going to take her out now." She felt a tugging sensation and a strange pressure on her spine, but just as quickly, it was gone again.

"Happy birthday, little girl," the doctor said.

"She's out?"

Ian peered over the sheet again as Mike squeezed her shoulder. "Don't worry—C-section babies always take a minute or so to start crying, but they're usually fine."

She felt like the worst mother in the world for not even noticing the baby wasn't crying. As the seconds dragged by, she started to doubt there even *was* a baby until she heard a tiny gasp followed by a series of shallow, short screams. Ian's hand shot to his mouth, and for the first time ever she saw him cry.

"Where is she? I wanna see her." It wasn't fair that everyone else could see while she was stuck behind the damn sheet.

A nurse walked over, holding up a naked, wrinkled creature covered in white goo, eyes clenched shut and toothless mouth wide open like some kind of bad special effects gremlin. Kat wrinkled her nose.

"Is she supposed to look like that?"

"Yes, she's perfectly fine. We're going to clean her up a bit and then you can hold her." The nurse turned to Ian. "Are you cutting the cord today, daddy?"

"What?" Ian jerked his head up. "Oh. Yes, I do. I mean, I am."

Kat clenched her jaw in sudden anger as he followed the nurse out of her line of sight. He got exactly what he'd wanted without having to do any of the work, and now he was off bonding with the baby while she was stuck waiting for the doctor to stitch her up again.

A few minutes later, the nurse returned with a cleaner, calmer bundle, and placed her in Kat's arms. She expected Lili to feel like a doll, but she was much heavier—and longer. She must've been folded into some really uncomfortable positions to fit inside her stomach. No wonder she was always kicking.

Everything felt surreal. Lili wasn't an abstract idea anymore. She was actually there, taking up physical space. This was the moment she was supposed to finally fall in love with her baby, but all she felt was the same sense of profound ambivalence.

CHAPTER 20

Wade

Wade's phone vibrated with a text from Ian as he shut down his work computer. *Mom and Dad are coming to the hospital around 5:30 if you wanna join.*

Perfect timing. He pulled on his coat and shoved his laptop into its bag when his desk phone rang, Betsy's name appearing on the screen. He hesitated, but figured whatever it was probably wouldn't take long.

"Oh, thank God you're still here," she said. "My computer's doing that loopy thing again."

When he reached the call center, he went right over to her cube without bothering to pull up a chair.

"Okay, what did you break this time?"

She swiveled around in her chair. "You know my computer hates me."

"No one could ever hate you, Betsy." He bent over her desk. "How's your grandson?"

"He's getting so big I can hardly believe it." She showed him a photo of the boy playing with trucks under the Christmas tree. "Before I know it he'll be starting school." She sighed, staring at the photo. "Sometimes I wish I could stop time so he'd stay little forever."

Wade stopped typing. That was it—the answer he was looking for.

Betsy frowned. "Is something wrong?"

"No—everything's fantastic!"

He bid her a quick farewell before rushing toward the elevator, his mind racing a mile a minute. He called Rob from the car.

"So I got this great idea for my game. Imagine there's a time machine. Except instead of traveling to the past or future, you can loop your consciousness to a specific time period—could be a day, a week, or even years. That way you could re-live the best part of your life over and over again, forever."

"That's depressing as hell, Wade."

"What? Why?"

"Have you *seen Groundhog Day?*"

"He was having a horrible day—this isn't like that at all."

"No matter how great your day was, it would still get old quick."

Wade scratched his head. "Okay, so what if your memory was reset every time so you didn't *know* you were in the loop? Then you'd always be happy because every-thing would feel like the first time."

"I still wouldn't do it," Rob said. "How do I know my best moments aren't still ahead of me? Plus, I've watched

enough sci-fi to know the machine would probably mal-
function and doom me to re-living the *worst* moments of
my life."

"Goddammit, Rob. It's just a game. Why do you always have to shit on everything?"

"You asked for my opinion. It's not my fault you don't
like it."

Wade pouted, but Rob was right. Time travel was one
of the oldest gimmicks in history, and there were probably hundreds of stories that had already done his idea
much better.

"Never mind. Forget I said anything."

"Calm down. Just because *I* wouldn't do it doesn't
mean it's not a good idea for your game. But I wouldn't
know, would I, because you refuse to tell me anything
about it. I'm still assuming it's about Jill, by the way."

"It's not about Jill!" He was so sick of hearing that,
even if it *was* partially true. "It's about my great uncle
trying to save my great aunt from Alzheimer's, okay?
Originally, the main character was a scientist trying to
develop a cure, but now I think it'd be better if he was
building a time machine. Because even if he saves her this
time, it's only postponing the inevitable. Eventually we're
all gonna die of something, whether it's Alzheimer's, or
cancer, or being hit by a fucking car."

The line was silent.

"There—are you happy?" Wade clenched the steering
wheel as he turned into the hospital's parking garage.

"I told you the entire plot of my game and you think it's dumb."

"Seriously. Calm the fuck down. I didn't say it was dumb."

"But you're thinking it."

"I was actually thinking it was pretty romantic."

Wade scoffed. "You're such a liar."

"I might be a dick, but I'm not a liar."

Fair enough. Wade sighed as he pulled into an open spot. "I gotta go. Kat had the baby this morning and I'm gonna visit them."

He signed in at the front desk and followed the receptionist's directions to the fourth floor maternity ward. Stepping off the elevator, he met his father walking toward him.

"Did you see them yet?" Wade asked.

"The nurse is helping Kat shower. Ian said he'll come get us when they're ready."

"Where's Mom?"

"She's in the waiting room down the hall." His father studied him over the rims of his glasses. "She's still upset about what you said on Christmas."

Wade stared at the tiled floor. He'd thought about calling to apologize, but let it go for so long he was embarrassed to bring it up again. "I'm not really mad at her. I'm just tired of everyone treating me like a little kid who can't handle anything on my own."

"If you want to be treated like an adult, act like one. Deal with your problems head on instead of throwing tantrums."

Wade balled his fist in his coat pocket. He wanted to argue his father's point so badly, but that would only prove him right. He stood up straight and tried to speak frankly, without any hint of whining or immaturity. "Do you hate me?"

The lines around his father's eyes softened. "Of course I don't hate you. You're my son." His voice cracked and he cleared his throat. "But you're also your mother's son, and I admit I often don't understand either of you. I'd try to teach you things like home and auto repair, but all you ever wanted to do was play. I once asked what you intended to do if you ever got a flat tire, but you only smirked and said you'd call a tow truck." A hint of a smile emerged. "You sounded exactly like your mother."

Wade laughed. "You grounded me for sounding like Mom?"

"I grounded you because I was afraid for you. You're smart and kind, but never seemed to live in the real world. It was my job to teach you to fend for yourself so people wouldn't take advantage of your trust." He shrugged. "If it's worth anything, I wanted you to visit Aunt Rita. Not every week like your mother had to see her grandmother, but at least a few times a year so you'd better understand the nature of life and death. But ultimately, Rita was your mother's aunt so I dropped the issue on the condition that you boys at least attend funerals."

He studied his father's face with fascination. They'd lived under the same roof for two decades, but there was still so much he didn't know about him.

"Dad, if you could relive one memory, what would it be?"

His father took off his glasses and rubbed the lenses with his shirt. "When I was 16, I spent the summer in Poland visiting my grandparents. Every Sunday I'd wake up at dawn, pack a lunch, and hike up the nearby mountain. I'd stay up there for hours, reading and looking out over the countryside, feeling at one with nature and my place within it."

Who was this wistful man and what did he do with Wade's father? "How come you never mentioned any of this before?"

"Because it was a profound personal experience, not a silly anecdote." Ah, there was his father. He slid his glasses back on. "I need to use the rest room. Go apologize to your mother."

Wade found her in the waiting room, gazing out the window at the lights in the street below. He pointed out into the night. "I think I see a UFO."

She glanced sidelong at him. "I *did* hear a report that radio signals were jammed for 13 minutes this morning."

"We should warn Ian. Don't want them accidently switching his baby with an alien." He took a seat beside her. "I'm sorry I yelled at you on Christmas. It was hard seeing everyone so happy with their spouses."

She wrapped an arm around his shoulder, pulling him closer. "You'll find another girl one of these days, and she'll be an even better match for you than Jill was."

He wanted to believe her, but it was looking more like he'd either have to settle for perpetual bachelorhood or start giving up the things he loved to become the boring asshole girls his age seemed to want.

"I know your birthday's not until Friday, but I want to give this to you today." She handed him a flat package wrapped in blue paper. Inside was a gift certificate to a print shop in downtown Scranton. He had no use for it, but thanked her all the same. She burst out laughing. "You're so polite, God bless you, but you have no idea what it's for, do you?"

He grinned and shook his head. "Not at all."

"It's so you can get cover art designed for that game of yours."

"That's... thank you." He stroked the raised print along the edge of the gift certificate, feeling over-whelmed. "I didn't know you knew about it."

"I overheard you talking with Ian and Jeremy. After you left, I asked them about it." She smiled. "I still re-member how you used to read to me from those video game manuals and show me your favorite pictures. Ian said you'd been working on this game for months, and that kind of effort deserves a nice package to display it in."

It was the most thoughtful gift anyone had given him. He hugged her. "Thanks, Mom."

"Look who I found," his father called out from behind them.

Ian had dark circles under his eyes, but the biggest grin on his face. "Who wants to meet the newest Dakalski?"

They followed him into a dimly lit room, a privacy curtain hiding the hospital bed.

"Kat's not up for visitors yet, but she said I could bring you in for a few minutes as long as we stayed quiet." He tiptoed behind the curtain and wheeled out a cart with a plastic bin on top. "This is Lili," he whispered, placing the tiny bundle in their mother's arms. Wrapped up so tightly in blankets and a hat, she wasn't much more than a tiny round face with closed eyes.

After they'd passed her around and snapped a ton of photos, Ian gently lowered her back into the bin. "Thanks for coming," he said, "but I'm about to pass out myself. I'll call you guys tomorrow."

Heading back toward the elevator with his parents, Wade glanced into an open room where an old man lay unconscious in bed, wired to so many machines he looked like one of those old telephone switchboards. He wondered what was wrong with him.

"Oh, I almost forgot," his mother said, snapping him out of his trance. "I ran into Drew's mom at the supermarket last week and heard all about his upcoming move. How exciting is that?"

Wade stopped in his tracks. "What move?"

"To Manhattan." She looked puzzled, but then her hand flew to her mouth. "Gosh, I hope I didn't steal his thunder. I assumed he would've told everyone by now."

He hadn't known Drew was even considering moving, but then again, he'd been so caught up in his own shit lately that he couldn't remember the last time he'd called him.

"Did she say why he's moving or when?"

"Apparently he got a big promotion at work and they're transferring him. He's training in Scranton until the end of March and moving to his new place April 1st."

It sucked that Drew was leaving, but at least he had time to send him off right—maybe with a going away party. It might be their last chance to hang out as a group until who knew when. Maybe he could even get Rob to come.

CHAPTER 21

Eleanor

Eleanor adjusted her legs in the butterfly chair, trying to pay attention to *LOST*. She had no idea what
was going on or why she should care, but it was Natalie's
favorite show and she promised herself she'd make a
better effort to connect. On screen, a man in a yellow
hazmat suit appeared from a trap door, and Natalie and
Nick screamed in excitement from the twin bed where
they were cuddled up together.

"That's Desmond," Natalie reminded her. "The one
who had to push the button every 108 minutes."

"Oh, okay." Eleanor nodded, barely remembering.

"Natalie wants to have a hundred of his babies," Nick
said, elbowing her. "She'd drop me in a second if he were
here."

"Damn straight." Natalie stuck out her tongue and
Nick tackled her to the bed, pinning her in a headlock.
She shrieked and twisted out of his grasp, laughing,

before he pulled her in again for a kiss. Eleanor looked away, a dagger slicing clean through her gut.

It'd been six weeks since she left the note on Trent's door, but he still hadn't called. She spent the first few days wired, unable to eat or sleep, constantly on the verge of throwing up. After a week she started making excuses for him. Maybe he was on vacation. Maybe he was so nervous he needed more time to psych himself up. She even called her cell phone from work to make sure it wasn't broken. But as the weeks dragged by, the truth became painfully obvious—he wasn't going to call.

Everywhere she went, people walked around with phones practically glued to their ears, making all sorts of stupid jokes and plans, yet Trent couldn't even be bothered to text so much as a "sorry, but I'm not interested."

He was supposed to be different. He wasn't afraid to look into the abyss and ask uncomfortable questions, unlike most people who blindly traipsed through life without stopping to ponder what any of it meant. He was the only person who'd ever tried to get to know the real her, locked away beneath the awkward, shy exterior that everyone else assumed was the whole package. He'd shared his art with her and even kissed her, but apparently none of it mattered. She wasn't the exception. He ignored her like he did everyone else.

Her eyes welled up. She had to get out of there before Natalie and Nick noticed. "I'll be right back."

In the bathroom, she pushed up the window screen, sticking her head out into the frigid night air. Closing her eyes, she breathed slowly, letting the tears freeze on her face. She seemed to spend more time in Natalie's bathroom than her bedroom. By now, Natalie probably assumed she had some kind of chronic bowel problem, but was too nice to ask about it.

She opened her eyes. Parked across the street was a step van with the logo for *Scranton Flowers* painted on the side. It used to be that every time she passed a sign with the name *Scranton* on it, she'd feel giddy with anticipation, but now it made her want to punch a wall.

She should probably move. Her lease was up in a few months anyway, and if she looked on the bright side, it was the first time she had the freedom to start anew anywhere she liked without parents, colleges, or ridiculous high school crushes holding her back.

Shivering, she closed the window. No more endless mountain winters, that was for sure. She pictured a map of the United States in her head. Maybe someplace in California where it was warm all year round. She always did want to visit the Winchester Mystery House.

It'd been her favorite story in the *Ghosts of America* book. Sarah Winchester, the widow of the man who invented the Winchester rifle, was convinced she was being haunted by the ghosts of all the people her husband's rifles had killed. In order to stay one step ahead of the ghosts, she built scores of additions onto her house, including staircases that led to nowhere and doors that opened over two story drops. But in reality, Sarah was just a lonely old widow with too much time and money, and too little construction know-how. At least she'd *had* a husband once.

Natalie's laugh echoed through the vent, snapping Eleanor out of her trance. They were far from best friends, but occasionally hanging out with her was better than nothing. And if she moved again, that's exactly what she'd go back to—nothing—wandering from place to place like Sarah's ghosts, forever lying to herself about how things would be "different this time."

She shuddered. She'd rather kill herself. It probably wouldn't even hurt that much. Just down a bottle of painkillers and go to sleep. At least then she'd no longer be aware of the nothingness.

CHAPTER 22

Kat

Kat leaned over the bassinet, holding her breath as she wiped the gooey newborn shit out of the crevices with a paper towel. She'd been prepared to change diapers, but not for the sheer frequency of it—sometimes up to 10 times a day—or how often it involved changing everything else in the room, from the baby's sheets to her own clothing. Lying on the changing table, Lili waved her tiny arms and legs in the air, making fussing sounds.

Oh God, please don't cry again. It had taken 20 minutes to get her calm after changing her soiled pajamas and that was only 10 minutes ago. Abandoning the bassinet, Kat rocked Lili in her arms, hoping to head her off.

"Please don't cry," she repeated in a soothing, singsong voice. But Lili only scrunched up her face and wailed all over again.

Kat's head throbbed. It'd been a few hours since either of them ate. Maybe it was that simple.

She stroked Lili's soft, fine hair. "Let's go eat, okay?"

Baby in one arm, she clutched the railing as she carefully descended the stairs. Her incision site no longer felt like it was going to rip open every time she laughed or sneezed, but she still felt like an old woman when she walked, deliberately placing one foot in front of the other until she got wherever she needed to go.

Outside the kitchen window, the snow had finally stopped falling from the slate grey sky, but now lay two inches thick across the deck and patio chairs. If only she'd had the baby in spring or summer she could be out with the stroller in the fresh air instead of cooped up in the house for days on end.

Arm growing numb, she switched the baby to her other side before mixing a bottle. When it was done heating, she offered it to Lili, but she only pulled her face back and continued screaming. Kat closed her eyes, the searing pain in her temples seeping farther back and threatening to set her skull on fire.

"Come on, Lili. Please eat. Mommy has a headache and needs to lie down."

She adjusted the baby's positioning, and even tried preemptively burping her, but she still refused to eat. She peeked inside her diaper, but it was dry. Maybe she was cold?

She adjusted the thermostat before heading back up to the nursery and wrangling Lili's flailing limbs into a pair of extra thick fleece pajamas. Bouncing the baby in her tired arms, she paced back and forth until she couldn't take it anymore.

"What the fuck do you want?" she screamed, overwhelmed by a sudden and powerful urge to throw Lili to the floor.

Oh God. Tears welling up in her eyes, she plunked Lili into the still-dirty bassinet and hobbled out onto the deck, the frigid air burning her skin and lungs.

"Fuuuuuuuck!"

She grabbed a patio chair and hurled it off the side of the deck, screaming as the effort stabbed like a knife at her incision site. Clutching her stomach, she crumpled to the deck, suddenly aware of the snow's cold dampness creeping through her socks and pajama pants.

"Fuck," she muttered repeatedly, keeping pressure on the wound, afraid she'd ripped it open. Carefully, she turned down her waistband to check for blood, but didn't see any.

I need to get out of this house.

Shivering, she stepped inside and texted Ian. *I wanna go out to dinner tonight. Can you ask your mom to watch Lili?*

She threw her wet clothes in the washer along with Lili's dirty sheets before taking a long, gloriously warm shower. By the time she was done, Lili had cried herself to sleep, and there was a text waiting from Ian. *I'll call my mom when this class is over.*

She toweled off and peeled the old bandages from her skin. A full month had passed since the birth, yet she still looked six months pregnant—worse than that, actually, as her stomach had lost its roundness and now hung like a deflated balloon with that angry red gash along the bottom. She replaced the bandages and tried not to think about it. At least she'd finally stopped bleeding.

Determined to make the most of the night, she went all out, blow-drying and styling her hair, shaving, and putting on makeup before dressing in the one outfit that still made her feel pretty—a sleeveless black maternity dress that hid most of her imperfections.

By the time she was ready, Ian was due home any minute. She loaded the diaper bag with as many supplies as might be needed for a few hours, but then doubled the amount to be safe.

As she wrapped Lili in extra blankets, she woke up, her blue eyes gazing up as she made peaceful gurgling sounds. If only she could be this agreeable all the time, parenting wouldn't be nearly as frustrating.

"I'm sorry I yelled at you," Kat said, kissing her head and placing her in the carrier. "It's just hard to know what you want when you can't tell me."

When did babies start talking—age two? That seemed so far away. She didn't need in-depth conversations, but a simple exchange about toys would be a lifesaver right now.

"I know. Let's read a book while we wait for Daddy." Anything to give her a head start on verbal communication.

Rummaging through a box of gifts from her coworkers, she found a plastic bath book called *The Frog*. She set Lili's carrier on the couch and sat beside her.

"Here is a frog." She turned the page. "The frog hops." She turned another page. "The frog eats flies." She flipped ahead, only to find more of the same mind-numbingly simple sentences. "I'm sorry, Lili. This isn't really a story. Let's see if we can find something better."

She returned a few minutes later with a copy of *Harry Potter and the Sorcerer's Stone*.

"You won't understand this any more than the frog book, but at least this one might keep Mommy sane."

After the first chapter, she checked the time. Ian was over an hour late. Maybe Sister Augustine had kept him for a meeting. She tried calling, but only reached his voicemail. "Hey, where are you? Call me back when you get this."

She was a page and a half into chapter two when Lili started whimpering.

"Oh God. Please don't cry again."

Picking her up from the carrier, she felt something wet and warm on her hand a split second before she smelled it.

You've gotta be kidding me.

Stomach grumbling, she spent the next half hour cleaning up the baby and scrubbing down the carrier. Why was shit suddenly getting everywhere? She examined the bag of off-brand diapers, wondering whether it was bad luck or a bad product when she heard the front door open. She rushed to the top of the stairs, hoping nothing too terrible had happened to Ian, but he only plopped down on the couch and turned on the TV without even saying hello.

"Where were you?" she asked, hobbling down the stairs.

"I wound up eating at the sports bar with some of the teachers."

Anger boiled in her veins, but she tried to stay calm. "We had dinner plans."

"My mom was busy tonight. She said tomorrow would be better."

"I needed a break *today!*" She suddenly didn't care how angry she sounded. He deserved to get yelled at for this.

"What was I supposed to do? We can't take Lili to the restaurant, and we certainly can't leave her home alone."

"You could've called someone else—your Aunt Sally, maybe."

Ian threw his hands in the air. "Jesus, Kat. I didn't know it was that important to you."

"You didn't even call to say you'd be late."

"I didn't realize I needed to check in if I wanna go out."

Her blood pressure skyrocketed. Did he really not get it? "You're right. I *didn't* care about that stuff before. But we have a baby now, and every hour you stay out is another hour I'm stuck taking care of her by myself."

Ian scoffed. "*I'm* the one staying up with her half the week even though I have to go to work in the morning. At least *you* get to sleep in and take naps."

"I'd trade with you in a heartbeat. You have no idea how lonely it gets cooped up in the house all day with no one to talk to."

"No one makes you stay here by yourself. You could easily call a friend to hang out."

But there was no one to call. She hadn't spoken to any of her college friends since the wedding, her coworkers were little more than glorified acquaintances, and if she was being honest, the rest of her friends were really Ian's friends—she never hung out with them when he wasn't around and they'd probably dump her in a second if she and Ian ever broke up. Somehow Ian had become her only real friend, and with every passing day he was drifting further away.

Her lip trembled. "I don't have any friends."

Ian rolled his eyes. "Now you're being dramatic."

"Why? Because I'm daring to express an emotion other than complete and total happiness?"

Ian ran a hand through his hair. "Why don't you call Alicia?"

"Right. Because I would have so much in common with a housewife."

"Jesus, Kat. I can't help you if you're dead set on feeling sorry for yourself."

Her hands shook. Every time she tried to assert herself, he made her feel like a total basket case. "Fine." She grabbed her coat and purse.

"Where are you going?"

"Out to dinner. Because, unlike you, I haven't eaten all day and I'm starving."

She drove halfway to Casa Bella before realizing how pathetic it would feel sitting alone at a table for two, all dressed up with only her linguini and chardonnay for company. People would wonder whether she'd been stood up, or if she was some kind of sad, strange cat lady. Instead, she pulled into the Wendy's drive-thru and sat in her parked car, cheeseburger wrapper spread across her lap like the least romantic picnic ever.

She scrolled through the contacts in her phone, passing by the names of half a dozen girls who'd each been her very best friend at one point but might as well be strangers now. In every case, the friendship had blown up or faded away shortly after she'd hooked up with a new guy. She used to chalk it up to her friends' jealousy—either of the relationship itself or the fact that she could no longer devote a hundred percent of her time to them—but now she wondered whether it'd been her fault all along. Because, unlike Ian, she never made any real effort to keep those same-sex connections alive. She put them all on the backburner the minute a new boy entered the picture, and then became so preoccupied with him that she barely noticed her friends fading away until they were already gone.

It was always me. I was the asshole.

She considered calling one of her old friends to re-connect, but then felt a little sick. She was doing it all over again—only reaching out because she was on the outs with a boy. Had she ever had a real friend in her whole life, or was everyone she thought she cared about just a boyfriend-substitute, good only until the next real thing came along?

CHAPTER 23

Ian

Ian laid on the living room couch, holding a whimper-ing Lili to his chest, praying she'd fall asleep and not start crying. He knew he'd be tired once she was born but this was more like total mind-body exhaustion.

Back in the day, he could stay out late multiple nights a week and even pull the occasional all-nighter because there was always plenty of time to catch up on sleep over the weekend in glorious 8-10 hour stretches. But this was 24/7. Even when it was Kat's turn on the night shift, he still woke up every few hours when Lili cried, and it wasn't always easy to fall asleep again. Maybe part of him *did* go out with the teachers earlier that night to get away from it all. It wasn't fair to Kat, but then again, she expected him to be on all day at work, and then on again all night at home without a break in between. It was like having two full-time jobs.

They both needed a break, badly. Maybe his par-ents would agree to take Lili for a whole weekend. In the meantime, he should probably find a way to smooth things over with Kat. She didn't say a word when she got home from dinner, just marched upstairs and shut the bedroom door behind her. He usually bragged that she wasn't into flowers like other girls, but apologizing had always been easier when he didn't have to come up with creative alternatives.

Lili's breathing slowed and her head lolled to the side. Carefully, he moved her to the bassinet before returning to the couch and setting the alarm on his phone. Kat hadn't told him not to come to bed, but sleeping down-stairs felt like the safer option.

He awoke a few hours later with a pounding head-ache and a back full of knots. The bedroom door was still shut, so he took an aspirin and a shower before re-dress-ing in his clothes from the day before and praying no one at school would notice. Once there, he checked the sign up sheet on his office door. Thankfully, no one had requested a meeting during first period, which meant he had 40 minutes to nap before health class. He locked his door, folded his coat into a makeshift pillow, and curled up on the floor behind his desk.

Not five minutes later, there was a knock at the door. *Bloody hell.*

He opened the door to find Rob dressed in his Best Buy polo shirt. "What are you doing here?"

"Darryn's dropping out. I'm here to get the forms."

Ian shook his head. "Dropping out of what?"

"School, idiot."

His brain felt fuzzy. "What? Why?"

"I got a letter claiming I didn't pay last month's tuition. And now because I supposedly broke the billing contract, they're saying I have one month to pay the remainder of the year or they're gonna kick her out. Obviously I can't afford that, so at least this way leaving school goes on record as being her choice."

"Are you sure you paid the bill?"

Rob rolled his eyes. "Yes, I'm sure I paid it. The school never cashed my check."

"Did you ask the office to double-check? It probably got lost, or..." He suddenly remembered telling Sister Augustine about their family's money troubles, and his insides went cold. She wouldn't really go that far for her damn statistics, would she? He shook his head, refusing to believe it. "It doesn't make sense. If they kicked out everyone who missed a payment, the school would be half-empty."

"Regardless of what they usually do, the contract technically gives them the right," Rob said. "I might've tried to appeal, but Darryn doesn't care. She's starting work next week and plans to take the GED this summer."

Ian wanted so badly to explain about Sister Augustine's threat and the application to community he'd sent on Darryn's behalf, but it was pointless. If Sister Augustine had truly gone this far, an acceptance from community wouldn't mean shit now. And without any hard evidence in regards to losing the check, it would be their word against hers. With an acid taste in his throat he yanked open a filing cabinet drawer, searching for the papers Rob needed.

Even after Rob left, Ian felt so disgusted he couldn't concentrate on work. He called the front office and told them he was going home sick, but then napped in his office until noon. By then the worst of the anger had faded and he was left only with a dull sense of resignation. There was nothing else he could do for Darryn, so he might as well concentrate on something still within his control.

Sitting at his computer, he browsed the web looking for concerts Kat might like. There was nothing good in the upcoming weeks, but No Doubt was touring that summer. The show was still months away, but at least they'd have something to look forward to.

He drove home, tickets in his pocket, but when he opened the front door he heard sobbing from the kitchen.

Oh God, something happened to the baby.

"Kat," he called out, dropping his keys and briefcase and sprinting toward the sound. She sat on the floor, knees hugged to her chest, surrounded by plastic containers and everything else that had been on the kitchen counters that morning. On the stove, blue flames flickered beneath an empty burner. He turned it off and squatted down, hugging her. "What happened?"

"It fell."

A grease stain dripped down the wall toward a frying pan and half-cooked grilled cheese sandwich on the floor. This was all because of a sandwich? He was relieved yet worried anew. She was obviously much worse off than he'd thought. He hugged her tighter. "I'll make you another one."

She sniffled. "There's no more bread."

"How about an omelet?"

"We don't have eggs, either."

He stroked her hair. "Okay, new plan. You lay down while I take Lili and go shopping."

He bundled Lili in multiple layers of fleece pajamas and drove to the convenience store. Unstrapping her from the car seat, he realized his mistake—there were no shopping carts. He wouldn't be able to carry groceries if he was also carrying her, but couldn't leave her in the car, either. *Fuck it.* He unstrapped the entire car seat and carried it into the store, baby and all.

Walking through the narrow aisles, he set the car seat down every few feet to arrange more groceries around Lili, making sure none of them were weighing on or pinching her. She was awake now and questioning him with wide blue eyes so much like Kat's.

"Sorry Lili, Daddy needs his other hand to carry the milk."

As he neared the refrigerator cabinets, he caught a snippet of conversation from two teenaged boys in the next aisle.

"She totally squirted."

"No shit. Was it a lot?"

Peering around a display of Tastykakes, he recognized them from school. He didn't remember their names but they were both juniors.

"No, but it was fucking crazy. I've never seen it before."

"Was it that blonde from the party?"

"No, the dark-haired chick from the mall. We were parked down by the reservoir and the whole time she's screaming, and then this cop drives by and I swear he's gonna hear her, so I quick push her head down, and she..."

Ian's phone rang.

Shit.

He scrambled to turn it off, but the boys had already seen him. *Please don't recognize me.*

"Mr. Dakalski?"

Fuck. He forced a smile. "Hi boys. What brings you here today?" *Oh God, I sound like my dad.*

The one kid stood up straighter, holding a bag of chips. "Getting snacks."

"Is that your kid?" the other asked.

"Yeah." Ian suddenly realized how bad it must look that he'd been covering his daughter with groceries. They avoided eye contact for a few more agonizing seconds before he snapped out of it. "Well, I gotta go. See you in school," he said, brightly, before squeezing past them and hurrying toward the register.

He could almost feel them pointing and laughing behind his back. Any illusions he might've had about being the cool young teacher were shattered forever. When did he get so old and out of touch? Was that part of having a baby, or had it been coming long before? He looked at Lili, still so tiny and innocent. How old would she be when she figured out how lame he was—13, 10, 7?

Kat was asleep when he got home so he put Lili to bed and sat on the floor of the spare bedroom with his guitar. Over the past few months, he'd been able to piece together a few of his old songs, this time making sure to add the chords to the lyrics sheets so he'd never forget them again. Balancing the guitar on his thigh, he lightly strummed the strings, singing along softly.

"You should play more often. You're really good." Kat stood in the doorway wearing his Thrice t-shirt and a pair of orange and white striped panties.

He flushed. "How long have you been there?"

"Only a minute." She sat on the floor beside him.

"If you think *this* is good, you should've heard me back in the day."

"Do you have any recordings?"

"Most of the time we recorded directly onto Drew's parents' computer, but it crashed and we lost everything. There might still be a few VHS tapes floating around, though."

She smiled. "I'd love to watch them."

"My Aunt Sally had one of us playing at her block party. They booked a local band, but during one of the intermissions they let us go on stage and play a few songs. And by stage, I mean someone's front lawn. We gave her the tape because Greta loved watching it. She could barely walk but liked to sit close to the TV and bounce to the beat."

He grinned, remembering how stoked he'd been playing a real gig. "Most of the audience didn't care. They're standing around talking, and kids are riding by on bikes, all oblivious to the fact that there's a band playing right in front of them. But if you look closely at the very edge of the screen, there's this bearded fat man eating a hot dog and nodding to the beat."

Kat laughed for the first time in what seemed like forever. It was a wonderful sound and he couldn't help but join in.

"Yeah, I know. Our two biggest fans were a toddler and a fat man."

She leaned in, kissing him with more enthusiasm than she had in months. Letting the guitar slide off his lap, he held her face, reveling in her warmth. She reached for his belt.

"Are you sure that's okay?"

"I started the pill after I stopped bleeding. Just go slow and don't touch my stomach."

Afterward, he lay on the carpet with her head on his chest. Maybe being old wasn't so bad after all. He might not be having crazy sex in the backs of cars with virtual strangers, but he was with someone he loved and was building a life with, even if things had been far from perfect lately. That had to mean more, right?

CHAPTER 24

Wade

*P*ale shafts of sunlight streamed through the basement windows as the scientist helped his wife into the machine's cabin. After getting them both settled in, helmets strapped beneath their chins, he pulled the lever toward the "on" position.

The generator awoke, turbines picking up speed and producing a low metallic hum as the dashboard lights flickered on. Leaning over, he kissed her one last time before pressing the button.

Rapping his fingers against his bedroom desk, Wade watched the rough cut of his game's ending sequence again and again. The story felt much more meaningful with the time loop machine in place of a chemical cure, but something still felt off. Maybe the music wasn't conveying the right mood.

Minimizing the game window, he searched for better music online, but couldn't find anything closer to what he needed.

His phone vibrated with a text from Drew. *I'm not sure yet.*

Seriously? He'd been playing phone tag with the guy for two months now, but all he ever got were vague and non-committal texts, answered days after the fact. He didn't think he'd done anything to piss him off besides maybe slacking off on keeping in touch, but maybe he had.

He called Ian. "Have you talked to Drew lately?"

"No, why?"

"I'm pretty sure he's avoiding me, but I don't know why."

"Maybe you fucked one of his exes and didn't realize it."

"Very funny." Wade leaned back in his chair. "I wanted to throw him a surprise going away party, but he refuses to pick a date to hang out, and he's leaving in two weeks."

"Why don't you ask him if something's up?"

"I guess." It was the obvious solution, but Wade had a sinking feeling that confronting Drew would only push him further away. He looked at his laptop screen, not really in the mood to keep working. "You wanna come over and play something?"

"I can't. It's my night with the baby."

"Come on. I'm sure Kat won't mind covering an extra night."

Ian snorted. "You have no idea how much shit I'd catch for asking."

"So bring Lili with you. She can sleep in my room."

"Honestly, I'm exhausted. All I wanna do is finish the laundry so I can take a nap before Lili wakes up again."

Wade rolled his eyes. "When's your next off-night?"

"Friday."

"You wanna come over then?"

"Do you mind if we go to the movies instead so Kat can come with us? We could both use a night out."

"That's cool. You guys pick a movie and text me the time."

After ending the call, Wade sucked it up and texted Drew, figuring if something was wrong it would be better to get it out in the open before he moved two hours away. *It seems like you don't wanna hang out—is something up?*

In the kitchen, he filled a bowl of instant noodles with water. Before it even finished cooking, his phone vibrated with another text from Drew. It was the fastest he'd responded in months.

I'm sorry you got that impression. I've been extremely busy with work and packing for the move. The only time I'll probably have free is this Saturday after 8pm.

Wade felt immediately lighter, glad he'd asked. He texted Ian. *Party's on! Saturday @ 8 – bring Lili if you have to.*

He took stock of his food supply, which was danger-ously low. He could order pizza, but still needed to buy drinks and snacks.

Scrolling through his phone, he texted a few more friends about the party. Hopefully at least a few of them could make it, even with only three days' notice. He stopped when he got to Rob's name. It was a long shot, but he was on a roll. Maybe if he asked *really* nicely, he'd actually come. He should probably ask in person, though.

Rob opened his basement door and cocked an eyebrow at Wade. "Yes?"

Shit, he already suspects something's up. "Do you still have any of those old VHS tapes we made in high school?"

"Somewhere. Why?"

He might as well cut to the chase. "Okay, so don't be mad, but I'm throwing a going away party for Drew. I thought we could watch the tapes and reminisce about the good old days."

Rob moved aside to let him in. "Why would I be mad? You can hang out with whatever douchebags you want."

"I want you to come."

"Nope." Rob walked past him and flipped on the light to his walk-in storage closet.

"Hear me out—please?" Wade stood outside the closet while Rob rummaged through musty cardboard boxes.

"I'm listening."

"You remember that time Drew got put in third lunch all by himself? You had last period free, but got your schedule switched so you could eat with him even though it meant staying at school an extra 40 minutes every day."

Rob pushed aside a stack of board games without looking up. "And?"

"Look. I care about both of you, and you obviously used to care about each other. I know friends fight sometimes, but it's been almost a year."

Rob shoved a small box of VHS tapes at Wade's chest. "Keep them."

Wade gripped the box so tightly he almost crushed it. "Was Caitlin Jones really worth throwing away over 10 years of friendship?"

Rob scoffed. "You still think this is about Caitlin?"

"Isn't it?"

"No." Rob slammed his fist on his desk, a vein bulging in his neck. "It's about Drew Shafer being a lying, manipulative bastard who's gotten away with murder for years because none of you had the balls to call him out on his bullshit or back me up when I did."

He'd never seen Rob so angry before. "Okay, I get it," he mumbled. "Forget I said anything." All he wanted to do was bring his friends back together, not create entirely new rifts.

He trudged back to his car with the box of tapes, wondering what lies Rob was even talking about. Sure, Drew tended to stretch the truth, but it was always about ridiculously obvious things like his conquests with girls or how important he was at work. Plus, everyone *knew* he was exaggerating. It was more like a running joke that never hurt anyone.

But then again, it *was* odd that he'd dodge him for two months and then claim everything was fine. There had to be something else he wasn't telling him.

CHAPTER 25

Eleanor

Natalie sat on the edge of the desk, sipping coffee as she described the lake house her family rented every summer on Mount Pocono. Half listening, Eleanor lifted a document from the scanner glass and sealed it in air-tight plastic, occasionally muttering a "yeah" or "mhmm" wherever it seemed appropriate. Sometimes it was annoying when Natalie took breaks in the archive, but other times it was kind of nice. It made her feel like she had a friend.

Natalie's cell phone rang, but she ignored it after checking the screen. "I don't think I'm gonna keep seeing Nick."

Eleanor dropped the plastic sheet. "What? Why not?" She'd just had dinner with them at the coffee shop the week before and everything seemed fine.

"Our relationship feels kind of forced lately." Natalie shrugged. "All we ever do is watch TV and have sex."

Oh, is that ALL? Eleanor suppressed the urge to break something.

"We used to talk all the time when we were friends," Natalie continued. "But now it's like we ran out of things to say. And if we're this bored after only three months, that's a really bad sign." She played with her bracelet, the hint of a smile on her face. "I'm not that upset though, cause I met this new guy at a concert last week, and we talked for hours like old friends. We wound up making out, and we're going on a proper date this weekend."

"You cheated on Nick?" It was disgusting. After all that time they'd waited to be together, she was going to throw him away just because he didn't always have something to say?

"Don't say it like that," Natalie said, looking hurt. "I already feel bad. Nick's a great guy, but I think I needed to be with him to know that I *didn't* wanna be with him, you know?"

"I guess." Eleanor turned back to her computer. It was always so easy for everyone else, hooking up and breaking up like it meant nothing.

Natalie fiddled with her coffee cup. "Are you okay? You seem upset."

Eleanor shook her head, wishing Natalie would leave already. "I'm fine. I just have a headache." She rubbed her temples. "I think I'm going to sit in the dark for a few minutes to see if it helps. I'll catch up with you later, okay?"

Natalie seemed to buy it and closed the door on her way out.

Eleanor laid her head on her desk, hating herself. If Natalie thought *Nick* was boring, what could she possibly think of *her?* She was stupid to think they had a real chance of being friends. They clearly didn't share the same values. All they really had in common was the library. If one of them got a new job, Natalie would forget about her just as quickly as those girls in her photo album who promised to write but never did.

Needing air, she went upstairs. She was almost to the front door when Carmen called to her.

"Can you man the desk for a few minutes? Penny's in the restroom. She said it might be awhile, and I have a report to finish before we close."

Eleanor whimpered internally. It was always *something* with Penny. But at least the library was dead at the moment.

"Sure thing," she said, trudging behind the counter as Carmen hurried away, her high heels clicking on the tile behind her.

She tried to clear her mind of the negativity by alphabetizing returns on the cart. The bell on the front door jingled but she didn't look up, hoping whoever it was would pass her by without needing anything.

"Hey there." A young guy with shaggy dark hair set two books on the counter. "I need to return these."

"You can leave them there," she replied, looking back at the returns.

"They're late though. Like, *really* late." He laughed. "I'm kinda scared I owe a hundred bucks or something." He actually had a really nice smile.

Her face grew warm. "The fines are capped at five dollars per book unless you lose or destroy them."

"Really? That's awesome." He produced a small wad of crumpled bills from his back pocket, straightening one out before handing it over. As she rung him up, he looked at her a little too intently, squinting slightly as if he recognized her but couldn't place her. Feeling awkward, she looked away.

"Have you ever read that one?" He gestured toward *The Time Machine.*

"A long time ago."

"I loved the part where he goes to the end of time and everything's all slow and those giant crabs are crawling on the beach." His big brown eyes danced with enthusiasm. "I've seen the movie a bunch of times, and have the children's illustrated version, but neither of them showed that part. I wonder why."

She'd wondered the same thing as a kid. "Probably because it's too strange and depressing for most people."

"I don't think it's depressing at all. He knows how the world's gonna end, but doesn't give up trying to save it."

She never thought of it that way before. She handed him his change and receipt, but suddenly didn't want him to leave.

"Well, see you around." He walked toward the door.

Her stomach twisted into knots. He seemed like a nice guy, and was pretty good looking too, but he wasn't a regular, and if she didn't act right away she'd almost certainly never get another chance.

Natalie would do it.

"Wait," she called out. He patted his hoodie pockets as if checking whether he'd left something behind. She felt like she might throw up. *I can't believe I'm doing this.* "Would you want to hang out sometime?"

He titled his head slightly to the side, as if not quite comprehending.

I'm such an idiot. Of course he doesn't want to hang out. She stared down at the counter, face burning up. "You don't have to. It was just a thought." A ridiculous, dumb, pathetic thought.

"That sounds awesome, actually. When do you get done with work?"

Wait. He said yes?

Her mind blanked. It took a second to remember where she was or what was going on. "I can probably leave in like 10 minutes as long as I let my boss know."

"Awesome. I can wait for you at the coffee shop down the street if that's cool."

"Yeah. That's cool."

"Great. See you soon." He flashed his infectious smile again before leaving.

She paced the area behind the desk, panicking. Never expecting him to actually say yes, she felt sicker than she'd ever been in her life. She'd never been on a real date before, and had no idea what she was supposed to do. She didn't even know his name.

Pressing the back button on the computer, she pulled up his account. His name was Wade Dakalski. He was 24 years old and lived in an apartment in Dunmore.

She quickly exited the screen, wishing she hadn't found out even that much. *Stop stalking people! Go talk to him like a normal human being.*

The night air felt electric as she made her way down the street to the coffee shop, almost tripping multiple times as her shoes caught in sidewalk cracks. She tried to breathe normally, but her heart raced on a block ahead of her.

Calm down. This isn't that different from hanging out with Natalie. He's only one person and must already like you at least a little bit or he wouldn't have said yes.

She found him at a table for two, playing with his phone and leaning so far back in his chair that its front legs hovered an inch above the hardwood floor.

"Hey," she said, taking a seat across from him.

"Oh, hey." He snapped to attention, the chair legs clattering to the floor. He gestured toward a coffee cup on the table. "I got you plain coffee, but if you want something else, I can go get it."

"No, this is fine. Thank you." She took the warm cup in her hands, glad to have something to do with them.

"Good, cause I have a confession to make." He leaned in, lowering his voice. "I don't actually drink coffee, so I have no idea what most of that fancy stuff is."

She grew warm again, having him so close. "What's in your cup, then?"

"Hot chocolate." He leaned back, his arm draped over the back of the chair. "I've tried coffee a few times, but it never grew on me. I was at this pancake house down the shore with my family once and my mom couldn't stop raving about how great their coffee was, so I tried it, but it still tasted like balls." He blushed and laughed. "Not that I know what balls taste like or anything, but I'm guessing not too good."

She had no idea what to say to that.

He cleared his throat dramatically, and held out his hand. "Hi, I'm Wade. I swear I don't always talk about balls."

Laughing, she shook his hand. There was something endearing about his clumsy sincerity. "I'm Eleanor."

"Okay, Eleanor, so this might seem weird, but I swear I've seen you before. I just can't figure out where. Did you go to Keystone?"

Here we go again. "I'm new to the area, but I went to Dunmore High School for a month about 10 years ago."

"That's *awesome*, but I don't think that's it. I went to Holy Nativity, and none of the Dunmore girls I knew from the neighborhood were even half as pretty as you."

"Oh." She reached for a creamer, failing to suppress a grin. "Thank you." She dumped the little cup into her coffee and stirred it, trying to think up a question. "So, have you read any other good books lately?"

"Okay, please don't hate me, but I'm not really a book person. Those books I returned were the first I've read since college."

"It's okay. I love books, but I'm not really a book librarian."

He squinted at her. "What other kind is there?"

"There are lots, actually." She was always astounded no one seemed to know that. "I'm a digital archivist, which is mostly restoring old photos and documents with Photoshop, and organizing them in ways that make it easier for people to reference them."

"That's awesome." He twisted a plastic stirrer straw between his fingers. "I've been using Photoshop to edit graphics and stuff for the video game I've been making. It's pretty great."

"You make video games? Is that your job?"

"Nope. I'm in tech support, but the game is like a really huge hobby that I care about way more than my real job." He gestured freely as he explained a little bit about the premise and mechanics of design. He was so smart and cool, but not stuck up or judgmental at all, and the way he constantly laughed at himself made her feel more at ease.

"I don't know much about newer games," she said, "but I used to play Zelda and Super Mario at my friend's house when I was little. Actually, I think I liked her games more than I liked her."

He folded his hands in front of his chin, his warm brown eyes growing wide. "Oh my God, please marry me."

Her stomach lurched forward, but she managed to laugh it off. "Um, we should probably get to know each other better first."

He smacked his forehead. "You're right. What was I thinking? Everyone knows you're not supposed to propose until at least the second date." His eyes sparkled. For some reason, she didn't feel the need to look away.

"Why don't we go back to my place and play something?" he asked. "I've got plenty of old school games, or I can introduce you to something from the current decade."

She thought about Natalie and Nick at the bonfire. She wasn't ready for that. Or maybe she was. She didn't even know. It was all happening so fast, but she didn't want him to think she wasn't having a good time.

"Um, it's getting kind of late. Maybe we could hang out again on Saturday?" That would give her a few days to at least start processing everything.

"Yeah, that would be awesome. I'm doing something with friends that night, but I'm free all afternoon. How about Lahey? I heard they re-opened the mini-golf course for the season."

"Where's that?"

He dropped his mouth open in mock disbelief. "Oh my God, you really are new here. This is gonna be great." He passed his phone over the table. "Put your number in. I'll text you the address."

On the walk home, she practically skipped up the street, smiling and reliving the experience in her head so she wouldn't forget a single detail.

I asked out a complete stranger, and now we have a second date! I'm awesome! She laughed out loud at her use of his word.

Her phone buzzed in her purse and she almost jumped out of her skin. *I had a good time tonight,* the text read.

She smiled wide, feeling like a giddy fool as she texted him back. *Me too.*

CHAPTER 26

Kat

The apartment was cramped with furniture too large for the space and littered with brightly colored children's toys. On the far side of the room, JJ quietly built a tower out of wooden blocks while watching cartoons on TV. If only Kat could fast-forward time until Lili was old enough to entertain herself like that. "How old is he now?"

"Two and a half," Alicia answered, her long red ponytail swishing behind her as she closed the front door.

"Is he potty trained yet?" she asked, mentally pleading for a yes.

"I wish. We bought him a potty for Christmas thinking he might be into it if we treated it like a cool new toy, but he was totally onto us. We figure we'll try again after his birthday."

Kat forced a polite laugh as she set Lili's carrier on the couch. She'd only been changing diapers for two months but already it felt like an eternity. Doing it for three years was unfathomable.

"How are you and Miss Lili doing?" Alicia picked up a plush bunny from a dining chair and tossed it into the toy box before motioning for Kat to have a seat.

"We're great." The familiar lie slipped out before she knew what she was saying. She thought about correcting herself, but Alicia had already opened the fridge and started naming the drinks inside. "Iced tea is fine," Kat said.

Alicia reached up to a high cabinet and pulled out two drinking glasses, looking slim in her jeans and form-fitting t-shirt. Kat glanced down at her persistent stomach bulging from underneath her black maternity dress. Her doctor said it could take months to lose the weight, and even then she might never look the same. She didn't know whether to hate Alicia's good luck or be hopeful because of it.

Alicia unwrapped some kind of noodle casserole. "Did you guys do anything fun for St. Patrick's Day?"

Kat hadn't even realized the holiday passed. Without work to keep her on track, she was lucky if she remembered what day of the week it was.

"We decided to keep it low key this year," she lied, scooping casserole onto her plate. "Stayed in and had a couple of drinks. You?"

"We took JJ to the parade by St. Peter's. He cried most of the time. I think the crowds and loud music were a little much for him, but he loved picking up candy from the street and ripping apart the green lei we bought him, so all in all, a fairly successful adventure."

"Sounds fun." Actually, it sounded boring as hell. At family gatherings this was usually the point where she excused herself and found someone more interesting to talk to. But that was the whole problem. "So, I don't think Ian ever told me—where did you work before you had JJ?"

"A bunch of places—a pizzeria, a craft store, a supermarket."

"Did you go to college?" It didn't sound like it, but she didn't want to presume. Plenty of college grads were still working in food service or retail.

Alicia laughed. "If you count one semester as going to college."

"You didn't like it?"

"I liked the parties." She passed Kat a fork. "But then my ex got this really amazing gig touring the Midwest as a drum tech for a friend's band. I took a semester off to go with them as their photographer and never got around to going back."

In sophomore year of college, Kat had felt like a complete failure when a two-week virus set her back so far she had to drop Accounting—and that was only one class. "Do you ever regret it?"

"Not at all. It was awesome seeing the country and meeting all those people. We didn't have money for hotels, so we'd usually make friends during the show and crash at their places. One time we stayed with this Renaissance

Faire dude. He lived in this huge castle-shaped house and let us play with his costumes and stuff."

Depending on strangers seemed horribly danger-ous—what if that guy had been a serial killer?—but get-ting to see the country must've been life-changing.

Kat pushed the casserole around the plate with her fork, wishing she'd been allowed to fail more often as a child. To learn it wasn't the end of the world. Alicia was so much braver than she'd ever been and seemed ten times happier. If she'd had an easygoing mom like her, she might not have become such a mess. She swallowed hard, hoping she wouldn't ruin their budding friendship.

"I lied before."

Alicia cocked her head to the side. "About what?"

"I'm *not* doing great. I... I hate everything about be-ing a mom, and some days I even hate Lili." It sounded terrible out loud, but she felt so much lighter getting it off her chest that she kept going. "If I could travel back in time and stop myself from getting pregnant, I'd do it in a heartbeat."

Alicia rested her chin in her palm. "I know, right? Babies totally suck."

Kat blinked. "What?" She expected Alicia to kick her out, not agree with her.

"It's true. They're needy little bastards who never say thank you and cry every time you try to have sex. And even when they get older, you still can't have sex because now they walk in on you. And Heaven forbid you try to lock the door, cause they'll stand there sobbing until you let them in." She sighed. "Can you tell that's been happening lately?"

It was such a relief to know she wasn't alone. "How have you not gone insane?"

"Oh, I have." Alicia walked over to the counter and returned with a laptop. The screen was covered in deep gashes and several keys were missing.

"I had this thing for *three days* before JJ ruined it. I went in his room to wake him from a nap and there he was, carving into the screen with a pen. I lost it. I screamed at him until he cried, and then *I* cried because I felt like a horrible mom. He wasn't doing it maliciously— I think he liked the way the colors warped on the screen when he touched it. And the more I thought about it, I realized I wasn't even mad at *him*. I was mad at *myself* for being dumb enough to leave my expensive new computer in a place where my two-year-old could reach it."

I'm mad at myself too. And I'm taking it out on Lili and Ian.

"Did you and Jeremy ever fight about the baby?"

"Oh God, all the time. We still do sometimes, especially when we're both tired, but even when we're fighting I know we still love each other, and that helps a lot."

That wasn't exactly reassuring. "But it's still not the same as before?"

"It is and it isn't. We still goof around, but there's something different about it too, like we appreciate each other on a deeper level because we've gone through such a major, life-changing event together." She rested her chin in her hands. "It sounds silly, but sometimes I'll be watching Jeremy play with JJ or change his diaper, and I'll start crying because he's taking care of this person we created together, and I love him so much more in that moment. I think whatever we traded off in freedom is ultimately worth it because of that."

Kat held back tears, thinking about how often Ian went out of his way to do something nice for her, just because. She could deal with a screaming baby, or never losing the weight, but not losing him.

Driving home, she came up with a plan. She'd stop at the grocery store to pick up ingredients for a nice dinner, and later that night she'd apologize for the way she'd been acting. She'd explain that she was ready to stop feeling sorry for herself and start putting their relationship first.

Rehearsing out loud some of the things she might say, she was suddenly hit by a strong wave of nausea. She barely had time to pull off to the side of the highway and open the door before vomiting chunks of noodle casserole all over the road.

Head spinning, she leaned back against the seat. *What did Alicia feed me?* She hadn't felt this sick since—no, that was impossible. She was on the pill. Even if she'd somehow skipped a day, surely that wouldn't negate all the other days—would it?

She sped home and checked the birth control package. She was a day behind.

Fuck. Fuck, fuck, fuck, fuck, fuck.

Yanking open the drawer under the bathroom sink, she found the slim box with the extra test she'd bought last year. Hands shaking, she fumbled with the eyedropper. The test strip showed two dark lines almost immediately. She was pregnant.

She paced the bathroom, trying not to freak out. She may not have known her own mind the first time around, but there was no question now. She didn't want another baby—not now, and probably not ever, but definitely not now.

I need to think.

She tucked Lili into the bassinette and stepped outside, the cool wind soothing her warm skin as she paced up the street, her fingers pressed against her temples.

Ian would be devastated. He'd wanted the first baby so badly, not to mention how touchy he was about death. There was no way he'd agree to an abortion or forgive her if she had one. He might even want a divorce.

They'd have to hire lawyers and divvy up their possessions—maybe even sell the house. She might be able to afford the mortgage on her salary alone, but there was no way he could. And poor Lili would grow up living out of a suitcase, shuttled back and forth between homes per whatever schedule the courts imposed. Every week or so, Ian would show up to drop her off before leaving again. One day he'd surely get remarried—probably to some homemaker type who'd happily birth a dozen more of his children. And she'd have to stand by and watch as the man she loved made a wonderful new life with someone else.

No. I won't let that happen.

If they were going to have any hope of saving their marriage, Ian could never know. She'd schedule an appointment during his work hours the following week and drop Lili off at a daycare while she was gone. And while she was there she'd ask for a more foolproof method of birth control. Maybe one of those shots that last for a year or more so she could make sure this never happened again.

Feeling steadier with a plan, she turned the corner back onto their street, and noticed Ian's car parked in front of the house. Her newfound calm dissolved as she suddenly realized what a bad idea it was to leave Lili in the house alone.

Ian's gonna kill me.

Heart racing, she hurried up the street. He couldn't have been home for more than a few minutes. Maybe he hadn't noticed she was gone.

At the sound of the front door opening, Ian stormed out from the kitchen, clutching his cell phone, his eyebrows raised so high they practically flew off his forehead. "Where the fuck have you been? I was about to call the police!"

She winced. "I just went for a short walk around the block to get some air."

"And you left our two-month-old daughter home alone?" It sounded so much worse when he said it like that.

"I'm sorry. It won't happen again."

"What if she choked on her spit or the house burned down? She could've died!"

"I said I was sorry!"

"What the fuck were you thinking?"

"I was gone for less than 10 minutes. She's alone longer than that when I shower."

"What if I hadn't come home early and you'd gotten hit by a car?"

Kat threw her hands in the air, sick of hearing about all these worst-case scenarios. "Then I guess the baby and I would both be dead. There, I said it. Are you happy?"

"Of course I'm not happy."

"Well, neither am I. I tried to tell you I wasn't ready for a baby, but you didn't care. You kept going on about how everyone is scared and you've just gotta *jump in.*"

As soon as she said it she wished she could take it back. He took a step away and ran a hand through his hair, looking like a wounded animal. She reached for his arm, but he yanked it back.

"I'm sorry I ruined your life," he muttered, heading for the door.

"That's not what I meant. Please don't leave."

"I have plans with Wade."

"Cancel them."

"I can't talk to you right now." He slammed the door behind him, leaving her alone in the quiet of the living room.

CHAPTER 27

Ian

Shielding his eyes from the seizure-inducing lights above the concession stand, Ian scanned the crowd until he spotted Wade sitting on a bench on the other side of the lobby. He waved to get his attention, but the dumbass was too busy with his phone to notice.

"Excuse me," he muttered, weaving through a gaggle of teenage girls as they chattered on in annoyingly high-pitched voices, completely oblivious to the existence of other people. He clenched his teeth and resisted the urge to shove them into a wall. *This is why I don't go to the movies on the fucking weekend anymore.* And Wade fit right in with the crowd, dressed in his perpetual jeans-hoodie-sneakers combo and smiling to himself as he texted someone.

"What the fuck are you smiling about?"

Wade held up his phone and smiled even wider. "I met a girl."

Ian rolled his eyes. "Of course you did." And now he was going to talk about her all night.

"She likes old school video games."

"I don't give a shit." He checked his watch. "What time is the movie?"

Wade narrowed his eyes. "Why are you being such a dick?"

Ian shook his head. *Fucking unbelievable.* "Sure, everyone else gets to say and do whatever the fuck they want, but when *I* do, *I'm* a dick."

"What are you even talking about?"

He threw his arms in the air. "You know what? Fuck you, fuck the movie, and fuck every teenager on this goddamn planet." He turned on his heel and strode a few feet toward the exit before Wade yanked on his arm.

"Seriously, what the fuck are you talking about?" He looked worried. Good. It was about time someone worried about him for a change.

"My life is shit. All I wanna do right now is get so drunk I won't be able to think about it anymore."

"Okay. I'll come with you."

They walked to a bar a few blocks from the theater with just the kind of atmosphere he wanted—dark and empty. Sitting at a wobbly wooden table across from a shallow stage, they ordered a pitcher of beer. Ian downed his first glass in one long gulp and immediately poured another. Wade's eyes widened.

"Slow down, you're gonna kill yourself."

"Fuck if I care."

"Is this about Kat? You wanted to go to a movie specifically so she could come, but she's not here."

He downed his second beer. "My whole life I've had to be responsible for everything. Teacher assigns a group project? No problem—we'll fuck around for weeks while Ian does all the work. School running out of money? It's all good—we'll get Ian to do the extra work because he never complains. Don't feel like changing the baby's diaper? Fine—let her sit in filth all day until Ian gets home. Because it's completely believable that she always *happens* to take a shit the moment I walk through the door." Wade stared at him with a stupid look on his face. "You have no idea what it's like, do you? All you have to do is show up and everyone's impressed."

Wade scoffed. "No one's ever impressed by me. In case you haven't noticed, our entire family thinks I can't even tie my shoes without help. Mom's offered to help pay my rent twice even though I've never been late on it. And don't even get me started on the shit Dad says to me."

"She offered to pay your rent?" This coming from the woman who made it clear she couldn't contribute a dime to the down payment on his house.

Wade shrugged. "I said no."

"Unbelievable," he muttered, running a hand through his hair.

He always took his schoolwork seriously, didn't drink until he was 21, and hadn't so much as touched hard drugs or had a one-night stand. He'd wasted his youth following the rules, so sure it would pay off in a happy, secure adult life. Meanwhile, his idiot brother who never gave a shit about anything beyond having fun somehow reaped the rewards. Wade got good grades without studying, had a job where he earned a fuckton of money for doing nothing, and always got the girl.

"My life's a fucking joke, that's what it is." He started pouring another glass of beer, but Wade pushed the pitcher away.

"You've gotta be kidding me. You have the life the rest of us want. Hell, the only reason I proposed to Jill was because I saw how happy you and Kat were and thought I could make it happen for myself."

"But that's the problem," Ian said. "Kat's not the same woman I married last year. She's supposed to be my rock—the one who pulls me out of my head and reminds me that life doesn't have to be so fucking serious, but now I can't even get her to smile. And I try to put myself in her shoes—I mean, obviously no one *likes* changing diapers—but I think maybe some small part of me *did* assume she'd do the bulk of the childcare just because she's a woman. I know that's not fair, but still can't help feeling resentful about being with the one woman who isn't over the moon about babies."

He gripped a handful of hair. "Sometimes I lie awake at night and wonder, is this who we're doomed to be for the rest of our lives—her a bitch and me an asshole?"

"Okay, don't yell at me for saying this, but you *are* an asshole sometimes."

Ian rolled his eyes. "Thank you. That makes me feel infinitely better."

"It's true." Wade raised his voice. "You treat me like an idiot every time I bring up an idea you don't like, and even when you change your mind, you never admit you were wrong or say you're sorry."

"I apologize all the time!"

"No. You don't."

Ian raised his glass to his lips. "I'm not gonna argue this with you."

"Because you know you're wrong."

"I'm not wrong!" He slammed his fist on the table so hard he caught the attention of the group next to them. *Goddamnit.* "I'm sorry, okay?"

"Whatever." Wade turned his attention to his phone.

Feeling a breeze, Ian looked over his shoulder to see the place had filled up since they'd arrived. The back door was propped open for a man wheeling in a cart with steel-framed musicians' cases strapped to it. His heart felt like lead.

"Let's go to another bar."

Wade rolled his eyes. "Why? We just got here."

He motioned toward the stage where the man was unloading the cases. "Cause I'm not in the mood to listen to some shitty ass bar band."

Wade continued texting. "I thought you loved shitty ass bar bands."

"No. I love real bands who write music that moves people, not a bunch of old men in Hawaiian shirts covering *Margaritaville.* That's pathetic."

"Why is it pathetic if it makes them happy?" Wade snapped.

"Geez, calm the fuck down. I didn't know you cared so much."

"I care about a lot of things."

Ian squeezed his eyes shut and tried not to sound like an asshole. "I didn't mean to insult you, or even the band for that matter. I just meant that I, personally, wouldn't find it fulfilling." He watched the man unravel a microphone cord and plug it into an amp. "Sometimes I miss music so much it hurts."

"So start another band."

Ian scoffed. "The only other musician I'm still in touch with is Drew, and he's moving. Not that he'd wanna do it anyway."

"You don't need a band. People sing and play guitar by themselves all the time. You could record a couple CDs and take them to bars and coffee shops. Someone's bound to let you play."

"It's not that easy." He hesitated. "I sort of suck now. What if I fuck up and make an ass of myself?"

A waitress dropped a plastic booklet on their table. Wade opened it and grinned. "Well, here's your chance to practice." He slid the booklet across the table. "It's not a band, it's karaoke."

Ian picked up the booklet, palms sweating. "I'm not exactly prepared to sing right now."

"Just do it. If you fuck up, it won't matter. None of these people know who you are, and you'll never see them again."

He scanned the room, triple-checking whether that was true. Scranton wasn't exactly a big city, and the surrounding towns were even smaller. The last thing he needed was a coworker or some student's parent to see this.

He wiped his palms against his pants. "Karaoke never has good songs, anyway. It's always the same tired oldies and Top-40 shit."

"Excuses, excuses." Wade flipped through the pages. "If I can find something that doesn't suck, you have to sing it."

Ian crossed his arms. "I don't have to do anything."

"Look, they have an entire 'alternative' section." He flipped the booklet around and pointed. "Green Day, My Chemical Romance, The Smashing Pumpkins—I know you've seen at least half these bands live so don't even pretend you don't like them."

Scowling, yet secretly pleased, Ian studied the booklet for a few minutes before submitting his name along with the song code for Linkin Park's *Given Up*.

First on stage were two college-aged blondes in low-cut tops who giggled and leaned on each other as they butchered their way through some already terrible country song. The audience clapped and cheered, but it only made his stomach churn. They'd obviously come to watch cute girls and drunken weirdoes, not a guy with a halfway decent voice singing a serious song. As they finished singing, he fumbled for his wallet.

"We have to leave now."

"We're not leaving until you sing."

"Like hell we're not." He stood up too fast and his head swam with the alcohol, almost knocking him right back down again. He dropped a handful of bills on the table. It was probably too much, but he was too buzzed to calculate the total.

The emcee took the microphone. "Thank you, ladies. Next up is Ian D. Where is Ian D?"

All the blood drained from his face. *Second? They want me to go on second?*

"He's right here," Wade yelled, pointing at him.

The emcee caught his eye and held out the microphone. "Come on up, Ian."

Wade shoved him forward. A wave of vertigo passed through him as he stepped onto the foot-high stage in front of the colorful blur of faces watching and waiting for him to fuck up so they could—what, exactly? Boo him? Laugh at him? Stay completely silent as though he'd never performed at all? Would any of that really be so terrible?

As the intro started playing, he slid the microphone into the stand, gripping it with both hands. Ignoring the crowd, he fixed his gaze on the monitor. His voice came out gravelly and low as he stumbled through the first few notes. Making matters worse, the lyrics on the monitor raced forward two beats ahead of the music, throwing off his tempo. His face grew hot and tension built in his muscles until he thought he might explode. Near the end of the first verse he accidently glanced up at the crowd. Only half of them were paying attention, and a few were even smiling.

Fuck the monitor, I know the words.

Closing his eyes, he took a deep breath right before the chorus and then belted out the lyrics in perfect time with the beat, the song's electric energy flowing through him, creating an unreal hyper-awareness of being physically present and alive.

When the song ended, he jumped off the stage and jogged back toward the table as the audience clapped and cheered.

"That was awesome," Wade yelled, high-fiving him.

Every ounce of his being was on such heightened alert that the rest of the world felt like it was drowning in quicksand. He wanted to cry, or run, or jump off a goddamned bridge.

"I wanna do something dumb."

Before Wade could protest, he sprinted out the front door, the crisp night air surging through his lungs as his feet slammed against the concrete. All around him patches of fluorescent yellow and orange pierced the darkness, flooding out like a kaleidoscope from storefront windows and the streetlamps overhead. Coming up to an intersection with a red light, he reached for the traffic pole and swung his weight around it, propelling his body off in another direction, his heart thumping so fast it threatened to leap out of his chest. Up ahead he could make out the blurry silhouette of one of the University of Scranton's many statues, but before he figured out which one it was the acidic contents of his stomach lurched forward, splattering onto the pavement.

Gasping for air, he crumpled onto a nearby lawn, staring up into the backlit branches of a budding oak tree until Wade's face appeared above him.

"Feel better now?"

Unable to speak, he shook his head as Wade sat in the grass beside him, catching his own breath.

"I'm taking you home."

Ian closed his eyes and nodded.

Inside Wade's car, he reclined the passenger seat and curled up into a ball, his head spinning as Wade called Rob for help retrieving the other car. As they drove away, Wade grabbed a paper Wendy's bag from the back seat.

"In case you have to throw up again."

The bag smelled like old cheeseburgers, almost causing him to need it immediately. He folded it up and wedged it between the seat cushions. He'd been a dick to Wade all night, yet there he was, taking care of him without complaint.

"Tell me about the girl."

Wade glanced at him uneasily before focusing back on the road. "Maybe another time."

"I know you want to."

A goofy grin spread across Wade's face. "Yeah, I totally do."

"So who is she? What's she like?"

"She's a librarian."

Ian covered his face. "Fuck, that's hot."

"I know, right?" Wade laughed. "And the best part is *she* asked *me* out."

"What?"

"I know! Usually whenever a girl likes me she'll start hanging around all the time or going out of her way to do stuff for me, but never comes out and says it. It's always me who has to take the risk. And now I know why they don't—you wouldn't believe how much less pressure there is going into a date knowing the other person is genuinely interested and not just going along with it to be nice. I mean, you still have to be cool and funny so she doesn't change her mind, but it's completely different."

"So what did you guys do?"

"We talked at a coffee shop for a little bit, but she had to leave pretty early so we're going to Lahey tomorrow before the party."

"Did you kiss her?"

"No." He sighed. "I didn't really get a chance. Plus, she seemed kind of shy so I figured I'd play it safe and wait until the next date." As he parked the car, Rob appeared, grinning and banging on the driver's side window. Wade rolled it down.

"How drunk is he? Is he saying funny things yet?"

Ian flipped him off.

"Nah, he's more philosophically drunk."

"Even better. We should take him with us to get his car."

"He threw up, though," Wade said. "We should probably leave him here."

Ian ventured a glance out the windshield, his house looming above them. The living room windows were dark, but there was a light on in the master bedroom. He couldn't handle another fight without first getting some aspirin and sleep.

"Can you both stay and hang out a while? Please? We can pick up my car in the morning."

"Fine by me." Rob jogged around to the passenger side and opened the door. "You need help?"

"I'm fine." He steadied his weight against the car door. "The baby's probably asleep though, so everyone has to be quiet."

Inside, he turned on the TV and was passing out Game Cube controllers when Kat appeared at the top of the steps in her pajamas, arms crossed like a disappointed mother. Wade and Rob muttered quiet hellos, but Ian's blood pressure rose, and he forgot to be quiet.

"We're gonna play *Smash Bros.*"

Without a word, she went back into the bedroom.

CHAPTER 28

Wade

Eleanor sat in the passenger seat of her beat up car, ankles crossed on the dashboard, looking cute as hell as she stared off into the blue sky above the parking lot. Creeping up beside the window, Wade made a goofy face, holding it for so long his muscles started to hurt. He was about to give up when she glanced over and jumped like she'd seen a ghost. She laughed and covered her face as he opened the door for her.

"You were really out there," he said.

She brushed her hair behind her ear. "Yeah, I do that sometimes."

"You were thinking about me, weren't you?"

She glanced at her shoes, her face flushing lightly. "Maybe."

Holy fuck. She's so adorable she might kill me.

Suppressing the urge to kiss her right then, he wrapped her in a hug instead, her head barely coming up to his chin.

"You make me feel tall. I could get used to that."

She rocked on her heels. "So what's so great about this course that everyone always comes here?"

"I'd love to tell you it's like super high tech or something, but as you can see it's totally not." He pointed over the fence where a few scattered groups of mini-golfers clustered around the small greens. "The windmill hasn't worked in years, and the whole place could use a coat of paint, but we all grew up coming here so it holds a special place in our hearts. Come on, I'll show you around."

He reached for her hand and she let him lead her up to the building. That was a good sign. Whenever girls let him hold their hand they almost always let him kiss them.

Inside, they picked up clubs and balls before heading back out into the warm afternoon.

"So, where are you from, originally?" he asked.

"That's kind of a hard question." She set her ball on the green. "I was born in Lawton, Oklahoma, but I don't remember it. My dad was stationed there when he met my mom, and they got married a few months before I was born. We moved every few years—sometimes more often than that. So I'm sort of from everywhere and nowhere at the same time."

"Do you still go wherever your parents go?" *Please say no.*

"Nope. I stopped moving with them a few years back. I stayed at my college in Indiana when they went back down to Texas."

He tapped his ball toward the hole. "That's really far. How often do you get to see them?"

"I haven't seen them since they moved. We don't really talk much."

"Is that good or bad?"

"It just is." She shrugged. "What about your family?"

"My parents still live in the house where I grew up. I live like 5 minutes from them."

"So you're close?"

"Kind of, but not really." He missed his shot and took another. "I usually only see them on holidays and maybe once every month or so for some family thing. My brother and I are good friends though, so I see him a lot more than I do my parents." He bent down, collecting their golf balls. "Well, I used to anyway. He had a kid recently, so I hardly see him at all now."

"I'm sorry."

"I actually saw him last night for the first time in awhile, but it was kind of depressing. I always thought he and his wife were the perfect couple, but they're having problems. It makes me wonder whether any of us can truly be happy over the long-term, or if all good feelings are temporary." He couldn't believe he was telling her all this, or the way she looked up at him with her pale grey eyes, really listening. "Sometimes I wish I could go back to when we were kids and freeze time. Everything was so much easier then."

"I don't know," she said. "A lot of people seem to think that, but kids never really get a say in anything that happens to them. If your parents tell you to clean your room or pack your suitcase, you have to shut up and do it or risk catching hell."

Wade laughed. "I definitely caught a lot of hell."

She gave a half smile before turning toward the next green, the breeze playing with her long brown hair. She seemed to have a lot of sadness in her. He wished there was something he could do to take it all away.

Catching up with her, he hugged her from behind. "I wish I knew you back then. You could come play baseball in the park with me and my friends. I know they'd all love you. And even if you didn't really like me, I'd totally let you use me for my video games."

When she smiled, her whole face lit up. "Are you still friends with the same people?" she asked.

His good mood dampened. He thought about down-playing the situation to keep things light, but she'd been so accepting of everything else, and plus, it felt good to talk with someone who actually cared.

"For the most part," he replied. "But lately it seems like everyone's fading away. Like I said, my brother had a baby and one of my other good friends is moving to New York City for a job. That would suck on its own, but the worst part is I don't think he was gonna tell me. I only found out because his mom told my mom."

She kicked at the ground with the tip of her shoe. "Maybe he thought saying goodbye would hurt too much."

"I doubt it. I felt so bad about not keeping in touch, but when I tried calling him to hang out, he dodged me for two months. I'm supposed to finally see him tonight, but honestly, I'm not that excited. It feels like he's already gone and there's nothing I can do about it."

She swiveled the head of her club against the ground. "If you met him for the first time today—as the adult he is now, with no memory of him as a kid—would you still choose him as a friend?"

The question felt like a punch to the gut. He wanted to say *yes, of course*, but truthfully, he wasn't sure. A lot had changed since that day in middle school when Drew got off the bus with Ian and played *GoldenEye 007* with them all night. They'd been through so much together— hookups and breakups, late night conversations, and countless hours of gaming—but were those past connections still enough now?

Squinting at the mountains in the distance, he tried to imagine Drew without all the associated memories, but it was hard to separate them.

"I think I *would* still wanna be friends. Because he *is* a cool guy, and I'd hate missing out on a friend because I met him when he was busy or going through a rough patch. I think part of being a friend is knowing deep down that someone's worth your time, even when they occasionally get weird on you."

She touched his arm. "I hope he recognizes what a good friend you are."

It was just about the nicest thing anyone had ever said to him. Overwhelmed with the moment, he took her face in his hands and kissed her slowly, savoring the feel of her soft lips against his. Her body was stiff at first, but she soon relaxed into his embrace, wrapping her arms around his waist.

His phone rang from his front pants pocket.

Fuck my life.

He tried to keep kissing her, but she started laughing so hard she had to pull back. Thank God she had a sense of humor.

"Go ahead, answer it," she said, her grey eyes sparkling.

Keeping one arm firmly around her back, he fished his phone out of his pocket. "It's my brother." He rolled his eyes as he put the phone to his ear. "I hate you right now." He stuck out his tongue at her, and she giggled.

Ian ignored the greeting. "Kat says she feels bad about last night. She bought a bunch of fancy food for an early dinner. You wanna join us?"

"I'm hanging out with someone right now. Can I bring her?"

"Oh, how cute. Is it the hot librarian?"

"You're such an asshole." Wade pressed the phone to his chest. "You wanna have dinner at my brother's house after this?"

"Um... sure. Why not?"

He raised the phone back to his ear. "She's coming too."

"I bet she is."

"Hold on a sec," he whispered to Eleanor as he walked a few feet away, keeping his voice low so she wouldn't hear. "I swear to God, if you say anything stupid to her—"

"Relax. I'm not going to ruin your date. Just don't start fucking on my couch or anything."

Hanging up, he noticed Eleanor twirling her golf club and staring off into space again. Sneaking up behind her, he wrapped his arms around her and kissed her neck.

"What were you thinking about just now?"

She turned around in his arms, looking up at him. "How handsome you are."

"I'm totally not." He blushed, turning his face away for a moment before bringing it right back to kiss her again.

CHAPTER 29

Eleanor

Eleanor parked behind Wade's car on the flat residential street, her energy already starting to wane. She shouldn't have said yes to dinner. She didn't want the date to end, but once they stepped inside his brother's house, their intimate little bubble would burst anyway. What if his family didn't like her? What if she ran out of things to say and Wade realized she wasn't really that cool after all?

Wade tapped on her window and she rolled it down. "What's wrong? Did I park in a bad spot?"

"Nothing's wrong. I just wanted to kiss you again." He leaned in the window, pressing his lips against hers, his fingers playing with the hair at the base of her scalp. It felt amazing and not at all real.

Somewhere nearby, a man cleared his throat. "Are you guys gonna come inside or just fuck in the car all afternoon?" A taller, cleaner cut version of Wade with lighter hair stood in the middle of the lawn with his arms crossed.

Wade looked at her with a mischievous gleam in his eye. "I'm not exactly opposed to option two."

At that moment, neither was she. "It's probably rude if we don't at least say hi first."

"If you insist." He opened the door and took her by the hand as they walked toward the house. "Ian, this is Eleanor. Eleanor, this is my asshole brother, Ian."

Ian rolled his eyes. "Come on in. Dinner's almost ready."

The living room was gorgeous with a brick fireplace, plush couches, and a flat screen TV. In the corner was an infant swing.

"How old is the baby?" she asked, trying to make conversation.

"She's two months." Ian plopped onto the couch with a video game controller and unpaused the image on the TV screen.

Wade took a seat beside him and motioned for her to join them. He draped an arm around her shoulder, pulling her toward him. "Eleanor likes games too."

A surge of pride welled up in her chest.

Ian seemed unimpressed. "Like what?"

"Mostly Super Nintendo and a little bit of Sega," she answered.

Wade squeezed her tighter. "You didn't tell me about the Sega!"

She laughed, enjoying the feel of his body against hers. "I only just remembered. The rec room at one of the bases had one, but I didn't get to play much because there were always other kids using it."

"Ian, save your game and switch to multiplayer mode." Wade hopped up and opened the cabinet under the TV. "I wanna show Eleanor how to play a modern game."

Ian grumbled but did it anyway as Wade unraveled the cords of two more controllers. Rejoining her on the couch, he rested his chin on her shoulder as he touched each of the buttons in turn.

"The left stick moves your character, and the right one moves the camera so you can look in different directions. A is jump, X is shoot, and this trigger up here is reload."

She practiced moving around the mountainous desert terrain, but using two sticks at once was harder than it looked. She bit her lip as she tried to maneuver out from the ditch she'd fallen into.

"Don't worry, you'll get the hang of it in no time." Wade gently guided her fingers on the buttons until she was back on the main surface. "For now, try to keep the camera as still as possible. It's gonna be you and me against Ian. Whoever captures the flag and brings it back to their base first wins."

"Got it."

He cupped his hands to her ear, his whisper sending up the hairs on the back of her neck. "You concentrate on getting the flag. I'll keep Ian out of the way."

She sat up straight, leaning toward the screen as she snaked through the rocky hills, and laughing as Wade and Ian lobbed insults and grenades at each other. Every now and then, Wade glanced at her, grinning, and her whole body felt lighter.

"Dinner will be ready in a few minutes." A pretty woman in a tank top and long black skirt stood in the archway between the living and dining rooms.

"Hey Kat," Wade called out, cheerfully. "This is Eleanor."

"I'd shake your hand, but I don't wanna mess up your game." She sat in the adjacent loveseat, curling her legs beneath her.

"You have a beautiful home."

"It's kind of a mess right now, but thanks." She pulled a pillow into her lap. "How long have you known Wade?"

"Three days." It seemed at once much more and much less than that.

"And you agreed to meet his family? That's brave." Kat laughed, but her smile didn't reach all the way to her eyes.

"I guess."

The flag was perched on a platform up ahead. Wordlessly, she picked it up and started back toward the craggy cave entrance.

"Where did you meet?" Kat asked.

"At the library where I work."

"What were you doing in a library, anyway?" Ian raised his eyebrows.

Wade's face flushed slightly. "What? I read sometimes."

Ian scoffed. "Comic books, maybe."

"We have comics at the library," Eleanor said, feeling a strong urge to defend him. "I read some *Robot Chicken* issues awhile back. They were really funny."

Wade's face brightened. "See, that's why you're awesome, and he's not."

She hid behind a tank, watching as Wade's soldier punched Ian's from behind, sending him crumpling to the ground.

"Go, go, go!" he yelled.

She ran past the body and into the base where their flag still stood, and a box popped up declaring the game over.

"You did it!" Wade threw his arms around her and kissed her, knocking her back against the couch's armrest. It felt strange kissing in front of his family, but his enthusiasm was so contagious, she didn't really mind.

"How come you never kiss me like that anymore?" Ian asked.

"I kiss you all the time." Kat sounded hurt.

"Not like *that*."

The loveseat springs creaked. "I think dinner's ready," she said in a flat voice as her footsteps trailed off toward the kitchen.

Ian smacked Wade on the side of the head. "Seriously, what did I tell you on the phone?"

Wade rubbed his head. "You didn't say anything about kissing."

Feeling uneasy, she looked from one to the other, waiting for someone to explain what they were talking about.

Ian unplugged his controller and started neatly wrapping the cord around it. "Hey Eleanor, did Wade ever tell you about the *real* first time he met you?" Wade narrowed his eyes in a kind of dark warning, but Ian ignored him. "He saw you on the street once and jerked off in a men's room thinking about you."

Her face flushed deep red. As far as she knew, no one had ever done that before. She hoped it was true, but didn't want to look stupid for falling for it if turned out to be some sort of dumb joke.

"Really?" she managed to ask.

Wade scratched the side of his face. "Um, yeah. That's why I thought you looked familiar. I'm really sorry." He shot an evil look at Ian. "I was gonna tell you eventually, but not until we knew each other better so it wouldn't sound so creepy."

She grinned. "Don't be sorry. It's kind of flattering."

"Yeah?" His face relaxed.

"Well, isn't that wonderful?" Ian flung his controller onto the couch and skulked off toward the kitchen.

"Is he always in such a bad mood?" she whispered.

"He can be a dick sometimes, but it's usually not this bad." He helped her up from the couch. "I don't think either of them has gotten a full night's sleep since the baby was born."

Kat carried a bowl of salad into the dining room and dropped it unceremoniously onto the table as Ian followed with a tray of bread. This was going to be a long meal.

"I should wash up first," Eleanor said. "Where's the bathroom?"

"Upstairs on the left."

She set her purse on the sink and examined her reflection in the mirror, barely believing she was the same person she'd been a few days ago. She couldn't stop smiling. When had Wade seen her? She hadn't even thought to ask. Everything was happening so fast, but it felt good—normal, even.

Her phone vibrated from inside her purse. It was probably Carmen trying to get coverage for Penny. "Hello?"

"Hey. Is this Eleanor?"

She didn't recognize the voice. "Yes, who's this?"

"It's Trent Zarella. From high school."

Her stomach felt like it dropped all the way through her bowels and splattered onto the tile floor. She gripped the side of the sink. "Trent. Hi." Her throat felt suddenly dry.

"I got your note. Sorry if it's been awhile. I don't live at that apartment anymore, and my ex is terrible about forwarding my mail."

Ex-girlfriend or ex-wife? She shook her head. That wasn't appropriate to ask. Neither was how long ago he'd moved, whether he was seeing anyone new, or any of the other dozens of questions ricocheting through her mind.

"Oh, um, that's okay." Her voice sounded high and thin.

"How did you wind up in Scranton again?" he asked.

She sat on the closed toilet lid, head spinning. Of all the times he could've called. She tried to reach the deeper register she spoke with at work, but failed miserably.

"It's kind of a long story. I can't really talk right now, though. Would you want to get together some time to catch up?"

"Sure. I have a family thing tonight, but what about tomorrow?"

Family thing—as in kids or cousins?

She wiped her clammy palms on her face. "Yeah, that sounds great. Where do you want to meet?"

"If you're close to the downtown area, there's a nice bar on Jefferson Street with lights wrapped around the front poles."

"Yeah, I know it." She passed it every day on her way to and from work. "I can meet you there at 7."

"Seven it is." She could hear the smile in his voice. "See you then."

Hands shaking, she clasped the phone to her chin, trying to breathe. She had a date with Trent, but right now she was still *on* a date with Wade, and he and his family were waiting downstairs.

A lump formed in her throat. She liked Wade a lot, but barely knew him. Sure, they were having fun now, but what about when she ran out of things to say and he got bored with her like Natalie did with Nick? Plus, that exchange with Ian had been so strange.

What did I tell you on the phone?

You didn't say anything about kissing.

Was it a stupid joke, or did Wade really have a history of bringing girls over and doing more than that? She felt so sick she didn't think she could eat.

Go downstairs and say you're not feeling well.

In the dining room, Wade and Ian were already eating and Kat was nowhere to be seen. Grinning, Wade patted the seat of the chair beside him. She couldn't speak— just stood there lamely for a few seconds before bursting into tears.

Wade jumped up and wrapped an arm around her shoulders, guiding her to the couch. "What's wrong?"

"I don't know." She covered her face with her hands. "I'm so sorry."

"Is there anything I can do?" He rubbed her back and she sobbed even harder. She supposed it no longer mattered if he thought she was a weirdo, but still hated herself for letting him see it.

She wiped her eyes on her sleeve. "I think I should go."

"Are you gonna be okay driving?" His warm brown eyes were big and full of concern. She felt so guilty. She needed to say something—anything—to make him stop looking at her like that.

"I'll call you sometime." She sniffled.

"Sure. Get home safe, okay?" He hung his head the slightest bit as he opened the front door. He didn't believe her any more than she believed herself.

CHAPTER 30

Kat

Kat knocked on the door and waited in the gathering dusk, wringing her hands together. The idea seemed worse with every passing second. They *weren't* really friends, and this would be weird. She turned to go but then he opened the door.

"Kat?" Rob's brow furrowed as he glanced over her shoulder, probably looking for Ian. That was all the confirmation she needed, but she couldn't leave now.

"Hey," she said, trying to sound cheerful. She brushed a strand of hair behind her ear. "I know this might sound weird, but I lost my phone charger and was wondering if I could maybe buy one from you."

He leaned against the doorframe, studying her a little too closely from behind his glasses. Was her lie that obvious?

"Come in, I'll see what I have."

She followed him past the laundry room and into his bedroom where a disassembled computer sat atop his desk. She'd been there a bunch of times with the rest of their friends, but never by herself. It seemed eerily quiet.

"Let me see your phone." He examined the bottom port. "I might have something that fits."

He pulled the blanket over his unmade bed before switching on the light inside his walk-in closet. "Make yourself at home."

Sitting on the bed, she smoothed out the wrinkles in her skirt as he rummaged through cardboard boxes.

"What were you up to tonight?" she asked, trying to fill the silence.

"Installing a hard drive."

"Does that take long?"

"Not really. Why?"

"Just wondering. I don't really know much about what you do."

"I fix and sell computers. There's not much else to it."

She twisted her hands in her lap, ashamed that she'd known him for years but never really got to *know* him. "Why don't we ever hang out—just you and me?"

"I didn't think you were interested."

She felt even worse. Had her apathy been that obvious to everyone except her? She picked at the skin around her fingernails. "I've had a lot of time to think lately, and I realized I've been sort of a shitty friend to a lot of people. I wanna fix that."

He turned off the closet light and leaned against the doorframe. "Are you going to the party tonight?"

"I'll probably stay home. Ian took Lili to Wade's already, so maybe I'll actually get some sleep."

"You're welcome to stay and hang out. We could play video games, watch a movie, or whatever else you had in mind." His tone sounded like he was asking whether she wanted to hook up.

The blood drained from her face. Was that really why she was there—not to strengthen a friendship but to scout out some sort of backup plan in case things didn't go well with Ian? She stared at the wall, unable to meet his eye. He was a good-looking guy, and the prospect of starting over fresh did have a certain appeal. She felt sick. *What the hell is wrong with me?*

He seemed to sense her distress. "Have you eaten dinner yet?"

She shook her head.

"Come on. I'll buy you tacos."

On the way back from Taco Bell, Rob drove down a side street and parked in front of a low closed gate. A nearby sign read *Dunmore Reservoir #1.*

"What is this place?" she asked.

"It's sort of like a park. Come on."

They slipped past the gate and hiked up a hill toward a metal-framed footbridge suspended over the reservoir.

"We can't actually cross because there's a locked gate," he explained, "but there's a few feet of bridge before the gate where we can hang our legs over the edge."

She took a seat on the bridge, gazing at the reflection of the full moon on the water as it trickled softly over the rocks beneath them.

He handed her a taco. "So, are you gonna tell me what's wrong?"

"I did something massively stupid." She stared into her lap. "And if I tell Ian what it is, he's gonna leave me."

"Did you cheat on him?"

She blinked, slightly offended he jumped to that conclusion, but also guilty that the thought had indeed crossed her mind. "No. Definitely not."

"Then he's probably not gonna leave. I think he could forgive anything but that. Hell, he might even forgive that too."

"How can you be so sure?"

He chewed his taco thoughtfully. "Because he's a loyal bastard. Every time he got a hold of something even half-way decent, he'd cling to it for dear life, even when there was something clearly better right in front of him. And if that's how he treated video games and Pokémon cards, I doubt he's gonna treat you differently when you're hands down the best thing that's ever happened to him."

She stared at him, speechless, unable to believe how kind he was or how far out of his way he'd gone to help her. It didn't jive at all with Drew's opinion of him as an asshole who shit on people for fun.

"Why did you sleep with Drew's ex?"

Rob hung his arms over the metal bar. "I didn't."

She scrunched up her brow. "Wait—then why does everyone think you did?"

"Because I told them I did."

"Why would you do that?" She shook her head. "Now they all think you're an asshole."

He looked into her eyes. "Do *you* think I'm an asshole?"

"No. I always thought Drew was overreacting."

Rob looked back out over the water. "Even when we were kids, it was always the same thing. Drew would take something I said too seriously and get huffy until our friends convinced me to apologize. He'd make a big show of forgiving and forgetting, but six months later it would happen all over again."

He pushed up his glasses. "I would've ditched him years ago if I wasn't afraid of losing half my friends. But then Caitlin showed up at the wedding and I saw an out—something so outrageous he'd never forgive me." He shrugged. "I knew there was gonna be fallout, but had to trust my individual friendships were strong enough to handle it, and for the most part, they were."

It was exactly what she needed to hear. She threw her arms around him. "Thank you for making sense."

CHAPTER 31

Wade

The apartment echoed with shotgun blasts and the clicking of controller buttons as Wade riddled his brother's character with bullets. It didn't make up for the shit he pulled earlier but still felt good. Ian's phone rang and he paused the game.

"Is that Drew?" Wade asked. The party was supposed to start an hour ago, yet no one else had shown up, including the guest of honor.

Ian rolled his eyes at the screen before shoving the phone back in his pocket. "It's Kat."

"You're not gonna answer?"

"She knows I'm at a party."

Wade scoffed. "Yeah. Some party." He grabbed his phone and dialed Drew's number, but only reached voice mail. "Hey, I thought we were hanging out tonight. If something changed, call me. Actually, call me either way so I know what's going on."

He tossed the phone onto the coffee table and rubbed his face, wishing he'd told him not to bother coming at all. Stomach growling, he glanced over at the boxes of now cold pizza on the table.

"Fuck him. I'm eating." He went to the kitchen and stuck two congealed slices in the microwave.

Ian squeezed past the table, heading toward the bedroom. "Put some in for me too. I'm gonna check on Lili real fast."

Wade leaned on the counter, watching the slices cook as he went over the events of the afternoon in his head again. Everything with Eleanor had been going perfectly—until it suddenly wasn't. He wanted to blame Ian's bad attitude, but, truthfully, she didn't seem that fazed by anything he'd said. He debated texting to ask if she was okay, but decided against it. He was done playing stupid mind games with girls. She said she'd call. If she didn't mean it, he was better off without her.

There was a knock at the door. *It's about time.* He yanked it open and did a double take. "Rob?"

Rob looked past Wade into the apartment. "Where is everyone?"

"So far it's only Ian and me. I can't believe you're here."

Rob waved him away as he took a seat in the recliner and plugged his laptop charger into the wall. Wade couldn't help but smile.

"You want some pizza?"

"Sure."

He gave his slices to Rob before nuking up two more. His phone rang. It was Drew—probably calling to cancel.

Drew spoke quickly, his voice echoing a bit. "Hey Wade. I've been stuck on the phone all night with the cable company. The cable went out at my house, and you know how my mom is about watching her shows. I'll be over in a little bit." In the background, a door hinge creaked and the first few notes of *Mary Had a Little Lamb* played faintly.

Wade's stomach hardened. "You're at home *right now?*"

"Yeah, I'm about to hop in the shower." There was no hesitation in his voice.

"You know you don't have to come if you don't want to, right?"

"Of course I want to. I'll be there in about 20." That was roughly the amount of time it would take to get to his apartment from the sports bar.

Ian emerged from the bedroom as Wade hung up. "Was that Drew?"

"Yeah. He's running late," Wade said flatly before collecting his pizza from the microwave.

An hour passed before there was another knock at the door. "Come in," Wade yelled, not feeling like getting off the couch.

Drew was all smiles, dressed in a shirt and slacks as if he were going to work instead of to a friend's place to play video games. Whoever his new friends were, they must be fancy. His posture stiffened when he saw Rob, but he quickly recovered. "What's up, guys?"

Wade motioned toward the table. "We ordered pizza, but it's cold now because you said you'd be here at 8."

"I said I could be here *after* 8, not *at* 8." Drew smirked. *What was he, proud of himself?*

Ian slapped Drew on the back. "Come on in. I'll heat you up a few slices and you can tell us all about that new job of yours."

Drew followed Ian to the table. "Don't worry about the pizza. I already ate."

Of course he did.

Wade skulked into the kitchen, grabbing a beer from the fridge as Drew regaled them with the epic tale of how he went through three rounds of interviews and ultimately beat out six hundred applicants to get his new job.

Wade suddenly understood Rob's annoyance. Even harmless lies were still lies, and they were supposed to be better friends than that. He spoke up. "Were six hundred people seriously considered or did they just get that many resumes?"

Rob raised an eyebrow from behind his laptop as Drew twisted up his face.

"Does it matter?"

"It seems like you're exaggerating a little bit."

Drew leaned forward, tapping two fingertips on the table. "It's a very important position. It's in Manhattan."

Ian's phone rang again, and his whole body tensed as he checked the screen. "Goddamnit, this better be important." He stomped off to the bedroom, shutting the door behind him.

Without Ian, the room fell awkwardly silent. Drew pulled out his phone and started texting. Wade exhaled, shaking his head. *Fuck it.* Their friendship was pretty much dead anyway.

"I know you were at the sports bar when you called. I heard the pinball machine."

Drew stiffened the tiniest bit, but continued texting. "I told you I was home. You probably heard the TV."

"I thought the cable was out."

"The TV was still working. We just weren't getting all the channels."

Wade's insides tightened. Drew was clearly busted— why couldn't he admit the damn truth already? "If you don't wanna be friends anymore, just say so."

Drew scoffed quietly and shook his head, seemingly more annoyed at being taken away from texting than hurt by the accusation. "I'm here, aren't I?"

"But you don't wanna be."

"I don't know what else you want me to say, Wade. I told you what happened." His forced calm was unnerving. He was so determined to show he didn't care, but all that effort only proved he did, so why couldn't he give up the act and be honest about whatever he was upset about?

"Why did it take you so long to answer my messages?"

"I'm a busy person. I can't always text people back right away."

"You don't seem to be having a problem with that now."

Drew pursed his lips, obviously pissed off but still refusing to acknowledge it. Rob glanced back and forth between them, and, to his credit, was at least pretending not to be gleeful.

Wade kicked at the floor, feeling hollow. If he was no longer willing to put up with this kind of treatment from girls, he probably shouldn't tolerate it from friends either. But this whole thing with Drew felt so much sadder. He expected to break up with girls, but not his best friends.

"I think you should go," he said quietly.

"Fine. Tell Ian I said goodbye." Still texting, Drew headed out the door. That was it. Without any hint of sadness or remorse, he was gone—possibly forever.

Wade sunk into the couch with his beer, feeling numb as Rob continued surfing the web. Suddenly, there was a loud crash as Ian stumbled through the bedroom door, clutching the handle of the baby carrier and struggling to keep the diaper bag from slipping off his shoulder. He was white as a ghost.

"What happened?" Wade jumped up and tried to help him with the diaper bag, but he clutched it tighter, his hands shaking

"I have to go," he muttered, head down as he pushed past him. Whatever Kat called about must've been really bad.

"Maybe I should drive you home," Wade said.

"I'm fine. Can you open the door, please?"

He couldn't really stop him if he was determined to go. "Text me when you get home so I know you're okay."

Ignoring the request, Ian maneuvered the carrier and diaper bag out the door and stumbled down the front walk to his car.

CHAPTER 32

Ian

He should be angry. He should be screaming about how wrong this was and fighting for the life of his unborn child, but he just sat across the dining room table from Kat, his shoulders so heavy he couldn't even shrug.

She leaned forward. "Please say something."

Even if he could guilt her into having the baby, he couldn't make her like it. Any time they argued, she could throw it in his face like she had the other night— *you're the one who made me have this baby.* No matter what they did, nothing would be the same again.

His voice felt like sandpaper in his throat. "Do you still love me?"

The hurt in her eyes cut him to the core. "I love you more than anyone else in the word, *including* Lili." She twisted her wedding ring around her finger. "Because the older she gets, the more time she'll spend with friends, the same as we did, until she finally moves out and it's only the two of us again. I don't wanna wake up

one day and realize we don't know each other anymore—
or worse, that we don't *like* each other."

She swallowed. "My parents must've loved each other
once, but I can't remember a single time they kissed,
held hands, or even said something nice to each other.
I think I sensed from very early on that I was the only
thing holding my family together, and I don't want Lili
to feel that kind of pressure. I know I've been difficult
lately, but I've been trying hard not to feel sorry for myself. I think I'll be okay as long as we promise to always
put our relationship first—even above Lili."

Closing his eyes, Ian propped his head up with his
hands, his watch ticking softly in his ear. It was all well
and good that she was in the midst of a personal epiphany, but this wasn't a theoretical conversation. There was
an actual child involved. Their child. Lili's brother or
sister.

"If you think we can make it work with one child, why
do you assume we can't with two?"

"Because I'm not nearly as amazing as I want everyone to think I am," she said. "I have needs and limits like
everyone else, and I'm tired of pretending I don't."

He gripped his hair hard, his watch still ticking in
his ear. He ripped it off his wrist and threw it across the
room. Kat winced as it hit the wall.

"I'm sorry. I... I need time to think." Leaving her at
the table, he pulled his jacket back on and stepped outside for air.

She should've done it without telling him. It wasn't fair to put the weight on his conscience without giving him any real say in the matter. Trudging up the street, he desperately wished he could shut off his mind. Just once it would be nice not to have to think.

He kept walking until the darkened outline of the church rose up in front of him. Only a year ago they'd stood inside in front of God and everyone they cared about, promising to love each other forever while having no clue what that actually meant.

He climbed the short set of stairs to the side entrance and cupped his hands against the window, peering in at the rows of empty pews outlined in faint moonlight. High above the altar, the ever-burning candle flickered in its narrow chandelier.

As a boy he used to stare at it, wondering how it stayed lit for all those years without burning out. Once during mass, he'd told Wade how cool he thought it was, only to have his brother shrug and say it wasn't a real candle. Desperately wanting to prove Wade wrong, he'd slipped into the rectory before school the next morning to ask Father K. and was devastated to learn it wasn't always the same candle. They simply replaced it whenever it burned low.

Sitting on the steps, he dialed Wade's number. His brother could be annoying and childish, but he'd always been able to see through to the heart of any situation.

Within 15 minutes Wade arrived, walking over from the parking lot with his hands jammed in his hoodie pockets. "Did you and Kat have another fight?"

Wringing his hands, Ian stared at the concrete. "Is it hard being an atheist?"

"Oh. Um, not really. Why?"

"So it doesn't bother you to believe we live in a fucked up chaotic world for a few short years, and when we die, we're gone forever?"

Wade leaned on the railing. "I think that bothers everyone to some extent."

"How do you deal with it?"

"I guess I try not to think about it too much."

"But how can you *not* think about it when we're surrounded by reminders every day?"

"Probably because I accept it as fact. If that's the way the world works, and there's nothing I can do to change it, then there's no point in getting upset about it."

"When did you stop believing?" Ian asked.

"Around fourth grade. Except I didn't really stop, it was more like I realized I never believed it to begin with. The whole thing was full of contradictions and whenever I asked for clarification I'd get some different made-up sounding answer from every priest I asked."

Ian felt like an idiot. Even 10-year olds thought religion was bogus, but he could never seem to let it go. Head throbbing, he craned his neck toward the blackened sky.

"Kat's pregnant again. She wants to have an abortion."

Wade was quiet for a moment. "What do *you* want?"

"I don't even know." His voice cracked. "My rational brain knows it's the worst possible time, but my irrational heart doesn't care. That's my kid and I want it so badly it hurts." He groaned. "But then again, I keep wishing she'd done it without telling me, and why would that thought even cross my mind unless I didn't really want it either? And what if I let her have the abortion, and it turns out there really *is* a God and we both go to hell?" He swallowed hard. "Do you see what it's like being in my head? I can't trust a single thought I ever have."

Wade sat beside him. "Look at me. Life isn't like school, okay? It's not something you can pass or fail. And if there is a God, I don't think he's sitting in the sky with a red pen waiting to take away points every time you fuck up. He's probably got more important shit to do, like making sure whole galaxies don't spin out of control."

"But what if you're wrong, and that's exactly what he does?"

Wade shrugged. "If you're damned if you do and damned if you don't, you might as well do what you want."

Ian stared at Wade with his unkempt hair and that stupid hoodie he'd worn since high school. He was still the same goofy kid who laughed at his own jokes and annoyed the shit out of him, but somehow he'd grown into a compassionate and well-spoken man who understood himself better than anyone else he knew. He supposed it took living apart and not tripping over each other every day to notice.

"*You* were an accident," Ian said.

Wade shrugged. "Mom would never admit it, but it was pretty obvious once I found out Dad got a vasectomy three months before I was even born."

"I heard her on the phone one night in high school," Ian continued. "She thought we were at Rob's house but I forgot my X-Box controller and had to go back. Aunt Sally had just found out she was pregnant with Greta and was worried about starting all over again when Jeremy was almost out of high school. I overheard the whole story about how Mom and Dad got really drunk at a party, but managed to get it on before she started feeling sick. She thinks she threw up her birth control pill because a few weeks later she found out she was pregnant with you. She thought about aborting you because they'd only planned to have one kid and could barely afford me. But now she's so glad she didn't do it because she can't imagine life without her little boy."

He choked back tears. "I must've wished a thousand times that you'd never been born, but finding out you almost weren't scared the shit out of me. You'll probably never cure cancer, but somehow you wound up being my best friend. How can I deny Lili that?"

Wade blushed and punched his arm. "I know I'm awesome and everything, but if you never knew me, you wouldn't miss me. And even if you never have more kids,

Lili will have plenty of other friends. She'll be okay and so will you."

He threw his arms around Wade's neck, hugging him as hard as he could. "Thank you. I really appreciate that."

"Then stop choking me, asshole."

He let go, allowing himself a short laugh. "I'm sorry I fucked things up with Eleanor. It doesn't excuse what I did, but if it's any consolation, I only said that stuff because I was jealous. She couldn't take her eyes off you."

Wade sighed. "I don't know what she was upset about, but I don't think it was you."

"What did she say?"

"Nothing. Just that she was sorry and would call me sometime."

"That's... shitty." There wasn't really another way to say it. "What did you see in her anyway? She was kind of hard to get a read on."

"You mean besides the fact that she's so goddamned cute I think my heart might explode?"

Ian grinned. "I guess she's alright. Not really my type, though."

"She was so easy to talk to. I was telling her all this really personal stuff like I'd known her for years. I didn't feel like I had to be constantly funny, or smart, or interesting. I could just *be*. I guess I felt better about myself when I was with her."

Ian could relate to that. Kat was so smart and gorgeous he always felt more confident with her by his side.

If someone like her could love him, he might be worth something after all.

He traced a crack in the concrete with his finger. "I think I'd be okay with the abortion if it meant I got to have my wife back."

"What are you waiting for, then?" Wade said. "Go home and tell her."

He shook his head. "I can't. Not until I have a plan. I need to be absolutely sure something good will come of this—that in a few weeks we won't wind up stuck in the same rut again."

Wade nodded. "A very smart person once told me if I had a problem, I should write down any solutions that came to mind, no matter how crazy they seemed, and then cross out anything that sounded like a cop out or required someone else to change."

Ian shook his head in disbelief, feeling honored.

"What?" Wade asked. "It worked for me."

"No, you're right. I just... my brain is fried. Would you mind if I stayed at your place tonight?"

Wade stood up and stretched out a hand. "Come on. Let's get out of here."

CHAPTER 33

Eleanor

Eleanor re-read the same sentence over and over again, still having no idea what it said. Peering over the top of her book, she watched the bartender fill a glass and pass it to someone at the other end of the sparsely populated bar. She wiped her palms on her corduroys. It was ten minutes to seven. She'd purposely arrived early so Trent would be the one who needed to initiate conversation, but the wait was killing her. She hadn't been able to eat all day and now felt lightheaded on top of her nerves.

She sipped her ginger ale slowly as the bell on the front door jingled. A tall man wearing a red gingham shirt entered, but his hair was much too light to be Trent. She tried reading her book again, her spine aching. How people sat on these backless stools for hours at a time was beyond her.

"Eleanor?"

She whirled around, looking right up into a pair of impossibly ice blue eyes. Her heart stopped beating. "Trent." His close-cropped hair was a very pale brown, and his face much leaner than she remembered, but no one else could have those eyes. "You look so different."

"And you look exactly the same." He grinned, enveloping her in a tight hug, his muscles strong and defined. She rested her head against his chest. God, he was huge. He could probably break her in half if he wanted to.

He sunk onto the stool beside her, shaking his head as he looked her up and down. "I didn't think I was ever gonna see you again."

She clutched her glass. "I wasn't sure you'd remember me."

"I can't believe *you* remembered *me*. I must've read that note ten times to make sure I hadn't gone crazy." He ordered a beer. "Where are you living?"

"A few blocks from here. You?"

"Down in Wilkes-Barre."

"How long have you been there?"

"About a year." He shook his head. "I made the mistake of dating my boss. The breakup was so bad I had to get a new job and move in with my sister."

"Oh." All those times she'd gone looking for him had been for nothing. The envelope she found from Budget might've even been his separation papers. "So what do you do now?"

He rolled his eyes. "I sell phones."

"You don't like it?"

"Eh. The customers are morons, but it pays the bills. What about you?"

"I'm a librarian."

He grinned. "Why am I not surprised?"

She felt put off, but wasn't sure why. "What do you mean by that?"

"I don't know. Seems to fit your personality." He leaned forward, resting an arm on the bar. "So what happened all those years ago? Did you have to move for the Army or something?"

"Yeah." She played with her coaster, weighing how much to tell him. "My dad got last minute orders. I barely had time to pack before we left."

"Where did you end up?"

"Colorado Springs."

"Jesus Christ." He shook his head. "I tried to get an address or phone number from the school office, but they wouldn't tell me a thing—wouldn't even mail a letter *for* me."

"That's awful." She stared into her glass, feeling terrible. He cared enough to go through all that trouble, and she hadn't even said goodbye.

"You still haven't told me—how did you wind up back in Scranton, anyway?"

She shifted in her seat. "I moved here for the job."

He squinted. "Why would you move to Scranton to be a librarian? Can't you do that anywhere?"

Her face grew warm. "I wasn't happy where I was before. I needed a change."

He leaned in even further and her stomach fluttered. "But still—Scranton, Pennsylvania? Most people here are trying to get out."

"It was one of the few places I remembered being happy." She gripped her glass tighter. "I guess I hoped maybe if I came back, I could feel that way again."

"Did it work?"

"Not really." She swirled the ice around in her glass. "Sometimes I think I wasn't wired to be happy. No matter where I go, I always feel alone."

He nodded. "God, do I know what that's like. I was an outcast from a cliquey group of assholes from kindergarten all the way through high school. A few times it nearly killed me."

She didn't remember anyone picking on him, but then again, she couldn't remember anyone interacting with him, either. "I didn't realize it was that bad for you."

"No offense, but you weren't there long. Every now and then one of them would rebel against the group and start hanging out with me, but it always ended the same way. They'd realize it wasn't much fun being on the outside and go running back to the group, usually with a bunch of new lies to spread about me. At least they *had* that option. No matter how hard I tried to blend in, they always saw right through me and rubbed my face in it."

No wonder he didn't talk to them anymore. "Why didn't you tell me?"

He gave her a crooked half-smile. "Because I wanted you to like me." He twisted the beer bottle in his hands.

"I told myself it was good you left when you did, before some cool guy finally noticed you and turned you against me."

"Are you kidding? No guys were ever into me even the slightest bit."

He downed the rest of his beer and motioned toward the door. "There's something I wanna show you."

Outside, the chill air ripped through her thin sweater as she followed him around the side of the building, an overhead light casting an orange glow over the alley. He untucked his shirt and started unbuttoning it.

Her eyes grew wide as she quickly looked away. "What are you doing?"

"I promise I'm not being lewd. Look." Beneath his sleeveless undershirt, both toned arms were covered in colorful tattoos. She didn't know where to look first.

"How long did this take you?"

"I started on my 18th birthday, but the newest one is only a few months old." He laughed. "I'm kind of addicted."

She recognized the bleeding face with the computer circuit board under the skin. "I remember when you drew that."

"Yeah, a lot of these designs are really old."

So much space was already covered, but he was still so young. "Do you ever regret them?"

"Believe me, there's some I wish I never got, but they all represent who I was at a particular time whether I like it or not. I can't change the past, but I can make damn sure I never let myself become that person again."

She tilted her head to read a block of text when she saw a familiar image. "Is... is that my plow?"

He twisted his arm so the ink hit the light. It was definitely the plow, sitting alone in the overgrown field, its back wheel cracked. "I liked what you said about it. That it was broken but still had a purpose."

She couldn't believe it—one of her images emblazoned on his skin forever. "When did you get it?"

"About three years ago."

Her heart skipped a beat. They hadn't seen each other for seven years by that point, yet he'd still been thinking about her. She imagined him sitting in a darkened tattoo parlor, ignoring the pain as he attempted to be closer to her. "What sparked the idea?"

"I was really depressed for a while and my girlfriend didn't get it. She kept buying me presents and planning all these outings, but it just made me feel shittier for not being able to snap out of it. Then one day she flipped out, said she was tired of trying to cheer me up when it was clear I didn't *want* to be happy. I told her it wasn't her fault—this is the way I am—but she wasn't like you and didn't get it. She said if that was the case, she was better off finding someone who wasn't broken."

He scratched the back of his head. "I don't know. Something about the word 'broken' really bothered me—like I was an old toy or piece of furniture, instead of a human being. I didn't wanna be held down by it, so I decided to own it."

The orange streetlight buzzed above them as she waited for the rest of the story—the part where he talked about missing her and wishing they could be together—but it seemed like that was it. For someone who always felt so alone, he sure seemed to have a lot of girlfriends.

"Did you ever try to find me?" she asked. "You know, online or anything?"

"I searched a few times, but your last name's common and I didn't know where you lived, so it was like shooting in the dark." He stepped closer. "But I've been here this whole time. You could've looked me up whenever you wanted. So why now?"

She kicked at the ground, unable to meet his eyes.

"Because I didn't know how to deal with my feelings. I thought if I shoved them down and pretended they didn't exist I wouldn't get hurt. It didn't work, but I didn't know what else to do. By the time I grew up and moved out on my own, I was afraid it'd been too long and would be awkward. And if I never tried to contact you, I could at least pretend that somewhere in the world there was one person who still cared about me. But then one day I woke up in a dingy house surrounded by a bunch of girls I didn't like, and it felt like my soul was dying. I had to find out if there was a better life for me back here with you."

He grabbed her shoulders, kissing her hard. His hot breath tasted like beer, and her bones felt crushed under the pressure of his arms.

I'm kissing Trent Zarella.

But it felt nothing like that day in the abandoned house, or even Wade's more sensual touch.

Stop thinking about Wade. You have Trent now. For the first time in your life, you're getting exactly what you want.

But it didn't feel right at all.

Trent relaxed his grip. "I never thought I was gonna get to do that again."

"Yeah, me neither." She felt like crying. This wasn't how it was supposed to be. "Can we go back inside? I need to use the rest room."

She locked the door of the wooden stall and sat on the closed toilet lid, head in hands. She'd only hung out with Wade twice and didn't really know him at all. Did he think she was special or only some random girl to pass the time with until someone better came along? Even if he *had* legitimately liked her, there was no guarantee he still would after the meltdown she had at his brother's house. He probably wouldn't even miss her.

She sat up. It was the exact same thing she'd thought about Trent all those years ago, yet he was in the other room this very minute, caring so much he'd tattooed her plow on his arm. But that wasn't really about her. It was about him. He didn't want to be held down by his differentness, but it was all he talked about. It was also the main reason he liked her—because *she* was different too.

But when she was with Wade, she didn't feel different at all. It was like she forgot to be sad. Maybe that's what she needed, someone to pull her out of her dark insulated shell, not curl up and live inside of it with her.

She felt eerily calm. *It's happened. I've actually gone insane.*

She peered out the bathroom door. Trent sat by himself at the bar, beer in hand, watching the overhead TV. If she walked out the front door, he wouldn't notice. She shook her head. She couldn't do that to him. Not again. She climbed onto the stool beside him.

"Trent, I have to tell you something."

He tore at the label on his beer bottle. "This isn't gonna work, is it?"

She blinked. "I... how did you know?"

"Usually when girls are into you, they don't suddenly get quiet and run away to the bathroom after you kiss them."

Her stomach twisted. "I'm sorry."

"Was it something I said?"

Well, kind of, but not really. "I'm seeing someone else."

"Story of my goddamned life." He took a swig of beer.

"I left that note before Christmas. I didn't think you were going to call."

"Great. So my ex is still finding new ways to screw me over. She'll be so pleased."

It was scary how quickly his personality shifted. One minute he'd been a brightly shining sun, and the next he was a black hole sucking all light from the room. She felt sorry for his exes.

"It was still really good to see you."

"Uh huh." He wouldn't even look at her.

She didn't want to leave him like that, but didn't know what else to say. She left the bar and walked halfway home before she stopped turning around, expecting to see him following her.

Back at her apartment, she sat out on her little balcony, hugging her arms to her chest and staring at the city lights. If this night was going to get worse, she might as well get it over with. She dialed Wade's number.

"Hello?" At least he answered. That was a good sign, right?

"Hey. It's Eleanor."

"What's up?" He didn't sound upset. In fact, he seemed pretty calm.

"I'm sorry about yesterday. An old friend called while I was in the bathroom and it dredged up a lot of memories I wasn't prepared to deal with. You were really kind to me though, and that meant a lot."

"Are you okay now?"

"I think so."

"Good." He didn't try to make her feel guilty, or demand extra details or apologies.

"Do you want to come over sometime soon?" she asked. "Maybe we can watch a movie or something."

"That sounds awesome."

CHAPTER 34

Ian

Having borrowed them from Wade, Ian's shirt and slacks felt both loose and tight in all the wrong places as he knocked on the open office door. "Sister, may I have a word with you?"

Sister Augustine motioned for him to take a seat, but he remained standing.

"This won't take long." He slid an envelope forward on her desk. "It's Darryn's acceptance from community. I thought you might like to have it for your records."

"Is that all, Mr. Dakalski?" She didn't flinch, just folded her hands on top of the desk, her beady eyes daring him to say anything else. Any doubts he might've had about whether she'd purposely lost Rob's check disappeared in that moment, making the next easier.

"I wanted to come back and work at this school because I received an excellent education and have fond memories of my time here. I learned more than I expected over the past two years, and I'm grateful for that opportunity. However, my family will always be my number one priority and right now they need me."

He placed a second envelope on the desk. "I'm resigning—effective immediately."

Reveling in the warmth of the sun, he carried a cardboard box of office supplies up the front path to his house. He may have just made the biggest mistake of his life, but he could worry about that later.

Inside, the house was quiet. Lili was asleep in her bassinette and Kat dozed in the recliner beside her, a blanket pulled over her lap. Sitting on the armrest, Ian rubbed her shoulder. As soon as she saw him, she threw her arms around him.

"I was so worried when you didn't come home."

"I'm sorry, Kat. I promise I'll never stay away like that again."

"Are you okay?"

"I'm fine. But I have to tell you something." He held her shoulders lightly, looking into her eyes. "I quit my job today."

"What?" Her eyes grew wide. "Why?"

"So I can stay home and take care of Lili when you go back to work."

She sat up, shaking her head. "But what about your career? Aren't you worried about money?"

He burst out laughing. "I'm scared as hell. But I did the math, and as long as we're careful, we can afford to live off your salary until Lili's old enough to start school. Plus, it'll give me time to work on my music."

"What about the other thing?" She glanced down at her stomach.

He nodded. "Make the appointment. We'll get someone to watch Lili so I can be with you the whole time, just like the birth." He stroked her cheek. "I was also thinking we could hire a regular babysitter, maybe every other Saturday night, so we can go out and do something together, just the two of us." He reached into his jacket pocket and pulled out the No Doubt tickets. "Maybe something like this."

Tears streamed down her face. "I thought you were gonna leave me."

"These past few days I've questioned pretty much everything I've ever believed, but I never once considered leaving." He kissed her. "You say you're not amazing, but you are. You're the most amazing person I've ever known."

CHAPTER 35

Wade

*P*ale shafts of sunlight streamed through the basement windows. Covered now with a tarp and thin layer of dust, the machine sat motionless, dashboard dark. On the workbench two helmets rested on a neat coil of wires.

At an outdoor café, the scientist's wife sat alone under an umbrella, silhouetted against the bright orange sunset she faced. Joining her, the scientist took off his fedora, and kissed her before sitting beside her and taking her hand.

Wade held the duffel bag behind his back as he stood on the landing of Eleanor's third floor fire escape, looking out over the city of Scranton and the mountains rising behind it. When she opened the door and smiled, his heart felt like it might burst in his chest.

"My God, you're beautiful." He kissed her slowly before pulling back, barely able to contain his excitement.

"I have a surprise for you." He pulled a jewel case from the bag. "It's my game. I finished it last night."

"That's so cool. Congratulations." She took the case and laughed when she saw the smiley face he'd drawn on the disc with permanent marker.

"I was gonna wait until I had a real cover made, but I was too excited."

"How does it feel to finally be done?"

"It doesn't feel over yet." He laughed. "I'm not sure what I'm gonna do with all the extra free time."

"Maybe you'll make another one."

"Or I could hang out with you." He grinned, marveling at the way her grey eyes reflected the bright blue sky.

"Let's play it right now," she said.

Inside, he set up the X-Box before kicking off his sneakers and sitting on the floor in front of her futon. Controller in hand, she sat between his knees, leaning back against his chest. Wrapping his arms around her shoulders, he kissed the back of her neck as the opening image appeared on the screen.

Book Club Questions

1. Which character did you admire most or least? Why?

2. Did your opinions of the characters shift depending on whose viewpoint you were reading?

3. How did parental relationships continue affecting the characters even after they'd grown up and moved out?

4. In what ways did the characters learn to take responsibility for their own choices and happiness?

5. Do you agree with Wade's epiphany that friends and lovers should be held to the same standards? Are you more likely to put up with poor treatment from one group as opposed to the other?

6. In what ways have your own friendships grown or changed after losing a shared experience like school?

7. In what ways did Kat and Ian adhere to and/or subvert stereotypical gender roles in their marriage? Do you think it's possible to avoid these issues entirely?

8. Is honesty always the best policy? Were there times characters were justified in lying?

9. Each character struggled with outdated beliefs about themselves, each other, and the world. Have you ever found a belief similarly hard to let go of, even when there was mounting evidence you could be wrong?

10. Eleanor often reflected on the information and people lost to history. Were there any unanswered questions that stuck with you? Why do you think the author chose to leave them open-ended?

Acknowledgements

Ever since I was a kid it's been my dream to publish a novel. I'd like to take a moment to express my heartfelt thanks to the people who helped make this dream come true:

All the friends who supported my art over the years by coming out to listen to my music, helping bring my films to life, and encouraging me along the grueling (but exciting!) adventure of writing my first novel.

Fellow author Holly Lisle, whose *How to Revise Your Novel* course taught me about "The Sentence," drastically improving the way I write fiction forever.

My super awesome editors, Alana Saltz and Naomi Hughes, for helping level-up my novel to meet the final boss of publication.

My Mom and Dad, for making sure I grew up with access to books and a good education, and always supporting my art, even when they didn't understand what the heck I was doing or why.

My husband, best friend, and fellow novelist, Fred Almengor, for being such a phenomenal sounding board for all things writing-related, cheering me on during bouts of self-doubt, and generally being the most intelligent, fun, and caring person I know. I love you.

About the Author

Lynn Almengor holds a BA in Video Communication from Arcadia University, and previously wrote/directed guerrilla-style independent films. Because her parents were right about art rarely paying, she also works as a Web Producer in her hometown of Philadelphia, PA. When not writing, Lynn can usually be found playing video games, watching "bad" movies, or goofing off with her husband and their four ferrets. This is her first novel.

Follow her online at www.plaidcoreproductions.com

CPSIA information can be obtained at www.ICGtesting.com
Printed in the USA
LVOW07s2002130916

504435LV00010B/987/P